To the memory of my grandparents,
Emma and Arturs Lietuvietis.

Song of

LATVIA

LATVIA 1940

Winter let go slowly that year as the rivers and lakes thawed, froze, and thawed again. Heavy snow, dark with dirt, melted into the rivers and swirled downstream, emptying into the Baltic Sea. One day it was winter. The next day the ground was no longer hard and the storks arrived, nesting and mating on barn roofs across the countryside. The air smelled of newly growing grasses and ferns. Wild daisies bloomed. The flat landscape was broken by white birch forests, limbs covered in glossy green leaf buds. And in the middle of June, a different kind of winter arrived.

CHAPTER ONE

*M*ija wanted to push her way down the tiers through the other eight thousand singers and run to the train station. She could be home in a couple of hours. Tapping a foot, she studied the empty podium far below.

The opening ceremonies should have started twenty minutes ago. Latvia's president should be giving the welcoming address. Or at the very least, the conductor should be there explaining the delay.

"I don't know why they didn't cancel the Song Festival. With much of the continent at war, it's not the right time."

Mija's sister-in-law Laima, standing next to her, said, "You think our tiny country will be drawn in?"

Mija raised her eyebrows. "Why wouldn't we be?"

"Well then, it's exactly why we're here. Latvians sing. We rise up and sing. That's how we survive."

"Then I hope we start singing soon."

Laima patted Mija's back. "Nothing's going to happen today."

Mija stared at the fifty thousand spectators sitting on wooden benches fanning out in a semicircle on grassy acres. The audience looked like small lumps of multicolored clay. Minutes ticked by and the buzz of speculation increased to the level of frenzied wasps.

Behind her she heard, "The president is sick." From below, someone else said, "The car bringing him from Riga to Daugavpils had an accident." Then there were the more outlandish rumors such as the president and conductor were still in the restaurant where they'd had dinner, got drunk, and forgot the time.

A voice boomed and echoed over the loud-speakers, startling everyone into silence. "Good evening. This is President Ulmanis speaking to you from Riga." The disembodied voice apologized for not being there. Mija strained to hear the words, stiffening in anticipation. Ulmanis continued. "Earlier today, Soviet troops overran a guard post on the border between our two countries. There were casualties and the Russians took prisoners."

Mija's breath knotted at the back of her throat and bile rose from her stomach. She forced herself to swallow it. Her immediate worry was her husband Aleks, a colonel in the Latvian Army. Ulmanis continued to speak but words intended to reassure did not. He finished with, "The present situation demands that I stay in Riga. We must continue with calm and reason. You remain in your place and I'll remain in mine."

Dead silence lasted only seconds before the crowd was abuzz again. Mija said, "Aleks will be called back to Riga even though he has another week of leave. I should go home. My children need me."

As Laima said, "But . . ." the conductor appeared and tapped his baton sharply on the podium. The crowd quieted as he leaned into the microphone. "You heard the president. Our place right now is to stay here and sing." He straightened, lifted his baton, and nodded.

Laima patted Mija's hand and whispered, "We stay."

The orchestra, sitting on rows of chairs below the singers, played the first notes and on cue, the harmonious sound of united choirs filled the air. Mija sang the well-rehearsed songs. Her mind went other places. She could still get the next train home. On the other hand, her mother lived with them and so did the maid. Whether Aleks was there or not, her two children were safe on their small farm. But what if foreign tanks were moving through their country right now? Their farm was close to one of the main roads going from the Russian border to the capital of Riga.

The first song was over and the audience gave them a standing ovation. The conductor waited for the crowd to settle down before raising his baton for the next song. And so it continued. As the evening went by, Mija discovered that singing in unison with her countrymen soothed her soul. Laima was right. Song festivals were the heart of Latvia.

Following tradition, the audience rose from their seats and joined in the final song, "Dievs Sveti Latvia" (God Bless Latvia).

> God bless Latvia,
> Our beloved fatherland,
> Do bless Latvia,
> Oh, do bless it!

> Where the Latvian daughters bloom,
> Where the Latvian sons sing,
> Let us dance in happiness there,
> In our Latvia!

WITHOUT MISSING A BEAT, the orchestra started from the beginning. The scene in front of Mija blurred as tears welled up. She took Laima's hand. Then Laima reached for the hand of the person on the other side. That woman took the hand of the next person. Soon all the singers on every tier held hands. Mija raised her arms high, bringing the other two along. The singers around them followed. On tier after tier, arms raised. Hot tears slid down her cheeks. She hoped the sound of Latvians united in song reached heaven. Twice was still not enough. Mija prayed, "Please, God, keep us out of another war." The third rendition complete, arms lowered slowly.

The conductor's voice cracked as he said, "I

declare the song festival over and pray that we all travel safely."

Mija wiped her cheeks and took a deep breath. She hugged Laima and said, "I'm glad you talked me into being part of this."

Laima rubbed away her own tears. "Me too."

The midnight sky was a dusty violet, sparkling with yellow stars. In orderly fashion tinged with a sense of urgency, the audience left the park for home. The singers always stayed to eat, drink, sing, and dance until morning. This time, instead of merriment, there was the rustle of troubled voices. Some wanted to leave. Most said no, leaving would be wrong. They talked about the president's speech and speculated on what would happen next. They talked about the last world war and their own War of Independence, fought more than twenty years ago. Latvia had gained its freedom from Russia then. Some said it was the same thing all over again, and if they didn't get involved immediately, they'd be under the Russian yoke once more. Others said no, it's a different time. Russia wouldn't dare.

MIJA AND LAIMA BECAME separated from the rest of their town's choir as they made their way toward the food tables where fiery torches on ten-foot poles marked the area. Mija said, "I don't think Aleks wanted me to come."

"Did he say that?" said Laima.

"No, but I could tell he was worried."

Laima looked askance. "Do you think he keeps information from you?"

"There are lots of things he can't tell anyone, not even his wife."

"I suppose so, but I don't think Aleks would let you go into a dangerous situation."

"Not knowingly." Mija hesitated for a moment, head bent. "Still, we have great cause to be worried, what with the Russians crossing the border and killing people. No good can come of it."

"My dear sister-in-law, everything is under control. The president said so. Now let's get some food. You'll feel better on a full stomach." Laima's bravado kept Mija from saying more.

The singers tramped along crisscrossing paths from one end of the park to the other. Young and old, married and single, they walked, talked, and fretted. And then someone started singing. Others joined in. Soon the park resonated with a melodious mix of voices.

The singers wore traditional costumes. Each town had their own colors and patterns. Women wore ankle-length skirts of handwoven wool in stripes or plaids. Blouses were made of hand-sewn creamy linen that had been bleached in the sun. Close-fitting vests matched their skirts. Young maidens' heads were adorned with cloth crowns, alive with bright beads, while plain white caps marked married women. Men wore linen shirts and tan or gray woolen jackets and pants.

Competing aromas of steaming sauerkraut, grilled sausages, potato salad, cheeses, and cakes made Mija's mouth water, and she filled her plate with a good sampling. Next, they stood in line for mugs of home-brewed beer and walked again, looking for their group. Mija drank her beer in long swallows. Here and there, they ran into someone they knew from a neighboring town and said a few words of greeting.

Her beer almost gone, Mija decided to go home after all. Why should she stay? They'd been invaded. She needed to see her children and hug them. That was reason enough.

She stopped and turned to Laima. "I'm going home."

CHAPTER TWO

Laima shook her head. "There are no more trains until morning."

"Oh. You're right." A gust of cool air blew across Mija's back. She shivered and took the last gulp of beer, then realized Laima had said something. "I'm sorry. What did you say?"

Laima uncharacteristically stamped her foot. Beer sloshed and spilled onto her hand. "I said, worrying won't change anything. What aren't you telling me?"

"The killing started. The nightmares will return." Mija lifted her empty mug and sighed.

"Nightmares?" Laima asked.

"The last war. Soviet soldiers."

"We were so young then, barely in our teens. What did we know of war? For me, living so close to the coast, the war was far away. I never even saw a soldier. The worst thing I suffered was lack of food from time to time."

"They raided our whole area."

"What happened?"

"They were real beasts, I . . ." Mija shook her head, "I don't want to talk about that. Let's get another beer."

"Here, take mine. I'm not thirsty." They traded mugs and Mija took several swallows.

Six young men, arms linked together, swayed side to side as they walked, singing the slow refrain, "Dievs Sveti Latvia," over and over in deep voices. The sound grumbled like a funeral dirge. Mija and Laima stepped to the side to let them pass.

Laima said, "Maybe we should talk about what happened. We could find a quiet spot and sit."

"Thank you but . . . maybe another time." Mija shook her head again.

"When you're ready, I'll still be here." Laima knew Mija couldn't be pushed.

"I wonder what happened to our group? This park is so big. Maybe we should find a spot to sit. If they walk by, we'll see them."

Laima noticed a group of four men coming up behind them and said, "Come on, we have to move." Laima got out of the way in time, but Mija didn't quite make it. The man on the end stepped on the hem of Mija's long skirt. The delicate wool of her great-grandmother's precious handiwork ripped several inches. Tired, tense, and now angry, she whipped around and said, "You drunken good-for-nothing—"

The man's words slurred into hers. "'Scuse me, sorry." As he stumbled against Mija's shoulder, the stench of his breath, heavy with cheese and beer, drifted into her nostrils. She stepped sideways to get away from him.

"Mija?" The man's knees buckled as he took several unsteady steps backward, away from the path, and bumped into a linden tree. His outstretched arms kept him upright as he slid down the trunk and sat down among the gnarly roots.

He had wavy black hair and a slight bump on his otherwise straight nose. Mija walked a little closer and looked into his pale blue eyes. "Peters? Can it be you?"

"Omigod, Mija. Yes, it's me." He stared up at her with a silly grin.

At that moment, the sun popped up over the horizon and everything became brighter. Peters closed his eyes.

"I've never seen you drunk before."

"Yes, I'm drunk. And my head hurts." As Peters lowered his head into his hands, a lock of hair escaped onto his forehead where beads of perspiration trickled down.

"Haven't you heard?" As he looked up at her, his grin turned into a grimace. Her eyebrows lifted in question. "They've attacked. We're done for. Bombs are next." Peters scanned the empty sky as though there were already planes circling. He wiped his forehead with his sleeve and used his fingers to push his hair back into place.

Laima gently touched Mija's arm. "Aren't you going to introduce me?"

Mija tapped her head with the heel of her hand. "I'm sorry. Laima, this is Peters. Peters grew up on the farm next to my parents where the Jekabsons live now. Then he went off to university, his parents moved away, and I never saw him again. Recently, I heard he was the mayor of Velsaine, but I don't know." She smiled, "Do you think the people of Velsaine would be crazy enough to vote in a drunkard as their mayor?" Peters grunted a laugh.

Laima said, "A pleasure to meet you. I don't know about you two, but I could use some coffee. I'll go get it and also some bread."

Peters said, "Thank you. I take my coffee black."

"Ah, just like Mija. I prefer a little cream." As Laima walked away, Peters patted a grassy spot next to him. "Here, sit."

Mija hesitated. She didn't want to get grass stains on her skirt. As if he read her mind, Peters took off his jacket and laid it down beside him. "Please, sit on this. I'm not ready to stand."

She sat down and arranged her skirt around her ankles, fingering the torn hem.

"I'm sorry about your skirt. I'll be glad to pay to have it repaired."

"No matter. If you remember, my mother is a pretty good seamstress. She'll patch it up so no one will even know it was damaged."

"If you're sure." He cocked his head. "Remember the hours we sat in the park when we were teenagers?"

Mija nodded. "Yes, of course. And then you

graduated from high school the year before me, went off to university and I never heard from you again." At the time, she had thought they were more than friends and had always wondered what happened.

Peters scrunched up his forehead. "I wrote you a letter during my first week of college. A long one. You never wrote back."

"What? I never got a letter." Mija's eyebrows raised as high as they could go.

"And I thought . . ."

"Peters, really? You really wrote to me?" She put a hand on his arm.

"Of course." He slapped his knee. "I was devastated when you didn't respond. I assumed you had a new boyfriend."

"I did not. And I was crushed that you never wrote and assumed you found someone else too."

Peters took her hand from his arm and held it in both of his.

"All these years . . ." He gave a slight shake of his head. "During the years since, whenever I ran into someone from Gulepils, I asked about you. I know you're a history teacher, that you married a colonel and have a twelve-year-old daughter and five-year-old son."

"Why didn't you send a second letter? Come to visit?" Mija struggled to make sense of this revelation.

"I was young and stupid, I guess. I just assumed . . ."

Mija sighed. "Me too."

"As for visiting, I barely scraped by during those years. My parents moving back to Tukums sealed it.

They took over my grandparents' farm when my grandfather got cancer. He died in a matter of months. At university, I worked to make ends meet and couldn't afford to go home. I couldn't even go back for my grandfather's funeral."

"You were always very determined. So, you graduated from Stockholm University?"

"In economics." Peters sat up a little straighter. "With honors."

"Wonderful. Did you change your mind about law school?"

"No. Circumstances changed it for me." He turned away from her for a moment. "Let's talk about something else."

She took a long breath. "Tell me more about yourself. Are you married? Children? I've heard almost nothing about you all these years. I recently learned by chance that you were the mayor."

"I am married. We have two boys, six and four years old." He gave her hand a light squeeze. "You look good, Mija, the same as I remember."

Mija blushed. "That's the beer talking."

A little bird, a white wagtail, ran along the ground, stopping a few inches from Peters' crossed feet. True to its name, the bird wagged its tail up and down and then flew off.

Peters said, "Look at that. Birds aren't afraid of us. Why should the Russians be?"

"When did you become a pessimist?" Mija turned her head away.

Peters touched her chin with the tips of his fingers and turned her face back to him. "But you don't disagree. I feel your concern. I still know you."

"Yes, you know me." The gangly boy had turned into a solid, handsome man. All of a sudden, she wanted to stay here with Peters and pretend they were teenagers again and not think about anything else. Then she was horrified at her thoughts. She was worried and wanted to go home. At the same time, the memories of her days with Peters came back so strongly that if she could, at this very moment, she might have chosen to go back to the past, to her teenage years with him, to the beginning of Latvia's freedom, when all things seemed possible. She had known peace, contentment, and joy in his company. Her eyes closed. She could smell the wild daisies from their childhood park all over again.

Peters returned her to the present with, "And you still have the most beautiful green eyes."

Mija hadn't felt butterflies like this in a very long time. "I wish I'd bumped into you earlier. We could have spent more time catching up."

His eyebrows furrowed in a familiar way. "We have time, don't we? When are you leaving?"

Mija looked at her watch. "I guess we do. I'm taking the nine o'clock train." She was surprised the hour was still so early.

He stared at her. She wanted to look away but couldn't. Mija studied Peters' face as if some answer there eluded her.

Laima returned, holding a small tray with three coffee mugs and a plate of golden raisin bread slices. Peters jumped up and took the tray. Mija stood and brushed some grass off the back of her skirt.

"Why don't we go to the picnic tables?" said Laima.

Mija said, "Yes, let's." They walked toward the field of wooden tables and benches. "Peters, I didn't even know you sang and here you are. How did you—"

"Get here? Let's say I can carry a tune, and I've always loved the song festivals. My town's group needed another tenor about a year ago and I joined then. How about you?"

"I was a last-minute replacement for old Velda. She got sick and Laima convinced me to fill in. Laima's the one with the voice though. She's been singing in the festivals for years."

"What a stroke of luck that you're here and we ran into each other." He smiled.

She couldn't help smiling back. "Yes. And at the very least, it's been a momentous occasion."

Peters lost his smile. "And now, we wait."

Mija frowned. "Wait for what? No. Now we dry the tears and fight back. The border attack is a sign of more to come. If we don't fight back, and quickly, we'll be occupied again in no time."

Peters said, "We're outnumbered by how many? Where are we going to get help?"

Mija shrugged. "I don't know. But I do know this.

We have to fight back."

They reached the picnic area and found an empty table at the end of the first row. Mija and Laima sat next to each other and Peters took a seat across from Mija. She noticed the shadow of dark stubble on Peters' chin and looked down, focusing instead on taking a bite of bread.

"Good coffee," he said.

Laima and Peters kept the conversation going about mundane things like farming and even cooking. Peters liked to make soup, and soon he and Laima promised to exchange recipes for meatball soup. Peters was also going home by train and walked with them to the station.

The platforms were so full it was hard to stay together. Peters held Mija's hand and Mija held Laima's until they reached their train. Peters hugged Laima goodbye first, a friendly, social one. His hug for Mija was tender and longer, reminiscent of a prior time. Nostalgia hung in the air between them. As Mija started up the steps, Peters touched her back and said, "I visit Gulepils once in a while. May I call you then?"

She turned to him. "That would be nice."

"So, until then . . ."

"Until then."

He took her hand again, brought it to his lips, and gave it a light kiss.

CHAPTER THREE

Their train car was nearly full but they found two empty seats in the next to last row.

Laima said, "Do you mind sitting at the window again?"

"Of course not. I love looking out the window."

Peters stood outside, waving to Mija. She waved back. At first, she thought maybe he was trying to tell her something or perhaps she'd forgotten something. She felt the hidden side pocket in her skirt. Her tiny change purse was still there.

Laima said, "Is that Peters?"

"Yes. He'd better get going or he'll miss his own train."

"It can be hard to say goodbye to an old friend."

"I still can't believe I ran into him."

As the whistle blew and the train lurched forward, Mija waved a last goodbye.

Laima said, "I think I'll close my eyes for a minute."

"Me too." But Mija was not the least bit sleepy.

As the train worked its way from the city into the countryside, she stared at the changing landscape and listened to the clickety-clack of the wheels. The houses got fewer and farther between. They reached the first farms. Fields of newly planted crops flowed past and then forests of white birch trees showed up a few meters from her window. Next, a small lake shimmered with sunlight. A barn appeared and Mija watched a white stork lift out of its nest on the roof. The long, black-tipped wings beat faster and faster as it rose and disappeared.

Laima's head fell onto Mija's shoulder, and she snored a little with every third or fourth breath. She moved closer to Laima to better prop up her companion's head. Mija twisted the long ends of her woven wool belt. When the two pieces were intertwined all the way to the end, she untwisted it and started all over.

Mija dozed and the past images she feared the most returned. She was twelve, the age her daughter was now. Her father and brother were at a neighboring farm, helping to bale hay. She saw the Russian soldiers through the front window as they marched toward the farmhouse. Mija had run inside to fetch a cloth for her mother, who had cut her hand on the edge of the hoe. Her mother and older sister, tending the vegetable garden, had their backs to the approaching men. Mija was confused, not knowing if she should stay where she was or run to her mother. She stayed.

As the soldiers, a group of about ten, approached

the women, Mija saw their sneering faces and heard them yell, telling her mother and sister to get undressed. She heard her mother scream, "Take me, leave the other one alone." The response was raucous laughter as they surrounded the women. The leader strode up to her mother and ripped her dress at the neck. Another soldier went for Mija's sister, Anna. Both women screamed. A third soldier put up his rifle as though to shoot and yelled for them to shut up. The first soldier pushed her mother to the ground.

Mija decided to hide. She went out the back door and ran to the vegetable cellar, only a short distance away and not visible from the front. She struggled with the door but got it open enough to get under it and felt her way down the steps in the dark. Down there, she couldn't hear anything and was glad. In the far corner, she burrowed into a pile of potatoes until she was covered, but still had a small space to breathe. So much time went by that her arms and legs cramped, but still she didn't move. She heard the tramp of feet above and someone threw the door open. Mija held her breath.

"The same old rotten potatoes down there, nothing more," yelled the soldier.

Another yell came from further away, "We could use some potatoes."

A third voice yelled, "We already have too much to carry."

An argument broke out and Mija thought for sure she would pass out. Then the leader yelled that they were all a bunch of monkeys fighting about rotten potatoes, and if anyone wanted any, they could carry them themselves. That ended the argument and the cellar door slammed shut. She gulped in long breaths.

The sound of tramping feet got quieter and then disappeared altogether. Mija didn't move for what felt like hours more. The musty smells of dirt and potatoes lined her nostrils and filled her lungs until she felt damp from the inside out. When she heard her father yelling her name, she clambered out from under the potatoes and pushed open the cellar door.

"Mija!" He ran to her and grabbed her in a bear hug. "Did anyone hurt you?"

She hugged his waist. "No, Papa. I hid as soon as I saw the soldiers. What about Mama and Anna?"

"I put them to bed and sent Feliks to get Doctor Liepins."

As the months went by, Mija's sister retreated into a shell of her former self. If Anna had to talk, she spoke in a soft monotone. Mija sometimes heard Anna muttering to herself, but the words were never clear enough to understand. Less than a year after the attack, Anna got sick and was gone in a matter of days. The doctor said she died from pneumonia. Her mother never talked to Mija about the attack just as Mija never told anyone that she saw the beginning of the brutal assault.

Mija kept the nightmare of that day locked inside. Once in a while, something triggered the memory and she relived it instantly. Her thoughts revolved around her inability to stop what happened. She thought, I should have taken Papa's rifle and shot them. *I was a coward for hiding*. She didn't think about how badly they were outnumbered, or that at the tender age of twelve, she did the best thing she could do by saving herself.

Two long years after the day Mija hid in the vegetable cellar, the war was over and Latvia was free. Treaties were signed. The country flourished in its newborn democracy. The war became a distant memory. Until now.

The whistle blew and the conductor walked through their car yelling "Jaungulepils, next stop Jaungulepils." There would be one more stop before Gulepils. The train neared the station and several people rose to leave. Their car was about one-third full. Mija's legs and arms were stiff from sitting. When the train started again, she moved Laima's head against the back of the seat and wiggled into the aisle.

She walked to the front, turned, and started back. A man sitting in the third row said to the man next to him, "I believe they had the invasion planned all along. So many Soviet tanks in Riga this morning . . ."

Every inch of Mija's skin broke out in a cold sweat. "Excuse me, sir. Did you say tanks in Riga?"

"Yes, tanks. And plenty of Soviet soldiers. I walked by them myself on my way to the train station."

"Any fighting?" Mija asked.

"More like celebrating. Hundreds of people were cheering them on. Idiots! If I hadn't already been leaving, I would have made plans to leave." He shook his head.

My god, was Peters right? Are we done for? "Surely only a small minority would welcome the Russians. May I ask where you're going?"

"To my parent's farm in Elste. I was going home for my cousin's wedding. But now . . ." He shook his head. "No, I'm not going back to Riga."

"Good luck to you," Mija said.

"And to you, madam."

Mija returned to the rear and slipped past Laima without waking her. She sat back and pressed her hot cheek against the cool window. *No, not again! This time they will not hurt my family. They will not hurt my children. I will shoot the bastards point-blank in the face.*

CHAPTER FOUR

*M*ija hugged Laima and got out of the taxicab. Her property sat at the edge of the city limits, abutting the countryside, while Laima's house and farm were in a more rural area three kilometers down the road. Mija ran up the brick path to the white stucco two-story house she and Aleks had built. Rose bushes grew on either side of the front door. They already showed deep-red buds. Soon there would be fresh roses in a crystal vase on the dinner table. Mija loved her roses and tended them with great care. Before every winter, she packed burlap around them and bound them with strong cord.

She opened the door to the sound of her son Ints screaming, "I'm going to get you!" He came running down the hall. Her daughter was already at the top of the stairs and ran into her bedroom, slamming the door.

"Stop, right now," Mija said and Ints jumped to a stop in front of her. He held a paring knife, sticking straight out.

"Give it to me." His shoulders sagged as he handed her the knife. "What are you doing with this?" With her free hand, she steered him by a shoulder into the living room.

"She made me."

"Your sister gave you the knife?" Mija pointed to one of the chintz chairs for him to sit and she sat on the matching one, facing him, on the other side of the marble fireplace.

"She tied me to my bed and spanked me." He rubbed his hip as though it hurt.

"For no reason?"

"No," he said, staring up at the ceiling. He sat still except for his fingers, which drummed against the arm of the chair.

"Where is everyone?"

"Lize's upstairs."

"Yes, I saw her. I meant your grandmother and Hortense."

Her mother Anete wasn't good with discipline and the maid Hortense wasn't much better. The children tended to run wild if neither parent was home, but this was beyond anything Mija could have imagined. Mija called out for the women. Anete came huffing from the kitchen, wiping her hands on a dishtowel. "I'm sorry. I was kneading the bread. Hortense is out in the chicken coop gathering eggs."

Mija stood and hugged her mother, "No need to apologize, Mama. Where's Aleks?"

"He was called back to Riga. This morning he took the early train."

"All right. Go finish the bread then."

"Did you hear?"

"Yes, the president spoke to us from Riga."

"What's going to happen?"

Mija gave her mother another hug. "I don't know, but I'll keep you safe."

"What if they come after us?"

"Mama." Mija nodded her head toward Ints.

Anete brought a hand to her mouth. "Oh, sorry."

"Soldiers are nowhere near here. Please, go back to the kitchen." Anete wrung her hands as she shuffled away.

Lize and Ints were told to stay in their rooms until supper. Mija took a hot bath and put on her favorite dress, a flower print. The softness of the worn cotton gave her comfort. She dabbed her favorite fragrance, Lily of the Valley, behind her ears.

Downstairs, the smell of baking bread filled the air. Through the kitchen window, Mija saw Anete picking rhubarb in the garden. That meant fresh pie for dessert tonight. Mija boiled water and made a cup of tea. She carried the sturdy white cup into the living room. With the children upstairs, the house was quiet, too quiet. She turned on the radio and sat on the dark green sofa while music played softly in the background.

Both old and new scenes came to mind: her

childhood war experience, Peters in high school, her husband Aleks in his uniform, running into Peters at the song festival, her fighting children. *Where had the years gone? And how did we move in a circle back to war?*

Anete walked in with her knitting and sat on the rose-colored chair where Ints had been. "Bread's ready if you want some."

"In a minute." Lack of sleep had caught up to Mija and even the thought of fresh bread wasn't enough to get her up. She sipped on the chamomile tea.

Since Mija's father died, Anete was always knitting an afghan, no matter the season. He had died in a freak accident a few months after Mija's wedding. He was out by the barn chopping wood, making the great piles of logs needed for heating the farmhouse all winter. The ax must have slipped because his hand was chopped off and he bled to death where he fell.

Anete's afghans all had green in them, her husband's favorite color. Some were solids. Others had stripes of light green, dark green, and white. They lay on the backs of the chairs and sofas in the living room and the sunporch. More filled the wooden trunk that was used as a coffee table. The clicking of her needles could be heard over the radio.

Mija expected the fighting would slow down as the children got older, but instead the bickering continued to escalate. A knife! What if Ints had stabbed his sister? What if he had fallen and stabbed himself? This had been going on since Ints started to walk. No form of punishment for either child made a difference.

She thought about her own brother, Feliks, married to Laima. Feliks was ten years older than Mija, and as youngsters, they almost never fought. Lize, seven years older than Ints, should have more sense. What if Mija hadn't walked in?

She put the cup down, took her shoes off, tucked her legs up and rested her head against the back. The next thing she heard was her daughter yelling, "Get away from me, you little brat!"

"Rat-ta-tat-tat. I shot you. You're dead."

"That's a piece of wood, not a gun, you idiot!"

Mija opened her eyes and saw them running toward the kitchen. In that split second, she decided Aleks was right. Lize would go to boarding school in the fall, to Velsaine Gymnasium, a one-hour train ride away. Aleks had always wanted to send both children to boarding school when they were twelve, and Lize had turned twelve in April. Lize would be safer at boarding school if war broke out. Soldiers wouldn't be likely to show up and cause trouble at a school. Mija wouldn't tell her now. She'd wait until Aleks was home. They'd tell her together. No, that wouldn't work. There was no way to know when he'd be home. She'd have to take care of this herself.

THE NEXT MORNING, she made Lize's favorite breakfast of porridge sweetened with strawberry jam. Lize ate the sticky mixture, and Mija poured herself another cup of coffee. Ints came in and Mija sent him out to the chicken coop with Hortense and Anete to help them gather eggs and promised to fry some for him.

She sat down next to her daughter. "Lize, remember your friend Vija?"

Lize swallowed and said, "She wasn't my friend. Her mother is your friend. And then she went away to boarding school last year."

"Well, yes, but you like her and you've spent a lot of time with her over the years. She was old enough to go to Velsaine last year. It's an honor to go there. You have to be accepted."

"Why are you telling me this?"

"Your father and I would like to send you there too."

"You want to send me away?" Lize dropped her spoon into the half-finished bowl.

Mija sighed and took another sip of coffee. "It's one of the most prestigious schools in Latvia. You'd be with other students your age. Remember all the stories your father told you about going away to school? He had many good adventures. Let's at least apply. We don't even know if they've filled all the spaces for the coming year."

"I'm not sure I want to. Can I think about it?"

"You can think about it while we wait to hear from them."

Lize finished her porridge in silence. That afternoon, Mija filled out the application which had been in the desk since the spring.

Uneasy days went by in slow motion. Gulepils was hours away from Riga by train and was not yet touched by troop movements. There was no sign that anything was different. But Mija heard things on the radio, and every few days, Aleks called from his office. As usual, she felt that he was keeping things from her.

Mija started each day early, in her vegetable garden, pulling any new weed sprouts from the soft, black earth, watching the radishes, potatoes, carrots, and other vegetables grow millimeter by millimeter. She also kept an herb garden with dill, parsley, and garlic. There was nothing better than a summer salad with fresh-picked lettuce, cucumber, and dill, all mixed with a dollop of sour cream. Aleks loved the radishes best and ate them plain. But Mija didn't know if he would be home to eat any of her radishes this summer.

One morning, she heard disturbing news and could hardly wait until Aleks' next call, which came later that day. As soon as she heard his voice, she said, "The radio said two hundred thousand Soviet soldiers are in the country and tanks are patrolling the streets of Riga. And further that Latvia's parliament voted for the country to become a Soviet republic. Why didn't you tell me? What's the army going to do?"

"I planned to tell you today. We can't do anything. Our hands are tied. Don't worry, once the Germans are defeated, the Russians will leave," said Aleks, his voice crackling across the wires. "I'm losing you. I'll call again soon. Take care." There was a click and then silence. He was gone. She dropped the receiver into the cradle. "Don't worry," he had said. How could she not?

A letter came informing them that Lize was accepted into Velsaine Gymnasium. Mija planned to take Lize shopping in Gulepils, stop for tea, and tell her then, but Lize walked into the living room while Mija was reading the letter and saw the envelope.

"Well? Did I get in?"

"Yes, congratulations."

Lize made a face. "I still don't know if I want to go. I want to talk to Papa about it."

"Of course. When he comes home."

"I want to talk to him on the telephone. Today."

"You know we have to wait until he calls."

"Then I'm going to Asja's."

"Not today. I need your help to weed the strawberry beds."

"You never let me do anything." Lize clenched her fists.

"That's not true. You can go to Asja's tomorrow."

"I'm going to the barn." Lize stormed out.

Lize didn't come back by the time Mija was ready to weed so she went looking for her. As Mija neared the barn, Lize walked out leading Big Z, named for the white zigzag on his forehead. He was saddled up. Lize put her foot in the stirrup and mounted. Mija's yell, "Stop, wait," was lost in the breeze as Lize spurred the horse and rode toward the road that led to town. A dusty trail grew up behind the horse's hooves.

Mija shuddered. Where is my headstrong girl going? Will I have to drag her kicking and screaming to

Velsaine? A taxicab appeared in the space Lize and the horse had occupied and stopped. A man got out, dressed in a black suit. The taxicab backed up and drove away. Mija walked forward, curious, and as she neared him, realized it was Aleks. He didn't look like himself. His face was a frozen mask. Her legs went weak and she waited for him to reach her. He grabbed her arms, pulled her close and kissed her. His lips were cold. He pushed her back but didn't let go of her arms.

He said, "Yesterday they deported President Ulmanis. Last night General Borsteins shot himself in the head."

Mija wrinkled her forehead. *Am I dreaming?* She stared into Aleks' shell-shocked face and asked, "Shot himself?"

Aleks pulled her into a hug and talked into her ear, "It's chaos in Riga. I resigned from the army rather than join the Reds."

CHAPTER FIVE

*I*n the shadowy light before day took over from night, Aleks drank the last of his coffee and placed the mug in the kitchen sink. He walked slowly down the hall and up the stairs, as if he wasn't quite ready for another day to start. Since he'd left the army, his days blended into his nights, and his life was a shapeless stream of radio voices. During the middle of the night, he often woke up and still heard the radio voices in his head, telling him about the new Soviet Socialist State and all the new rules that were for his benefit.

At the top of the stairs, Aleks walked past his and Mija's bedroom door where light spilled out onto the dark wood floor. Mija must be reading. He walked past the bathroom, past his son's room, and opened the door to the last bedroom. Lize slept on her stomach, a pillow on top of her head. One hand stuck out of the covers, fingers curled. She mumbled something unintelligible as Aleks touched her shoulder and whispered her name. He picked up the pillow. Lize turned onto her back, groping for the missing pillow, then opened her eyes, scrunched and blinked.

"It's not morning yet." She sat up and yawned. Frowning, she asked, "Am I being punished again?"

"No," Aleks managed a smile. "You did a good job repairing the chicken coops. Today is for fun. We're going mushroom picking."

"Ooh." Her frown turned into a genuine smile. This was an annual ritual with her father.

"Meet me downstairs. Hurry. And wear a warm sweater."

A BLANKET OF DARK clouds prevented the sun from shining on father and daughter as they walked side by side, carrying woven baskets. There had been rain off and on for the past week, the kind of weather mushrooms lie in wait for. They followed the stream that ran behind the barn and through fields broken with copses of various trees. About twenty minutes later, they reached a particularly large copse and entered it.

Tall skinny birch trees gave way to a mixture of pine, aspen, and oak. The light dimmed to a dark shadow. They picked their way so as not to trip over the knobby roots that grew into one another and were so twisted that it was impossible to tell which root belonged to which tree.

At last, Aleks heard the forest instead of radio voices in his head. He heard scampering and then saw the squirrel. A clattering of wings came from above, and he looked up but saw nothing except a murky tangle of branches and leaves. The chilly air made him shiver. He should have listened to his own advice and worn a sweater over his cotton shirt.

"There, Papa, there are some," Lize said as she stopped and pointed to a carpet of white mushrooms.

"Yes, Lize, good. They're perfect for pickling. We also need to find the golden ones today, the chanterelles. Your mother wants the white ones for pickling, and she'll dry the golden ones for later."

He helped Lize pick the white mushrooms, reminding her to break them off by holding them close to the bottom and moving them from side to side. The first batch went into Lize's basket. A beating tap-tap-tap broke into their work. Lize pointed to the bird perched sideways on a bare tree trunk.

"It's a pretty bird," Aleks said. He admired the black and white feathers, the red head, and the long pointy beak.

"It's a woodpecker, Papa, a white-backed one," Lize said. "And that tree is dying or done for."

"How do you know so much?" Aleks asked.

"Mama, I guess. She knows everything about the forest. And she told me that woodpeckers attack trees that are already dead or dying."

"She knows a lot. All I know about the forest is

how to pick mushrooms."

"Tell me again, Papa, about the first time you went mushroom picking by yourself."

The woodpecker stopped tapping and turned its head toward the sound of their voices. Aleks watched the bird fly away, its harsh trill fading as it disappeared beyond a pine tree. He turned back to Lize as he rubbed the tip of his left thumb with his index finger.

"Are you sure you want to hear that old story again?"

"Yes, yes," Lize said as she bent to pick the last mushroom. She sat down on a fallen log, set her basket on the ground, and looked up at him in anticipation.

Aleks smiled a half smile, sat down beside her and began. "Mama told me not to take the knife. My grandma gave it to me when I was ten. Mama and my brother Max and I spent that summer with grandma and grandpa at their cottage in the country. The knife had been my Papa's. Closed up, it fit in my palm, so it was easy to hide in my pants pocket. I loved the ridged wood of the handle. And the blade was sharp as could be. My grandpa had honed it on the sharpening stone."

"Papa, the mushroom picking," Lize said, with a smile.

"Yes, yes." Aleks looked around at the trees, composing his thoughts and started again. "For the first time ever, Mama told me it was my job to go mushroom picking the next morning. She said in a stern voice that I was now old enough to go by myself, but I was not old enough to use the pocketknife if I was alone. I slept in my clothes. I kept waking up and got up before anyone else. My brother and I slept on the sun porch on two folding cots. I had to be quiet not to wake Max. I put my shoes on and then accidentally kicked the pail by the door."

Liza laughed, "Papa, this story gets longer every time."

He smiled. "Pail in hand, I went running to the woods. I had forgotten the knife was in my pocket. I tripped on a branch, fell on my side and felt the shape of the knife. I didn't want to waste time taking it back, so I kept going. As the sky lightened, I walked deeper into the forest and found the mushrooms. I wasn't very good at the picking, though, and they kept breaking off at the cap. I knew Mama and Grandma wanted the stems as well and decided it would be easier to use the knife. I opened it and sliced the mushrooms off at the very bottom, next to the dirt. By the time the pail was almost full, I guess I got careless. Somehow my fingers got too close to the bottom of the mushroom and I sliced off the tip of my thumb."

"Can I see?"

Aleks lifted his hand toward her and Lize felt the white scarred area with one finger.

"I was more scared of Mama than of the blood. I couldn't let her find out. And I thought, what would Papa do? What would a brave soldier do? I ripped off a piece of my shirt and wrapped my thumb and tied it tight using my teeth. Soon the white cloth was red. I stood there in the woods and held my hand up high for a long time. Even after the bleeding stopped, my thumb still hurt. With my good hand, I closed the knife and put it back in my pocket. With my bad hand in the air, I finished filling up the pail and I walked home like that too. Until I got close. Then I put the bad hand in my pocket so no one would see. Mama never found out, but I did get in trouble for ripping my shirt."

"You were very brave, Papa," Lize said.

"I don't know about that. Let's find some chanterelles now."

Father and daughter stood up together to continue their search.

Telling Lize the mushroom story took him back to his own childhood. His father had died during World War I. He hadn't died in battle. He died from typhus in a Russian prison camp where hundreds, or maybe thousands, of Latvian soldiers rotted away in one winter's cold, ice, vermin and maybe their own misery. His father's legacy to his family was one war medal and some gambling debts. Aleks' older brother Max died of measles complications the winter after Aleks turned eleven. From then on, he lived under two shadows. One was his father's sacrifice for his country, and the other was his brother's legendary brilliance. Max had been a child prodigy in both music and mathematics. Aleks had to work hard for his marks and didn't stand out in anything. At the age of twelve, his mother sent him away to board at a military school.

Mija was delighted with the full pails Aleks and Lize brought home. That evening, the family enjoyed a hearty beef stew flavored with both kinds of mushrooms. After everyone else was in bed and the radio was turned off, Aleks sat at the living room desk with a glass of vodka. He took a large swallow, flinched as the bitter liquid slid down, picked up his pen and began to write.

THE JOURNAL OF ALEKSANDERS ADAMSONS
27 August 1940

If something happens to me, I want to leave a record. If I survive, I want to keep this for the future. I never want to forget what has happened to our country.

It's been a little over one month since the president was deported. In a sham election, the communist party took over. They've already nationalized the banks and all businesses and confiscated the property of all organizations, including churches. Religious practice is forbidden. All privately owned land exceeding thirty hectares will be broken up and distributed who knows how.

Thank God Mija and I own only five hectares. Thank God Mija went to the bank and withdrew all our savings at the beginning. She put the money in her black wooden jewelry box, the one her father made for her, and we buried it in a far corner of the barn. Her necklaces and bracelets are now in her underwear drawer, underneath, where they can't be seen easily.

How can anyone believe the propaganda that we are better off like this? I am so angry I want to punch something. On the one hand, I can't believe our army didn't put up a fight when they came in. On the other hand, how could we? They bulldozed over us with their tanks and manpower. Does anyone believe that when the war is over we will be free and the Reds will leave? If they do, they are crazy.

Mija doesn't say a lot, and I don't know what to tell her. I don't want to worry her more by telling her what I think and all I know. I've never seen her grow such a big garden, and I've never seen so much canning and drying and storing in preparation for the winter. She keeps her mother and Hortense busy from morning till night. Hortense doesn't have enough time to do her regular chores. Mija's beside herself with it, as though our house will be cut off from the rest of the world soon. Will it?

The Latvian army is being incorporated into the Red Army and it makes me sick. Did my father die for nothing? I don't want to die for nothing. It's hard to know what the right thing is. You need to hold on hard to your own life. If you don't hold on to your purpose, your ideals, is there a reason for living?

The one good thing I see is while the Reds are winning, we won't be bombed. They want our land and our ice-free ports. But the people aren't safe. They're not safe from the secret police. They're not safe from being arrested and deported for any little thing. I know how it is in Russia, and the same has started in Riga— arrests in the middle of the night and deportations to Siberia.

I feel so isolated. I need to do something, find out more than the lies from the radio and newspaper. I can't go back to Riga or I'll face the same fate as President Ulmanis. I'll be arrested and deported. I saw my name on the secret list, the one sitting on General Borsteins' desk when I found his body. His name was also there. I burned the list in the ashtray before I called anyone. I wonder how long it will be until they come looking for me? Why can't I bring myself to tell Mija? Am I protecting her or hurting her? She's not fragile. I've always known that.

I was so happy the day we married. Such a beautiful and strong woman and so independent, nothing like the other girls I knew. My regret now is that I didn't take her to Paris for our honeymoon. I let her talk me into waiting until the summer but she became pregnant with Lize right away and we never went. "We need to save for a house now," Mija said, and I went along with that too.

ALEKS STOPPED WRITING and lit a cigarette, blew the smoke upward, and pushed the chair back from the desk. He finished the vodka in a few short sips and poured another glassful. He took a deep drag on the cigarette and thought about the night he met Mija and how taken he was. He'd been afraid of girls before he met her, preferring the company of his military friends and talking about women rather than talking to them.

Their honeymoon was a weekend at the elegant

Riga Hotel. They had a perfect view of the opera house from their fifth-floor room. He was so afraid, afraid of touching her, not knowing what to do, afraid he wouldn't know how to please her. They got into bed dressed, he in his cotton pajamas, she in her silky, long nightgown. She was so soft in his arms and she smelled so good, like a flower. She wrapped her arms around his neck. His went around her shoulders and they kissed. Soon they removed each other's nightclothes and for Aleks, it seemed natural to explore every part of her body with his hands and his mouth and she did the same with him. He tried to control himself and then she was guiding him on top of her and inside of her and he climaxed and almost screamed but bit his tongue instead. She moaned in pleasure and afterwards, they lay side by side, her head on his shoulder, without any covers on. They pulled the covers up and slept like that, naked, folded within each other. When they woke up the next morning, their arms and legs were still intertwined and they made love again. He decided he was taking her to Paris when the war was over.

He stubbed out the cigarette and wrote:

A shortwave radio would help me learn the truth about what is going on. Tomorrow I will find one and learn how to operate it. That husband of one of the teachers at Mija's school has one. Maybe he can help me get one or make one. I can't remember his name but Mija will know. Why didn't I think of that before? I'm a dummy. I sit here doing nothing. Tomorrow I will do something.

He carried the journal out to the barn and dug a hole in the dirt in the farthest corner, not far from where Mija's jewelry box was buried.

CHAPTER SIX

*T*he days cooled in a stutter as autumn approached. Some were dark and windy, while endless clouds rolled across the sky, bringing raindrops that blew sideways before they found their way to the earth. Other days were hot and sunny, with the heat rising in waves. Crops were ready for harvesting. Farmers still used the old-fashioned method, scything by hand. Neighboring groups of farmers worked together bringing in hay, wheat, barley, oats, and rye. The sunburned men toiled in faded overalls and plaid shirts with their sleeves rolled up. The women, wearing flowered cotton dresses and white aprons, prepared food for the mid-day meal that they ate together.

Ints turned six the last week in August. Mija had a small party for his birthday, inviting Laima and Feliks, her teacher friend Ester along with her husband Edmunds, and a married couple, Harijs and Ilze, that she had grown up with. She also invited Ollie, another childhood friend. Ollie was a bachelor and acted as a second uncle to Mija's children. He always came with presents, often chocolates and oranges, both rare commodities.

Laima baked Ints' favorite cake, chocolate with buttercream icing. Mija made vanilla ice cream. After everyone had their fill of cake with ice cream and fresh strawberries, Ints went outside to play with his present from his parents, a German shepherd puppy he named King. Lize soon followed. The adults settled down on wicker sofas and chairs with their coffee or tea in the large glassed-in sunporch.

Lize sat on the front step. Ints sat on the lawn while the puppy ran around him in circles, stopping now and then to allow Ints to pet him. The dog was Aleks' idea. Mija hadn't wanted to get one.

Aleks had said, "Every boy should have a dog. I always wanted one. It's the best thing for a six-year-old. It'll teach him how to care for another living thing."

"That's true. At the same time, we're occupied. We don't know what's going to happen. We don't know if we'll be starving soon. Another animal is another mouth to feed."

Aleks wouldn't listen to her, and Mija finally gave in.

Mija was brought back to the conversation when she heard Laima say, "I have an announcement." She beamed. Feliks, sitting next to her, had a protective arm around her shoulder.

"We're going to have a baby!"

Mija covered up her shock with a closed mouth smile and said, "That's wonderful. When?"

"In about four months."

Mija said, "You waited so long to tell us. You know how to keep a secret, don't you? That will be around Christmas."

"Just after. Maybe a New Year's baby."

Mija was both happy and sad for her brother and sister-in-law. During the past seven years, Laima had suffered three miscarriages. A new baby during normal times was a wonderful thing. A new baby during wartime was worrisome.

Ilze asked, "Are you hoping for a boy or girl?"

"All I want is a healthy baby."

Feliks rubbed Laima's shoulder and said, "Me too."

Laima was thirty-six, one year older than Mija, and had been getting thicker in the middle the past couple of years. Mija hadn't noticed until now that Laima's rounded belly was holding a baby. Now that she knew, it was obvious. She asked, "Have you thought about names?"

"A little. We'll think more about that closer to the time." Laima patted her stomach. "The baby already started kicking. And I love it."

THE SKY OVER MIJA'S world had not yet been pierced with warplanes. The streets in their town had not yet felt the rumble of tanks. But the news on the radio and in the newspaper left no room for optimism. She kept her small handgun and a box of rounds hidden on the top shelf of her bedroom closet, covered with her oldest sweater. Her father had taught her to shoot as a teenager, both pistols and rifles, but she was more comfortable with the smaller weapon. Mija thought about teaching Lize to shoot but decided she wasn't ready for that kind of responsibility. Maybe next summer.

On the first Saturday in September, Mija, Aleks, and Lize traveled by train the thirty kilometers to Velsaine. Mija and Lize sat side by side while Aleks sat behind them.

Lize asked, "What if the other girls don't like me?"

Mija answered, "You've never had a problem making friends."

"What if I don't like them?"

"There will be plenty of girls. You'll make lots of friends. Don't worry about things before you need to." Mija gave Lize what she hoped was a reassuring pat on the hand.

"If I don't like it, I'm coming home."

"Wait at least three weeks before deciding."

"A week."

"Two."

Lize frowned. "And no more."

Mija thought, I'm glad Aleks is sitting behind us and can't hear this.

The boarding school was a short walk from the

train station, but because of the big suitcase and two smaller bags, they hired a taxicab to drive them to the imposing U-shaped, three-story former castle that sat on a hill at the edge of town. A German Baron had built it in 1879. Many red brick chimneys of varying heights and widths broke the roofline. Below the chimneys, dormer windows sat in a neat row.

For a few hours that Saturday, Mija concentrated on settling her daughter in her new surroundings and refused to think about war. She was pleased with the large room Lize would live in.

"Mama, I don't want to stay here." Lize stood by a bed and crossed her arms.

"You'll be fine," Mija said as she continued to unpack the suitcase and organize clothes in a tall six-drawer chest. Aleks was in the administration office on the ground floor finishing the paperwork. Classrooms were on the second floor, dorm rooms on the third.

Lize's room was painted a cream color; the hardwood floor was stained dark. There were four chests, four single beds, and four nightstands. The light oak furniture was arranged against the walls around the room, leaving the middle open. A green and yellow patterned rug filled the space. Since the room was in a rear corner of the building, there were windows on two walls. Two of the beds were under the shuttered windows. Lize and a girl named Astrid were the first to arrive and each took a window bed. If they stood on the bed, they could look down on the forest that spread out behind the school. Astrid had already unpacked and gone to explore the building.

"And look at this room. I have to live here with three other girls."

"This room is much bigger than your room at home," Mija said. She hugged her daughter and said, "Let's see how you feel in two weeks." Lize wrinkled her straight nose upward and tossed her long brown braids.

The uniforms bothered Mija. Consisting of navy skirts, white blouses, and red scarves, they reminded her of the communist youth group uniforms. The students would start wearing them on Monday, the first day of school. Saturday was moving-in day and Sunday was orientation.

Astrid came skipping in. She was a slight girl with long red hair woven in two braids twisted into buns on each side of her head. Against her pale skin, the freckles on her cheeks and nose looked painted on.

Astrid smiled at Lize and said, "Let's go for a walk."

Mija said, "Go ahead, Lize. I'll finish unpacking."

"Come on," Astrid said, "we can get some ice cream."

On this day, people could still walk to the store and buy ice cream and other sweet treats. There was still enough flour and sugar and milk and cream and eggs.

Mija and Aleks had plans for dinner that evening with Peters and his wife Ingrid. Mija had called Peters the week before. With trepidation, she got the operator's help to find his telephone number and he answered on the second ring. "Hello Mija," he had said. "How nice to hear from you. Yes, it's terrible what has happened. No, I don't know what I'm going to do now. Wait and see, I suppose."

Dinner was at the Black Cat Restaurant located on one corner of the town square. The sign above the door was a black metal cat looking down, tail raised in a half curl. The hostess said, "Follow me. The rest of your party is already here." She led Mija and Aleks through the main dining room into a back room that was small and cozy, holding several tables and chairs. A painting of an impressionist sunset hung above the fireplace. Peters and Ingrida were seated with another couple at a table for six. Mija was relieved to see the strangers. She had worried about the four of them sitting and talking, certain it would be awkward. Mija had told Aleks that Peters was a childhood friend and had not gone into detail, nor had Aleks asked. The third couple turned out to be Astrid's parents.

Peters explained that he remembered after Mija's phone call that Astrid, who lived in the town, would also be going to the boarding school, so he invited her parents to join them. "Klara and Leo own the best clothing store outside of Riga."

Klara said, "You're too kind, Peters."

The conversation flowed around Mija as she studied the others. Peters, about an inch over six feet tall, wore a serviceable but worn gray suit and blue striped tie. Aleks, at five-ten, was slightly taller than

Mija. He sat straight and stiff in his brown suit and solid brown tie. Ingrida had blond hair with dark eyes, slanted eyebrows, and high cheekbones, an unusual combination. Could there be Tartar in her background? Klara and Leo were intriguing in that they were older looking with light hair. Mija wondered how they had a daughter with red hair.

"What do you think, Mija?" said Aleks. Mija heard the last word, her name. She gave him a look she hoped said "Help me out."

Peters said, "I doubt if Mija likes that painting at all."

"You're right." She smiled. "Impressionists are interesting, and that's a lovely painting, but I wouldn't buy one for my home."

Mija concentrated on the conversation the rest of the evening and hardly tasted her food. The subject of war and occupation didn't come up. Everyone knew that talking about these things in public could get a person arrested later.

By the end of the evening, Mija found out why Astrid didn't look like her parents. Astrid was the daughter of a young couple who had worked as a cook and horse trainer on the estate of Leo's parents. Neither had living relatives. The mother died giving birth. The father fell into a deep depression and was unable to care for the little girl. Leo and Klara, unable to have children of their own, offered to adopt the baby and told her father he would be welcome to visit any time. But soon after signing his child over, he left the area and was never heard from again.

THE FOLLOWING WEEK, the public schools opened. As she had for the past ten years, Mija would teach history at the town's only elementary school. Ints would be in the first class. Two new teachers, both communists, were brought in from Russia. They spoke limited Latvian and spoke Russian to each other. A rumor went around that another communist would replace the principal soon. Still another one was that next year they would all be required to speak Russian and use Russian textbooks.

MIJA AND INTS ARRIVED home from school one day toward the end of September. Ints, as usual, went outside to play with King, and Mija went through the mail her mother had left on the desk in the living room. She ripped open the letter from Lize and devoured the straight rows of black ink words.

Dear Mama and Papa,

Astrid is very nice and so is Edita, but I can't stand Dagmar. She thinks she knows everything. Some of the teachers are strange, especially Miss Kronberga. She's a chubby lady with a lisp. Her teeth stick out and she spits when she talks. Some of the girls whisper that she is a communist and to be careful what we say. She's in charge of a play we're putting on next month. I'm going to be in it. They keep us busy from morning until night. We even have to sit and do homework every evening after dinner. I miss you.

Lize

Thank God, Lize is fine. Maybe I made the right decision to send her there. But still, a communist teacher and impressionable young minds. And what kind of play are they putting on? Propaganda?

She sat down at the desk and wrote a letter back, asking lots of questions, including one about the play. She censored her words in case the letters were opened and checked. All mail sent to the students went to the main office first. Someone could easily go through it.

When Lize comes home for Christmas, I will explain to her about being careful what she writes.

CHAPTER SEVEN

*I*t had been snowing for weeks, the fluffy kind that piled up fast and blew into big drifts. Even the trees looked like they were made of snow.

Because the Soviets had banned religion and holidays, churches were closed and the cemeteries next to the churches were all but abandoned. Only the very old or those staring death in the face themselves visited their loved ones buried there. Any celebrating was done inside, in secret. The windows were covered with dark draperies or taped with black paper so that any passerby who might be a party member or a snitch wouldn't see a lit candle or smiling face. Any presents would be homemade, as store shelves were empty.

At Laima and Feliks' farm, in the living room of the two-story log cabin they had built and lived in since they were married, a sparse three-foot pine branch was fastened upright on a stand inside the painted wooden wardrobe usually reserved for coats. The branch was not decorated but there were presents tied to it for Lize and Ints, an apple for each and some hard candies Laima had made. Without careful rationing, there would not have been any candy. But even so, Laima only had a quarter cup of sugar left. She'd been working all day today, Christmas Eve, making the food for dinner, which included the traditional peas, beans, and barley sausage. There wouldn't be a pig's head this year; they were saving the pig until they were in absolute need.

Mija was bringing gingerbread cookies. She had used the last of her sugar for this special treat. Gingerbread cookies were one of the few things she enjoyed baking. As good as she was with gardening, she didn't like cooking much, except for stews. She would throw in a little of this and a little of that, using up leftovers and adding a few fresh vegetables or meat, depending on what was available.

Winter in Latvia meant that day blackened into night by midafternoon. A multitude of white stars and a low silver moon lighted their way. Mija sat beside Aleks in the front seat of a large sleigh that had been passed down through several generations of her family. The sleigh was painted in a green and yellow design depicting the ancient Latvian signs of the sun, moon, and stars.

Mija gripped the tin of cookies as Aleks spurred the horse to go faster. Sitting in the back seat, Lize and Ints howled with delight as the sleigh flew over the snow-covered road. Their grandmother, Anete, sitting between the children, covered her eyes with one mittened hand and clutched the edge of her seat with the other. The bells on the horse jingled in time to the clip-clop of his hooves.

They reached the farm and Aleks stopped the horse midway between the house and barn. The passengers clomped through the trampled snow path to the front door while Aleks unbridled Big Z. Mija breathed in the crisp air and exhaled a streaming white cloud. Her cheeks were redder than they'd been in months.

A beaming Feliks greeted them at the front door. "Come in, come in. Merry Christmas!" The children stamped their feet before entering and Mija inspected each set of boots. On her approval, they entered, removed their boots, set them in a row beside the door, and walked in their wool socks. The women did the same and they all handed their coats to Feliks. Laima waddled in from the kitchen.

"It smells wonderful," said Mija. "Here." She handed the tin to Feliks.

He said, "Cookies?" Mija nodded. He started to open it. "I think I'll have a taste."

Laima said, "Then we'd have to give one to the children right now too. Let's wait until after dinner, silly goose."

Feliks took the cookies and coats to the kitchen, hanging the coats on hooks beside the back door.

"Where's the tree?" asked Ints, looking around

the living room.

Lize gave him a look as if he was rude to ask such a question.

Laima opened the wardrobe door to reveal the hidden treasure. Both children jumped up and down and clapped in glee.

Before they could ask, Laima said, "The treats are for the two of you. Go ahead, you can take them down."

As Mija hugged Laima, she noticed her sweaty face and damp back. "How are you feeling?"

"Well, I've been on my feet all day, so they're a little swollen, and my back hurts." She put one hand on her lower back and grimaced.

"Could you be in labor?" asked Mija.

"The baby's not due for another week."

Mija said, "My labor was in the front, but I've heard the pains can be in the back too. You should sit down."

Anete chimed in. "My labor was in the back all three times."

Mija put her hands on Laima's shoulders and steered her to the big chair that Feliks liked to relax in. Laima's ankles were so swollen that her legs went straight down into her feet. Mija pulled off Laima's shoes.

"Ah, that feels better," said Laima as she wiggled her toes and clasped her hands over her belly.

"What did the doctor say last time?" Mija asked.

Laima moaned and held her lower back with both

hands. Lize stood nearby watching quietly. Ints was already eating a piece of candy.

"I haven't been to the doctor since September. The fee is too high. We'll get the midwife when the time comes." Laima stretched out her legs. "You still have your teaching job. All we have is our farm, and we got a notice that most of our land will be split up in the spring. I don't know how we'll survive." Beads of sweat were prominent on Laima's forehead.

Mija frowned. "Why didn't you tell me? We would have helped."

Laima shrugged. Just then Feliks and Aleks entered. They looked so serious that Mija assumed they'd been talking about the war. Aleks was obsessed with his short wave radio. He had set up the unit in a corner of the hayloft and fashioned an antenna on the barn roof, disguising it with an abandoned stork's nest. The radio, sitting on a makeshift wood plank desk, along with an old wooden chair, were hidden behind several bales of hay. He spent every day there and kept records in some kind of journal that he wouldn't let her read. He did tell Mija that hundreds of people in the bigger cities were disappearing every month. Some were killed. The luckier ones were exiled. Unheated cattle cars took them to the frozen Siberian wastelands. He also told her they were better off staying where they were and not making trouble with the authorities.

Mija timed Laima's pains, but they were irregular and then stopped.

Laima said, "Let's eat now. Everything is prepared."

Mija said, "That's a good idea, but you stay put. I'll bring you a plate."

"I'm not hungry."

"Then I'll bring you some apple cider."

Mija and Anete set up a buffet on the rectangular pine kitchen table. Everyone filled their plates with more food than usual and spread out in the living room. Feliks tended the crackling fire and the room was warm. Ints went back for more. He was growing so fast that his pants were too short. Mija didn't know where she would get him bigger ones.

Laima's pains started again. Mija was sure this was labor but said nothing, not wanting to alarm anyone. The men chatted about the cold weather and walked around the room in a circle. Ints followed them, eating his apple. Lize sat on the floor by the wardrobe, playing with her little pile of candies. Anete was inert on her spot next to Mija on the sofa.

All of a sudden Laima said, in a low voice, "Mija, come here." Mija bent her head down close to hear her better. "It's getting worse and now the pain is both in the front and the back."

"Nu, let's time the pains."

Mija sent the men and children to the barn with the apple cores to give the horses a treat. She sent Anete to the kitchen to clear up the food and wash the dishes. Mija talked in a calm voice about her own birthing labors. Mija tracked the time using the minute hand on her watch. The fire crackled and spit. The pains were five minutes apart.

Laima held one hand on each side of her stomach, "I can hardly stand the pain."

Mija said, "Relax, breathe in and out, in and out, and think about something else."

"I can't." Laima's face was covered in sweat.

Mija yelled toward the kitchen, "Mama, go get Feliks." Anete came running in for her boots and yanked them on. She ran out the door without a coat.

"When did the pains first start?"

"I don't know. I first noticed the backache yesterday morning when I woke up. I didn't think it was labor."

"If you've been in labor that long, the baby may be coming. But it's hard to tell with first babies."

The others came running in helter-skelter. Mija told Aleks to take the children home. She added a firm "Now." Aleks promised them hot chocolate. Feliks ran to the telephone on the little table in a corner of the living room to call the midwife. The line was dead. He had no choice but to hook up a horse to his sleigh for the trip into town to fetch her.

Laima moaned, "I feel something wet." Her face was white.

"Maybe your water broke. Mine did with Ints. Nothing to worry about. Let's move into the maid's room." Laima had given up her maid right after the occupation began. They couldn't afford to feed an extra mouth. The small room was on the first floor, behind the kitchen.

As Mija helped Laima stand up, clear liquid gushed

down her legs and onto the floor. Laima's knees buckled and Mija held her up by one elbow as she yelled for Anete. Anete ran in from the kitchen, and on Mija's orders, held Laima's other elbow. Mija led them through the living room, then the kitchen, and into the bedroom. A single bed stood against the longer wall. With her free hand, Mija grabbed the edge of the blanket and threw it toward the foot.

"Let's get you settled." She eased Laima into a sitting position. "Mama, bring me a nightgown and some clean sheets."

Laima said, "My nightgowns are in the top right drawer of the big dresser."

Anete left without a word, her face expressionless, as if she had turned into something mechanical.

"Oh, help me. God help me," Laima moaned.

"What is it?"

"I want to push, my stomach is pushing down."

"Try to relax." She didn't want to frighten Laima so said nothing yet. In Mija's own experience, when she felt like pushing, the baby was about to come out. *Why did I wait so long to tell Feliks to get the midwife?* She helped Laima lie down. *Why isn't my mother back?*

"Do you mind if I take a look? I need to see if the head is crowning."

Laima nodded. Mija saw a circular dark something. "I see the head. It's okay to push. Squeeze my hand."

Laima screamed and Mija winced at the crushing pressure on her hand. *I don't know what to do. Where is*

Feliks with the midwife?

Between screams, Laima panted. "My stomach is pushing itself. What's wrong?"

"Nothing, your baby's ready to be born. Let it happen." Mija wiped Laima's face with an edge of the sheet. "Good Laima, good. The baby's head is coming."

Laima's screams turned into moans. Mija removed Laima's hand from her own so she could position herself better. The baby's head slid out and the body soon followed. She had reddish-blue skin, a full head of black hair, and her eyes were tightly shut.

Mia said, "What a beautiful girl." She turned her head to the door and yelled as loud as she dared. "Mama, whatever you're doing, stop, I need scissors. And a piece of rope or string." With her fingers, Mija cleaned mucous out of the little one's mouth. The baby moved her arms. Then she kicked her legs and let out a tiny wail. Anete came running in with scissors but no rope or string. She said, "I left the nightgown in the kitchen."

"Rip a piece of sheet."

Laima said, "Extra sheets are in the wardrobe, right over there."

Anete found one, made a cut and ripped off a long piece.

"It still hurts, I need to push again."

Mija said, "No. Relax. No more pushing. It's all over."

"It hurts even more." The baby started crying.

Mija felt the paralysis of indecision. She cut the umbilical cord in a daze. At least she knew how to do that. And she held the crying, naked baby.

She examined Laima. Something else was coming, but not a baby's head. *Oh my god. Can it be? Is that a baby's bottom? A second one and breech? God almighty. I can't do this. I must do this. How can I? I'm not a doctor for god's sake. Why didn't we send for the midwife earlier?* "Hold on, Laima. Hold on."

A memory came back. *There was a breech birth Zana witnessed in the hospital, and she talked a lot about it.* Zana was her roommate in Riga while Mija studied to be a teacher. *Come on, remember. Zana talked about it for weeks. I should have been paying better attention. Something about the position of the woman. Yes, they made her take a very strange position to get the baby out.*

As she thought about how to proceed, she told Anete to get a towel. Anete ran out and was back in moments. With the towel, Mija wrapped the baby and handed the bundle to Anete. "Go to the living room. Sit by the fire, hold her close, and sing to her. Bring her back if there's a problem, if she stops breathing. Don't take your eyes off the baby." Anete cradled the infant and walked slowly, cooing.

Laima yelled, "What's wrong?"

Mija moved a little closer to Laima and asked, "Did anyone tell you there might be two babies?"

"No. Oh my god."

Where was Feliks with the midwife? Mija sat down on the edge of the bed. She took Laima's hand between

66

her own. "Listen closely. There is another baby and it's breech." She stroked Laima's hand. "But it's going to be okay."

Laima sobbed, "I . . . I can't do this."

"You have to. I'm here. I know what to do. Remember me talking about my nurse friend Zana?"

Laima nodded slightly, tears streaming.

"She assisted at a breech birth and told me all about it. Have you ever seen a cow give birth?"

"Of course," Laima grumbled. "I grew up on a farm. But this is different. The pain is too much. I'm going to die." She turned her face to the wall and screamed some more.

Mija continued stroking Laima's hand and waited for the screaming to let up.

"You're not going to die. Look at me. You must follow my instructions."

"Why did I want a baby anyway? No one told me labor would hurt this much." Laima screamed again.

Mija couldn't think of anything comforting to say. But something had to be done about this second baby and fast. "You can scream all you want in a minute but right now, pay attention."

Mija stood up. "Turn around and get up on all fours, like that cow. Here, I'll help you." She put her hands on Laima's shoulders.

"I can't," Laima cried. And then she let out a low guttural scream. Mija rolled Laima onto her side.

Laima screamed, "I can't."

"Yes, you can." Mija's used firm pressure to turn

Laima further. "Get up on your hands and knees. Now. Get up."

Laima managed to get on her knees, then on her elbows. She screamed again and then groaned, "Oh, God, please make it stop!"

"Try to relax."

Laima lowered her head to the mattress.

"Can you lift your head up?"

"No. Oh God, make the pain go away."

Mija lifted Laima's head so she could slide a pillow under her forehead. The higher she could get Laima's head, the better. Or at least that's what she guessed. She prayed she was doing it right.

"Oh God, please let this be over. Let me die." Then Laima screamed into the pillow.

Mija prayed silently and moved to the foot of the bed to see if anything had changed. The buttocks had moved out a little. Oh God, how am I going to get her through this? *I'm not a doctor. What if Laima dies from my stupidity? No. I will get this baby out. And Laima will not die.*

Laima screamed and panted. "The pain is too much!"

As gently as possible, Mija eased the baby's buttocks out a tiny bit and then a tiny bit more. Intent on her mission, she barely heard Laima's screaming and moaning. After what seemed like an eternity, the buttocks were most of the way out.

Now what? Now what do I do? God help me, what do I do now?

As if in answer to her prayer, the buttocks moved

out all the way and then the tiny legs popped out. Laima screamed again, even louder and longer.

Oh my god, I have to get this baby out.

Without thinking further, Mija moved the lower body slightly toward Laima's stomach. Mija wanted to yank the baby out but told herself that wasn't right. She had to let it happen naturally.

"You're doing well, Laima. Push, one more push and this will be over."

Laima let out another long wail. Her voice was hoarse. Then the head slid out and Mija, still praying, caught the baby. This one was even smaller than the first one.

Mija heard Feliks yell from the kitchen, "We're here."

"Back here," she yelled as she cleaned out the mouth of the second baby. This one opened her eyes right away, scrunched up her mouth, and yowled. Relieved, Mija put the baby down and let her cry.

Laima was still panting. Mija said, "Are you all right?"

"I don't know. I feel like I'm in a nightmare. I'm tired. I want to sleep. I want to get up. I don't know what I want."

"All right. Breathe in and out. It's over. You did a wonderful job. It's another girl and she's just as beautiful as the first one. Turn around and lie down. But be careful. I'll help you. Wait, no, I don't know how to turn you with the baby still attached. Let's wait. You can lower your legs and rest." Laima's hair was matted with sweat and the bedclothes were soaked.

The midwife, Rasma, walked in followed by Feliks, holding the first baby. Anete was behind Feliks, carrying the nightgown Mija had asked for earlier.

"Wha . . .?" Feliks said, staring at the baby between Laima's legs.

Mija nodded. "Yes, two. The second one was breech."

Rasma said, "Goodness! How did you know what to do?"

"I'll explain later." Mija sighed. "I think God helped me."

Rasma took several instruments and a flannel blanket out of her bag. She cut the cord on the second baby. Then Rasma swaddled the tiny infant in the blanket and handed her to Mija. She told Feliks to heat water to lukewarm in a big pot and told Mija and Anete to wipe the babies all over with the warm water and then wrap them up again in something clean. Rasma helped Laima turn around and lie down on her back.

Laima cried quietly. "I have clothes in the nursery. Did I really have two? Did you say two girls? We only have one name. I'm so tired. But I want to hold my babies. Please."

Mija said, "Don't worry, we'll bring them to you in a few minutes. What a blessing, two beautiful babies, and on Christmas Eve."

Rasma said, "Christmas Day. It's after midnight."

Mija said, "Wonderful, even better. Tomorrow, or rather later today, I'll bring more clothes. I saved them from Lize and Ints. I have several boxes."

What Mija didn't say was that she was saving them for her own grandchildren. That was a fleeting thought and she felt guilty for thinking such a thing. She would think about today, not tomorrow, and be thankful that Laima and the babies were alive.

CHAPTER EIGHT

Aleks sat on the straight wooden chair at the plank desk in a corner of the hayloft. The shortwave radio was silent. He pulled the wool blanket tighter around his shoulders. Today was the first day of May, but this morning the temperature outside was almost as cold as winter. He fingered the edges of the pages as he reread some previous entries.

2 JANUARY 1941

The christening of the twins was yesterday. Pastor Ziedonis came to Feliks' farm since we are forbidden to go to church. They can't stop us from practicing our beliefs in our own homes. Not unless someone tells. Then the secret police come and arrest you and take you away in a black van.

We stood in the living room in front of the

fireplace. Just our two families were there, Feliks and Laima, Mija and me, and Lize and Ints and Anete. Laima's family lives far away, close to Ventspils on the coast. Mija and I are the Godparents. I held the quiet one, and Mija rocked the crying one while the pastor said the words of blessing and anointed their foreheads with water. Their names are Rita Lizebete and Ruta Lizebete. They are so tiny, they look like dolls. Mine felt lighter than a doll. She was so still that I kept looking at her chest to make sure she was breathing.

Afterwards, we shared a one-layer cake the size of a tart. Laima said she made the biggest she could with her last bit of sugar. For our gift, Mija and I brought dried mushrooms, two jars of strawberry jam, and a jar of honey. Anete took apart one of her afghans and knitted the twins matching sweaters and hats.

Food is scarce. I don't know how we will last the winter, even with all the extra things Mija canned and dried last summer. The vegetable cellar won't last either except maybe the turnips. I'm the only one who likes turnips. Even Ints, who eats anything, doesn't like them.

15 JANUARY 1941

The rumor is that another 300 were deported from Riga to Siberia and another 100 jailed. The prisons must be overflowing. I feel helpless, but if I show my face anywhere and am stopped, I will be arrested.

10 FEBRUARY 1941

More deportations, another 200 from Liepaja. My old army friend, Colonel Andres Ezers, was arrested last week. We were promoted to Colonel at the same time. He doesn't have a family and stayed in Riga after the occupation. What would I do without the shortwave radio? I keep a log at the back of this journal. One list is of how many deported on which dates and another list is of those I know are dead with their names and dates of death. I wonder when they'll come looking for me.

24 MARCH 1941

Mija came back from visiting Laima so disheartened. She doesn't think the twins are growing as they should and says Laima is getting too skinny. Well, Mija is getting too skinny, too, and so is everyone else. We eat every day, three meals, but the portions are too small. The cow stopped giving milk last week, we don't know why. She's been giving less and less. We probably have to kill her because we also have the two horses to feed. It's a good thing the dog doesn't eat much. Ints takes such good care of King. My poor son is growing taller but skinnier by the day. He gets the biggest rations, but they are still not enough. His skin looks gray. His two front teeth fell out, baby teeth, so he whistles when he talks. He has pants that are long enough now. Mija started a clothing exchange in the school. The pants are too big in the waist, but he cinches his belt tightly. His shirts are long in the arms, so he rolls the cuffs up. He looks like one of those orphans I used to see on the streets of Riga.

1 APRIL 1941

I hope the Germans beat the Russians and win the war. War is being fought everywhere else in the world. Here we are merely occupied and strangled. Another 350 deported yesterday. When will they stop? When there are no more Latvians?

I don't know how Mija can go to school every day and teach history. The principal was replaced with a communist last week, a portly man from St. Petersburg, she said. He has a gold front tooth. Mija keeps teaching so that nothing is suspicious about us. The money is worthless, and besides, we cannot buy anything because the store shelves are empty. Within months after the occupation, the Russians had taken whatever we had and loaded up trucks that drove straight to the border. And in our small town, there is very little black market. We would have to go to Riga for that. The bakery is open, but sometimes the people wait in line all day for nothing. Then they go back the next day and wait again.

We have rationed our own flour well, I think. We have enough for a number of weeks yet. Thank goodness for the additional flour Feliks gave us last fall. Either Hortense or Anete bakes a loaf of bread once a week. Still, we don't have enough for the five of us.

10 APRIL 1941

If Lize was not away at school, we would be out of food. Her letters come punctually once a week. Lize complains about the small rations in one sentence, but then in the next sentence she says she has enough. She assures us she is not starving. Mija writes cheery letters back.

What I wouldn't give for a spoonful of jam or honey. But there is none for the adults. Mija gave much of her supply to Laima to help keep her strength up so she could keep nursing the babies. The rest is for Ints.

I don't like turnips so much anymore. I hope we have an early spring. This year I will help Mija with her garden. She has so many seeds dried and waiting from last year, we should triple the garden. Or more. We will plant as many seeds as we have, even if all five hectares are used up. I'll become a farmer, plant wheat and barley like Feliks, and we will become self-sufficient. The people in the towns and cities must be even hungrier than we are.

ALEKS STOPPED READING. He picked up his empty cigarette case, opened it, closed it, and slammed it down. He smoked his last cigarette months ago. He drummed his fingers on the desk. No more vodka, either. And no coffee, just chicory or very weak tea, a whole pot made with just a few leaves.

I must be crazy, writing all these things down. If anyone finds this, my family will be in jeopardy. But the writing is all I have. I have to keep writing my truth. Besides, we're in danger no matter what as long as the Russians are here. If the Germans ever come to Latvia to fight, I'm going to join them. Any chance I get to fight against the communists, I will take it. I will kill as many communists as I can.

He picked up his pen and wrote:

1 MAY 1941

Ints lost three more teeth in the last two weeks. Mija says at least they are baby teeth. The new teeth have not come in yet, so between his clothes and his mouth, he looks like a little old man. I gave him my father's pocketknife to cheer him up, but he didn't seem interested and left it on the kitchen table. He's not doing very well in school, Mija says. None of us are doing well. Who can do well when they are hungry? The sky is almost always gray. Will there be a spring and summer this year? Every day I look for a stork to come and settle on our barn roof for good luck, but so far nothing.

ALEKS PUT DOWN HIS PEN and sighed. He was so tired. He thought about Mija and how she always kept her spirits up. *When was the last time Mija and I were close? Months ago, maybe right after Christmas? Well, it would take too much energy. After the summer crops are in and we have enough food to eat, and we are not hungry, then I will take Mija in my arms and kiss her and hug her and we will be together again.*

Should I write about the partisans? No, I don't dare. I should tell Mija, though. I took a chance and went to town that day last week. I couldn't get any food. Everyone was skinny like us and had dark circles under their eyes. The good part is that I ran into Harijs. He even had black market tobacco and cigarette papers and rolled them himself. We sat on a bench in a corner of the park where no one could hear us and smoked cigarettes. I got dizzy after the months without tobacco. Harijs is part of something called the Home Guard, and a group of them has been hiding weapons and rounds in the woods. They're planning an uprising against the communists the minute there is an opportunity. I hope and pray that the Germans come and rescue us. In the meantime, I'm going to join the Home Guard. The next meeting is tomorrow night. Finally, I'm going to do something. Should I tell Mija or make up a lie? I will tell her. That way, if I disappear, she'll know why.

The shortwave radio started making noises and he reached for his headphones.

CHAPTER NINE

*L*ize heard a train whistle in the distance and ran faster. She'd been running for over twenty minutes, all the way from Asja's house. She kept checking behind her as though someone was chasing her. She ran around the next corner and reached the lane to her home.

MIJA STOPPED PRUNING her rose bushes to wipe her brow with the back of her hand. At that moment, she saw her daughter come running around the corner. She threw the shears into the dirt, and as she ran to meet Lize, pulled off her gardening gloves and stashed them in her apron pocket.

"Mama, no, not here, in the house!"

Mija could see how frantic Lize was. She took her hand and they ran together. Inside the front door, Lize said, "Lock it!" Mija turned the bolt.

"What happened?" Mija asked.

Mija put her hands on Lize's shoulders. Lize gasped for air and started to cry, then sob. Mija reached around her daughter's shoulders and pulled her close. Lize sobbed in great big hiccups. Mija felt Lize's racing heart. *This isn't how it's supposed to be. These are the long days of summer, the days we should be enjoying the vast sky and the green grasses. We should be swimming in the lake, having picnics, making daisy chains. Instead, we are virtual prisoners in our own homes. Maybe I shouldn't have let Lize go out today. No bombs in Gulepils, it's easy to get complacent, even when you're hungry. No more!*

She took Lize onto the sunporch and sat her down on the wicker sofa. Mija took off her gardening apron. She pulled a handkerchief from her dress pocket, sat down next to Lize, and wiped her daughter's eyes. Lize's breath came out in ragged jerks, and she stared wide-eyed out the windows that covered three sides of the room.

"Okay, now tell me what happened," said Mija.

"We were in the barn."

"You and Asja?"

Lize nodded, "Yes."

"Then what?"

"They came." Lize wrung her hands. Another sob welled up.

"Who came?"

"Soldiers, Mama, soldiers."

Mija put a hand on Lize's shoulder, as much to

ground herself as to reassure her daughter. "Russians?"

"Yes! They took them!" Lize clenched her fists.

Mija fought to keep air in her lungs. She was twelve years old again and hiding in the potato cellar. Everything was dark. *No, I will not think about that. I am not a child, but Lize is. I must protect her.* She focused on Lize's face and brought herself back to the present. She put an arm around her daughter's shoulders. "I won't let anyone hurt you. Who did they take?"

"Her parents. Asja. Asja was barefoot. You know how she hates to wear shoes." Lize dropped her hands into her lap. Tears ran down her cheeks.

"You're safe now. Tell me everything." Mija rubbed Lize's shoulder.

"Where's Papa? The others?" Lize kept staring out the windows.

"Papa took Ints fishing. Grandma and Hortense are in the kitchen."

"Get Papa and Ints back. Get them home."

"Yes, of course, you're right."

Her daughter's insistence impelled her into action. The rest of the story could wait. She took Lize into the kitchen and told her mother and Hortense to make Lize some tea and toast and wait for her to return. Mija ran upstairs into her bedroom and pulled her handgun and rounds from the closet shelf. She loaded the gun, slipped it into one pocket and the box of rounds into the other.

What if they aren't at the lake? What if the soldiers got them? Don't be absurd. Soldiers couldn't have gone to the lake without passing by the house. In the distance she heard a plaintive train whistle.

"WE GOT ONE!" Aleks yelled as he helped Ints reel in the silver fish. "The fish are back!"

"Stop yelling." The words shot out from Mija as she reached them. Ints' dog came running over to her. She absentmindedly petted his head and said, "You have to come home."

Aleks looked askance at Mija as he took the fish off the hook and dropped it in the basket. "What's the matter?" he asked.

"Look, Mama," Ints held up the basket. "I caught a fish."

"That's good but it's time to go. You've been out way too long." Aleks opened his mouth to speak, but Mija looked at him with her eyes open wide, and he closed his lips tightly.

Mija hurried them home without an explanation. She didn't want to alarm Ints. Instead she talked to her son as if nothing out of the ordinary happened. "You did a fine job, Ints. We'll cook your fish tonight." King came along obediently, staying close to Ints.

As they neared the house, Ints said, "Go, King. Go wait for me in the barn." The dog looked up at Ints, who nodded his head, and King obeyed.

Inside the house, Mija shooed Ints upstairs to wash. "Scrub your hands well. Make sure to get rid of the fish smell, then change your clothes and come down to the kitchen."

As soon as Ints was up the stairs Aleks whispered, "What's going on?"

"In the kitchen, you can wash up at the sink."

Lize was calmer, sitting with red-rimmed eyes, nibbling on the last of her toast. Mija asked her to tell them what happened at Asja's. Lize spoke in a monotone as though describing something she was watching.

"Asja and I were in the barn playing with a newborn calf when we heard a loud engine. We ran to the barn door and peeked out. There was a black van. Two soldiers got out and went to the house and banged on the door with their rifles. Asja's father opened the door and her mother was right behind him and the rifles were pointed at their heads. 'Out,' screamed one soldier and pushed her father, then her mother with his rifle. He shoved them to the back of the van. Other people were already in there and some soldiers too. The one in charge yelled, 'Where's the brat? Tell me or I'll shoot you!' Asja screamed and ran out. I ran to the back of the barn and hid behind bales of straw. I heard doors slam and the van drove away. I waited a while, I don't know how long, to make sure they wouldn't come back, and then I ran home."

Lize's chest heaved with each breath.

Aleks paced around the small kitchen and said, "Don't be scared, Lize." Ints skipped in and almost bumped into his father. "Scared of what?" he asked.

Mija said, "Staying overnight in the barn at Aunt

Laima's. She wants you both to go for a visit and help plant her garden tomorrow."

"You big baby," Ints laughed and pointed at his sister. Lize gave him a withering look and drank the last sip of her tea.

"Go on, you two," Mija said. "Go upstairs and put some clothes together for a stay at the farm."

"What about the fish?" Ints asked. "I'm hungry."

"We'll bring it along," said Mija.

"Can King come?"

"Sorry, Ints. Not this time."

"Aw, please Mama?"

"Next time."

"Promise?"

"Yes."

"Okay."

Ints bolted out the kitchen door. Lize trailed after him.

"You'll stay with them, too, Mija," Aleks said. "While you pack, I'll call Feliks."

"What about Hortense and me?" asked Anete.

"I'll come back for you after I take the children," said Mija. "Pack enough clothes for a week and pack food too."

ALEKS WATCHED THE HORSE and carriage from the sunporch. His insides turned upside down. He wanted a cigarette, which he didn't have. He wanted a drink, which he also didn't have. He wanted to do something but could think of nothing. The horse and carriage became smaller until they were a dot and then disappeared. A few minutes later he heard an engine. Then he saw the black car with four people in it, pulling into their lane.

A RUSSIAN SOLDIER IN AN ill-fitting brown uniform and scuffed boots banged on the front door with the butt of his rifle and yelled, "Monkeys, get out here!" The three other soldiers stood behind him, rifles pointed at the door.

At the back of the house, Aleks slipped his slight body through the kitchen window, crouched down low and ran for the woods behind the barn. Anete scurried to the front door as Hortense closed the window behind Aleks and then followed her mistress.

Anete opened the door. "What do you want?" Her hand gripped the doorknob.

"Where's the colonel? And his wife and two brats." The soldier lifted his rifle and pointed at Anete's face. The other soldiers, standing behind him, also had their rifles trained on her.

"They're not here." Anete let go of the doorknob and stepped closer to the soldiers. She looked at the first one, right into his black eyes. "We're just two old women here."

The soldier scowled. "Too bad old hags aren't on my list."

Hortense stood in the doorway, crossing herself

and talking softly, "Dear God, please help us—"

"Shut up in there," the soldier yelled. To Anete he said, "Get over where my men can watch you." He waved the rifle toward the soldiers behind him. Anete walked silently, stopped in front of the trio, put her hands together, and turned her back to them. The lead soldier ordered two of the others to stand guard over her and the third to come with him.

"You," he yelled at Hortense, "take us around."

The soldiers overturned all the furniture. One soldier used his rifle butt to smash the glass face of the clock on the fireplace mantle. Hortense kept a tight grip on her small gold necklace. Her other hand was rolled into a fist.

"Where are they?" the lead soldier asked.

"They went to Jurmala yesterday," Hortense lied as she led them up the stairs.

In the master bedroom, the soldiers emptied every dresser drawer onto the floor. They stuffed Mija's jewelry into their pockets. They went through the other two bedrooms and then Anete's attic bedroom, ransacking the drawers but finding nothing of value. The lead soldier told Hortense to let go of her necklace so he could see it. "Too small. You keep it." He pushed Hortense back down the stairs and into the kitchen. Their rifles stayed pointed at her back as she packed all the food, a small bag of flour, a jar half full of chicory, and two jars of dried mushrooms into a box. With the tip of a rifle prodding her back, she carried the wooden box out the front door.

A "ruff-ruff" came from the barn and King bounded out into the sunlight, wagging his tail. The lead soldier lifted his rifle and shot. King fell, blood pouring from his neck. His body twitched twice and then was still. The lead soldier pointed to two of his comrades and told them to check the barn. He made Hortense walk to the back of the car and he followed her. He made her open the trunk and put the box of provisions inside. Then he used the butt of his rifle against her back to push her over to Anete.

"Put your hands up." He waved his rifle upward.

The soldiers came out from the barn and walked around the dead dog. One said, "Nothing in there but a skinny horse." The lead soldier said, "Check the wooded area behind the barn."

Tears mingled with sweat dripped down Hortense's face. Anete's face was white and bone dry. Gunshots rang out. Both women's arms stayed up. Hortense's hands trembled visibly.

When the soldiers returned, one said, "If he's there, I think we at least wounded him."

Another asked, "Did you see anything?"

"Movement in some bushes. We shot and then looked but didn't find anything except this." He held up a brown shoe. Anete's eyes widened. The soldier threw the shoe, which landed next to the dog's head.

Before they got back in the car, the lead soldier said to the women, "You tell that monkey colonel he can't hide from us. We'll be back. With hunting dogs." Then he shot into the air above their heads. Hortense

89

jumped. Anete stood still as a statue. "Next time, we'll shoot you too."

The black car roared away. Hortense followed Anete into the house.

"My God, what are we going to do?" Hortense put her hands together in a plea to the Almighty.

"That's right. Pray," Anete said. She uprighted her favorite chair, the one covered in rose chintz, and moved it to its proper spot next to the fireplace.

"Dear God, please help us."

"While you're praying, go bury the dog behind the barn, then cover the blood with straw."

Anete went to the black telephone on the desk in the living room and told the operator she wanted number 92, which was Laima and Felix's number. Laima answered and said Mija was on her way home. Anete explained what happened in as few words as possible. Laima promised to hide the children in the hayloft. Moments after Anete hung up the phone, Mija arrived and Anete recounted the story one more time.

As her mother talked, Mija's fears coalesced into a mountain crushing against her chest, and she expected her heart to stop beating. Instead, one heartbeat raced against the next one until her chest pounded in a staccato like a runaway horse's hooves. But all she said to her mother was, "Thank God the children weren't here."

"Thank God you weren't here as well. You're all on the list. To be shot. On sight. They said so."

An explosion of anger blew away the mountain of

fear. "I'm going to find Aleks."

"But the soldiers . . ."

"They won't be back that soon. Leave the house the way it is. Hitch the other horse to the back of the carriage and both of you go to Feliks' right now. Hide in the barn with the children. I'll meet you there. Get going, go as fast as you can."

Mija ran up to the master bedroom. A dress was not right for what she had to do. In the pile of clothes on the floor, she found Aleks' overalls and flannel shirt. He wore them last summer to help Feliks bale hay. The fit was not bad; she only had to roll up the sleeves and the pant legs once. She put on her wool socks and sturdy old gardening shoes and covered her hair with a bandana. The gun and rounds were safer in the overall pockets than they had been in the dress.

Downstairs, she took a dark green afghan and covered her shoulders like a shawl. Mija followed the stream behind the barn to the wooded area where the mushrooms grew. Her destination was the larger forest another kilometer away because she thought he'd go where there was more space to hide. But as she walked beside the white birch trees, she heard a voice. "Psst. Over here." Entering the woods, the bright sunshine faded to deep shade. The smell of pine resin was strong, and underneath there was the smell of bilberries.

"Where are you?" she asked in a loud whisper.

He popped out from behind a tree right in front of her. She screamed and he grabbed her and put his hand on her mouth. She swallowed the rest of the scream and pulled away.

"Are you crazy?" she asked and clutched the afghan tighter. She looked him up and down. She was damp where he had touched her and she realized he was soaking wet. Other than his missing shoes, he appeared to be uninjured. "What happened?"

"I lay in the water at the edge of the stream behind the barn until a little while ago, using a reed to breathe. Is everyone all right?"

"What's the matter with you, leaving my mother and Hortense like that? Two helpless women. What if the soldiers had shot and killed them instead of the dog?"

Aleks slammed his fist into the nearest tree trunk. "The bastards!" He hit the trunk again. "You need to know they're killing Latvians by the thousands." Aleks was shivering uncontrollably.

"Take your clothes off and wrap up with this afghan. And then tell me what else you know."

Aleks removed his clothes like a man on his deathbed. He wrapped the afghan tightly around himself and sat down on a large fallen tree trunk. Mija hung his clothes to dry on branches. Aleks sat there as if he was a petrified fossil attached to the log. Mija sat down well away from him.

"What about the people? You have to tell me everything. They came after me too. And our children. We could all be dead. I should have known. We would have gone into hiding. You put us in danger. Horrible danger. How dare you!"

Aleks shrank even further into the afghan. "I meant to tell you. I should have told you. There are lists of those who are to be sent to Siberia. There are other lists of those who are to be shot on sight. People have been disappearing all year. There are no old people or servants on the lists."

"Did you see these lists?"

"Not the new ones." He told her about the list in General Borsteins' office. "I was on the deportation list. I didn't know I was moved to the shoot-on-sight list. My god! I would have told you that."

"You should have told me anyway, and you shouldn't have left my mother and Hortense."

"They came in a car, not a van."

"So?"

"When I saw the car, I knew they were there to shoot me, not send me away."

Mija was quiet for a minute. "They were there for me and the children too. They would have shot all four of us. You should have warned me."

"I didn't know they were in Gulepils until you did, until Lize told us. I thought they were still miles away, towns away. I was going to tell you. I didn't know all of us were on the shoot-to-kill list. I would have sent you away. Far away." Aleks, still shivering, moved closer to her until their arms touched. Mija moved away from him.

He said, "The Soviet's plan has a method. They took Asja's family because her father Janis is the police chief. They won't come for Feliks because he's a farmer. Anete and Hortense are too old. But the information from the shortwave is not complete. I'm sorry."

"Now what?"

"I'll live in the woods. You go with the others. Hide in the barn at Feliks' house. I'll think of a way to get you somewhere safe."

Mija wrinkled her brow. "I don't think so. Where could we go? Russian soldiers are everywhere. Estonia is occupied to the north. Lithuania is occupied to the south. Russia itself is to the east. That leaves the Baltic Sea as the only escape route, maybe, if one could sneak past the Russian navy. Do you know of a way to escape by sea?"

"We would need time to plan such a thing. And money."

"We don't have either one. The children and Anete and Hortense should be safe for now. I'll stay here with you."

"No."

"Yes." She took the gun from her pocket. "Here. You'll need this."

"You keep it." Aleks closed his eyes and didn't say anything for a long time. He was still shivering. Mija sat, not knowing what to do. All she knew right now was that in spite of her anger, she couldn't desert her husband.

For their dinner, Mija gathered berries. As they ate, she and Aleks formed a plan. She needed to see her children and touch them to know that they were safe. She would go to the farm tonight and bring back food and other supplies.

At midnight the sky was purplish, as dark as it gets on a June night. Mija went by herself. It was about two kilometers to her brother's farm. From a distance, no one could see her easily but there was enough light for her to see the way. There was moderate cloud cover. A purple sky meant a storm was coming. Halfway to the farm, fuller, darker clouds appeared in the distance. And then she saw lightning. She walked faster. Mija kept a hand inside her pocket, clamped on the gun, ready to shoot before she was shot.

CHAPTER TEN

$\mathcal{M}$ ija stayed in the hayloft with her children that night. She sent Anete and Hortense to sleep in the house, one in the maid's room and the other on the living room sofa. Mija, Lize, and Ints settled onto a bed made of two down blankets on top of straw. Another down blanket covered them. One child slept on either side of her. Sleep did not come, so she turned from side to side, watching her children's even breathing. A steady rain beat on the roof. The thunder and lightning intensified. When the center of the storm was almost on top of them, fierce claps of thunder woke Lize and then Ints within seconds of each other. They sat up and Mija put an arm around each one.

Ints looked around. "Where's Papa?"

"Remember, I told you, he's waiting for me in the woods."

Ints said, "Why didn't he come?"

Lize said, "Is it because of the soldiers?"

Mija startled at the word "soldiers." "What do you know about soldiers?"

Her daughter said, "Well—"

"Did you hear something?"

Ints said, "Grandma told us."

"What did she tell you?" Mija could see from Lize's face that she was worried. Ints wore a look of confusion.

"I won't be angry. At either of you or at Grandma."

Lightning flashed, thunder boomed, and hail pounded the roof. Mija held on tighter to her children.

Ints started, "Grandma said the Russian soldiers are bad people and want to take us away and we have to hide from them." His voice rose as he spoke. "Is that true? Are they after us? And then Lize told me what happened at Asja's house. Soldiers took her whole family. Where did they take them?"

Mija looked at Lize, who was staring down at her lap. Lize said, "I thought he should know. He didn't take what grandma said seriously."

"Lize, he's six. But never mind. We need to all be aware and be careful and hide right now."

Ints asked, "Is Papa coming to hide with us?"

"Not now. It's safer for Papa and me to hide in the woods. And you're safer here with your aunt and uncle and grandma."

Ints asked, "And you'll be in the woods?"

"Yes, not far away."

Lize said, "I want to come to the woods too. I know how to be quiet."

"Yes, you do, you're a good girl. But it's too dangerous. You like sleeping in the barn, don't you?"

Lize said, "Not with Grandma. Or Hortense."

"But you need an adult here."

Lize sighed. "I am an adult. I turned thirteen in April."

"How about Uncle Feliks?" *I will ask my brother to sleep here with a rifle.*

Ints said, "Yes, Uncle Feliks."

Lize was silent, which was as good as an agreement. The thunder had moved away, and the hail was replaced with the patter of rain.

"Let's settle down and try to sleep."

Mija listened to the sounds of her children as their breathing evened out, Lize on her stomach, Ints on his side. The gun was still in her overalls pocket. Once the children were asleep again, Mija stowed the gun under her pillow. Sleep was a long time coming and even then, she woke up often.

The next morning, they all ate breakfast together in the house, hot oatmeal and wild strawberries. The food settled like a rock in Mija's gut. She asked Feliks to help her put together supplies, and when they were alone in the barn, she asked Feliks if he'd mind sleeping with the children for the time being.

"That's what I was thinking myself. And don't you think I should teach the children to shoot?"

"I don't know." Mija's stomach churned at the thought of her young son with a rifle in his hands.

Feliks chewed on his lip for a few seconds before replying. "He's old enough to learn about gun safety, yes?"

Mija nodded.

He said, "I think maybe he's big enough to handle my smallest rifle, which has almost no kick."

Mija was torn. "I want them to be safe." She exhaled. "All right."

They loaded Big Z with the supplies. She went back into the house and hugged everyone extra tightly.

Ints said, "Come back soon, Mama. And try to bring Papa." His eyes narrowed.

Lize said, "When will you be back?"

"In three days. But I don't know if Papa will be able to come. Both of you listen to Feliks and Laima and Grandma and Hortense. Lize, you can probably help Laima with the twins. Would you like that?"

"Yes, I already helped yesterday. I played with one while Aunt Laima gave the other one a bath."

"Good, that's good. And Ints, I'm sure you can help your Uncle Feliks."

"Yes, Mama, I helped yesterday with feeding the animals."

The children followed her outside. Mija gave them both another hug and got on Big Z. She waved several times as the horse took her away from the farm. She gave a final wave when she reached the road. They looked so small and vulnerable. She couldn't bear to look back again. Across the road, she kept the horse at a slow trot straight across the fields toward her new home in the woods.

At the edge of the copse, Mija dismounted, walked Big Z into the clearing, and loosely tied him to a tree. Aleks snored. She let him sleep where he lay on the ground, wrapped in the afghan while she unloaded and organized the supplies. For sleeping, she had brought a tarp and several blankets.

She was ready for him to move to the new bedding and called his name. He didn't respond and looked sweaty so she felt his forehead with the back of her hand. He was burning hot. He moaned at her touch and turned to the other side. She would let him sleep. Mija made a fire with some logs and twigs and boiled water for tea. She poured a cup for herself in one of the two tin cups she had brought and ate a piece of crust from the heel of a half loaf of bread. She took a carrot from the bag of food for Big Z. He chewed while she stroked his mane and told him how happy she was that he was with her.

Aleks was still not awake. Mija took the small shovel she had brought from the farm and went further into the woods to look for a place to dig a latrine. She was prepared to stay in the woods a long time. She could grow a small garden at the edge of the woods. If the summer passed and winter came and they were still here, she would dig an earthen cave to live in and cover it with foliage.

She was glad she left her house in disarray. If the

soldiers came back, they would not be as suspicious. Maybe they'd assume the family was already shot and cross them off the list. Even in the midst of this danger, it pained her to think that her vegetable garden would soon be overgrown with weeds.

Aleks didn't wake up until the sun was at its highest point and his forehead felt even hotter. She helped him walk to the latrine and then settled him down again in the new bedding.

He asked, "Where are the horses?"

"Biz Z is over there." She pointed in his direction and Big Z neighed. "Whitey is too old to live out here with us. I don't think he's going to last much longer."

"Who's Whitey?"

Whitey was their old horse, named for the white that banded his lower legs. How odd that Aleks didn't remember him.

"Whitey is our horse."

"I'm not old enough to have a horse. Mama said I would get one when I join the army."

Mija gave up trying to reason with him. She started the fire again to reheat the tea and got him to drink a few sips, but he wouldn't eat. For the next three days, Aleks slept and moaned or talked nonsense. Mija kept him as comfortable as she could and fed him as much weak tea and fresh water that he would take. But his fever didn't break. Mija thought about moving him to the farm but decided it was too dangerous.

That night the full moon and clear sky made for an easy trip to the farm. Even so, on her ride across the fields, her heart beat almost as fast as the horse's hooves beat against the ground. Once there, Mija left Big Z outside and strode through the back door into the kitchen first. Laima sat at the kitchen table, waiting.

"Laima, have you got anything to break a fever, some herbs maybe?"

"Why?"

"Aleks is burning up. I've never seen anyone so sick."

Laima said, "He has a fever?"

"His fever started the first night in the woods, and he's delirious much of the time."

"Let me see what I've got." Laima jumped up and was at the jelly cabinet in two steps. She took out a glass jar and unscrewed the lid. "Elderberries," she said, "they'll be the best." She poured some of the dried herb into a small paper bag. "Make each cup of tea using one-half teaspoon and give him one cup every hour. If this doesn't work, he'll need a doctor."

Mija took the bag. "Thank you. I don't think it's safe to get a doctor involved. Anything new on the war?" She put the bag on the table and sat down. Laima poured them each a glass of water and then, in spite of being skin and bones, dropped into her chair as if unloading a heavy weight. From long habit, they clinked glasses and sipped.

Laima said, "Nothing new on war, but Peters was here yesterday."

"What? Why?" Mija folded over the top of the herb bag several times.

A baby cried in another room. Without a word, Laima left and was soon back with one of the twins. Her little face was scrunched up. Laima sat down at the table again and opened her blouse. The little girl latched on and suckled.

Laima said, "The same day they came for Aleks, Peters was in Riga on town business and soldiers also rounded up people in Velsaine. His wife and sons are gone. Lize's friend Astrid and her parents are also gone along with a lot of others. Peters thought maybe Aleks would know something. None of the phone lines worked so he traveled here by horse. When he found your house deserted and in shambles, he raced here in a frenzy. He doesn't know if his own family is alive or dead and blames himself."

"Where did he go?" Mija methodically unfolded and refolded the top of the bag.

"He didn't say. I assumed he was going home. I told him you'd be back tonight and every third night after that."

"I hope he comes back. Where's Feliks?"

"In the barn. With his shotgun. Take this bell and ring it three times before you walk in. It's our signal that someone safe is coming."

THE ELDERBERRY TEA STARTED to help. Aleks sweated profusely each time he drank it. Three more days went by before his fever was gone. His face had deep hollows and bony ridges. His hair and scraggly beard sprouted white hairs among the brown.

Mija helped him wash up in the stream and change his clothes. While he sat on a log nearby, she made a thin root vegetable stew over a small fire. It was his first solid food, and he ate slowly.

"You're right," he said out of the blue. He stabbed his spoon down into the stew. "I'm a coward."

"What are you talking about? I never said that." Mija had eaten the last of her stew. She put the bowl down on the ground and turned to face him.

"I should have stayed with Anete and Hortense when the soldiers came." He ate another bite and dropped the spoon into the bowl. He reached for Mija's bowl. "At least let me take the dishes to the stream and rinse them."

"Wait," Mija said, "you explained about the lists. You would have been shot. It's not cowardice to save oneself in the face of certain death. But there's one thing I don't understand from that day. How did you lose your shoes?"

"I stopped for a minute to catch my breath and heard the soldiers. I took one shoe off and threw it as far as I could. My ruse worked. They shot in that direction and ran that way while I ran the opposite way. I took off the other shoe so I wouldn't make so much noise and then dropped it by accident along the way."

That night, Aleks wanted to go with Mija to the farm, but Mija said, "No, you're not strong enough yet." She turned to go.

Without saying anything, he put an arm on her shoulder. He hesitated a moment, then said, "Wait, let me tell you. You need to watch out for the Home Guard."

She turned to face him and said, "What?"

"Yes, maybe you'll see them. If not, maybe you should go to Gulepils tomorrow and look for Harijs." He took her hand.

"What are you talking about? What is Home Guard? What about Harijs?" She wondered if Aleks had lost his mind from the illness.

"Remember that evening a few weeks ago when I said I was going into town to talk to Willy about how to increase the power of the shortwave radio? I talked to him for a few minutes and then went with him to a meeting of the Home Guard. Harijs is in charge of all of Vidzeme. They're a group of partisans. They're getting ready to rise up in revolt the minute there is an opportunity, the minute the Reds start losing the war. They think they can help. They've done a lot already, even hidden arms in the woods in strategic areas. Harijs keeps a map. The closest place to us, from what I can remember, is about 10 kilometers away, toward Elste. They were planning to add more places to stockpile as soon as they got more weapons. If you went to Harijs' house, you could tell him what happened to us and then I could join them. Maybe they're ready to fight. I want to fight against the Reds." He leaned his back against a tree and his shoulders sloped downward. "They have an old cabin in the woods as their base of operations."

"Finally. You're telling me what I need to know.

I'll stay at the farm tonight and tomorrow morning I'll go look for Harijs. I'll come back here tomorrow night."

"Let me tell you how to get there." He gave her detailed directions to the cabin.

She looked him in the eyes. "Any more secrets I need to know about?"

"No, you know everything now."

She gave Aleks a pat on the shoulder. "Rest. There's plenty of stew for you to eat."

Mija didn't understand why Aleks continued to keep things from her. She had come to understand why he resigned from the army after he told her about the lists, and that he wanted to protect them from being deported or killed. Why didn't he trust her with that information from the beginning? Why didn't he tell her about the Home Guard before now? Questions, so many questions. She felt like something must be wrong between them, that he didn't trust her or thought she was too weak to handle the truth, and that hurt. Could they have been married all this time with so little understanding? She mounted Big Z and set him going as fast as he could go in the dark gray sky of the summer night.

As the horse took her toward the farm, she thought. *Would being part of an uprising like the Home Guard be a good thing? Or would it get us all killed that much faster? It's such a small group with so little to fight with. What good are a few guns against tanks? We have to be smarter instead of stronger. What is the best way to protect my children? Is there salvation for any of us?*

At Laima and Feliks' house, Peters had come back earlier and brought a surprise. Astrid, Lize's roommate from boarding school, was with him. They were sitting at the kitchen table with Laima. Peters stood up and pulled Mija close for a hug.

She said, "I'm so glad you're here. And Astrid, how wonderful to see you. How did you two get together?"

Peters said, "At a railway station, quite by accident."

Mija gave Astrid a hug and said, "I'm glad you're safe. I'm going to check on Lize and Ints in the barn, and then I want to hear everything."

At the barn, she rang the bell. Feliks waved down at her to come up the ladder. Lize and Ints were sound asleep in their corner bedding, so they whispered.

"Were you awake? It's the middle of the night."

"I don't need much sleep these days. I'll lie down and sleep soon."

Now that she'd seen her children with her own eyes, she could go back to the house and talk with Peters and Astrid.

Laima had set out glasses, a pitcher of water, and a small plate of pumpernickel bread.

Peters said, "Astrid, tell us what happened to you."

"You're my guardian angel," said Astrid to Peters, but her face was not smiling. She reached for another slice of bread.

Astrid sighed and finished chewing. Circles under

her eyes were as black as the bread and shiny, as though someone had punched her. She coughed often with a deep phlegmy sound. Between coughing and chewing, she told them her story.

"They came and took us by gunpoint. We had fifteen minutes to pack a suitcase. My parents and I were in the same cattle car with Ingrida and the boys. I couldn't stop coughing, and the two guards kept eyeing me. One asked my mother what was wrong. She told them I was very sick, that I had bronchitis, and then she told them they took me by mistake, as I was their servant girl, not their daughter. Since I don't look like them, I guess they believed it. The one guard opened the door enough to push me out."

Astrid took another slice of bread and continued. "I rolled down a hill but only had a few scrapes. I followed the railroad tracks back. When I heard trains coming, and there were a lot that day, I ran and hid. Still, I could see that the trains pulled cattle cars filled with people. At the first train station I came to, the stationmaster shared a bit of his food and water. He let me sleep on a bench. I was going to keep walking all the way back home, but then Peters showed up." Astrid coughed again.

Laima said, "How long have you had this cough?"

"Weeks," said Astrid, "but it wasn't so bad until after the train ride."

"We'll fix you up," said Laima. She went to the jelly cupboard and took out several jars of herbs and busied herself heating water.

"There's more news," said Peters. He poured a glass of water from the pitcher and drank.

"Nu, what? What more could there be?" said Mija.

"Plenty. The Germans are bombing Russia all along the Eastern front. They've crossed into the Baltics and even Latvia. They're in Liepaja. Can Riga be far behind?" he said.

"We'll be liberated," said Laima as she clapped her hands together.

Mija said, "Liberated from what? What makes you think the Germans are better than the Russians?" She wanted to take back her words as soon as she said them. "I'm sorry, maybe it will be all right."

"Isn't anything better than communism?" asked Laima. "The Germans won't take away our land and divide it up or take away our right to go to church."

Peters and Mija were silent.

Astrid had another coughing fit and couldn't stop. Laima finished making some kind of mixture with the hot water and herbs and handed her a cup of the herbal tea.

"Astrid, you'll sleep in the house until you're better."

By the time Astrid finished the tea, her cough had quieted. Laima took her to the living room and settled her on blankets on the floor, on the opposite side from the sofa where Hortense slept. The sound of a baby crying wafted from upstairs as Laima walked into the kitchen. She said, "Six months old and Ruta still doesn't sleep through the night. I'll nurse her upstairs.

Please excuse me."

Feliks came in. "I couldn't sleep after all. What I wouldn't give for a beer right now. This year I'm going to brew my own."

Mija told the men everything about the lists and the Home Guard.

Feliks wasn't interested in joining any uprising and knew nothing about the Home Guard. He said "I thank God every day that I'm too old to be conscripted into any army. I want the war to be over. I want to farm my own land in peace. And I hope the Germans win because then I won't lose my land. So far, I haven't received orders about how my acres are to be divided. I hope that means the Russians forgot about me."

"I don't think they forgot," Peters said. "They probably didn't divide up this part of Latvia yet."

Feliks asked Peters to stay with them to help with the planting and later with the harvesting. He wanted to plant all the fields this year, not leave any fallow. Peters agreed to stay through the summer, and they shook on it.

Peters also agreed to go into town with Mija the next day and help look for the Home Guard. Mija slept in the hayloft again. Peters bedded down there also, next to Feliks.

In the morning, Lize was happy to see Astrid but sad about Astrid's missing parents. After breakfast, the children went outside with Feliks to help with milking the cow and feeding the pig.

Mija and Peters fed the three horses before

saddling up Big Z and Feliks' horse Oscar for their trip into town. They trotted most of the 5 kilometers, wanting to get there as soon as possible, slowing down as they neared the first houses.

They visited Harijs' house first. His wife opened the door a few inches, said he wasn't home and she didn't know when he'd be back. She closed the door before they could ask anything else. They got back on the horses and made their way through the back streets in a different direction than they came. Even though the streets were fairly empty, they didn't talk. You never knew who might be listening through an open window. Mija was self-conscious of wearing the dirty overalls and plaid shirt and having her hair tied back with a kerchief. She felt dirty all over. She thought about having a real bath instead of cleaning up in the stream by the woods. Mija led her horse past the little white church where she and Aleks were married. She thought about that day for a moment, then shoved the memory aside. They rode past the cemetery behind the church, where her father and other relatives were buried, and followed a path into the woods until they came to a rundown cabin.

Before they had time to dismount, the door opened and Harijs came out. Mija said, "Hello Harijs. Aleks sent us. This is Peters."

Peters and Harijs remembered each other from school. Harijs was two years younger. She and Peters tied the horses to nearby trees. Inside, five men sat on the hard-packed dirt floor in a circle, studying a map.

Four of them remembered Peters to one degree or another. Peters knew Ollie best; they were in the same class.

Harijs said, "We're too far east to hear the planes. The only war we've seen is soldiers shooting innocent people. It's hellishly frustrating. But Willy says Liepaja has been bombed. The Russian troops, when they retreat, will use the main roads and the railroads. Our plan is to line the forests along the roads and take any shots we can as the troops go by. Without explosives, we can't do much against the trains."

"Yes," said Willy, "and we can use everyone."

Peters said, "I want to help, but my wife and sons are probably in Siberia. If I join in and I'm captured, they could take it out on them. Can I do something else?"

Willy said, "Do you know how to operate a shortwave radio?"

"No, but I can learn."

"Then you'll be the radioman. You can come with me when we're finished here and start learning today. I'll be going into the forest to fight. I want to see the faces of the soldiers who killed my best friend. I want to see them die."

Mija said, "I know how to shoot, but I have my children to think about. I'll send Aleks to you to do the frontline fighting."

Harijs asked, "How long until Aleks is recovered?"

"Soon, a few more days."

IN SPITE OF THE FACT that the Germans were advancing, Aleks wouldn't leave the woods. He said he didn't feel strong enough and wouldn't talk about it. Mija went back to the farm and told Peters that Aleks would come when the group left to fight. She hoped her words were true.

Peters and Feliks took turns standing guard at night. Peters worked with Feliks in the fields during the day and trained with Willy on the radio in the evenings. Aleks received orders to move to the forest on June 27. He said he was ready. They broke camp and Mija moved to the barn. She told the children about her handgun and made them swear over and over again that they would never touch her gun or Feliks' rifle without permission. Two days later, Aleks came back in the early morning and woke her up. They went outside to talk.

The grass was wet with dew. A trio of storks appeared from the south. Mija shivered in the cold morning air and hugged herself with both arms. Aleks put an arm around her shoulders.

"Look," said Mija. She pointed up with one hand. "They're back. I thought they weren't coming this year." One stork landed on the barn roof and the other two kept on flying north.

"Why are you here?" she asked Aleks. "I thought you'd be gone."

"The plans have changed. I'm going to Riga. I wanted to tell you myself."

"Why?"

"I want to be there when we're liberated. The Germans have taken Tukums. It's inevitable now, they'll reach Riga in a few days. We're going to be free."

Mija crossed her arms in front of her again and frowned.

"I thought you'd be happy," he said.

"I'll be happy when the war is over. You know how I feel. The Germans are no better than the Russians."

"Yes, we've had this discussion, but I haven't changed my mind, either. Anything has to be better than Communism. And the war is almost over, don't you see that?" Aleks tried to hug her, but she pulled away.

She said, "Now we have two armies all over us and no, I can't see the end."

"I have to go. I'm taking the mail train." He tried to hug her again and this time she let him.

She said, "Don't you want to talk to the children?"

"I think it's better if I don't."

"I don't agree."

"If you insist."

Mija shook her head. "No, never mind."

He reached toward her and touched her lips with his. His lips were cold and she drew away. He said, "Before long, we'll be back in our home. I'll help you with the garden. You'll see. Next winter we'll have plenty of food. You'll be all right when you're not hungry every day." He straightened his back and shoulders.

He put one foot in a stirrup and mounted Harijs' horse. Mija could hear him whistling for a few minutes. He reached the road, turned the horse, and then was gone from her view. Up on the barn roof, the stork added new twigs to the old nest that was still there from last year.

CHAPTER ELEVEN

As the train pulled into the Riga station, Aleks jumped off at the far platform to avoid the Russian guards at the main entrance. He slipped into the first building, which was used for mail transfer. The cavernous room was empty of people. Countless sacks of mail sat piled in huge mounds, covering almost every bit of space. Walking along the perimeter and out the front door, he merged into the crowd, continuing toward the main terminal.

The terminal was packed with men, women, and children. Aleks maneuvered himself inside the door into a chaotic scene of yelling, pushing, and shoving. He was to meet his contact here by the newspaper kiosk, which was on the other side.

He yelled into the ear of a man next to him. "What's going on?"

The man yelled back. "We can't get out the doors to the platform."

Aleks yelled into the ear of a man on the other side of him, "What's going on?"

The man yelled back, "German bombing getting closer. Russian pigs pulling out but won't let us leave." He shook his fist into the air.

Aleks nodded. With one hand in his pants pocket, holding his service pistol, he sidled along the wall toward the platform doors. Maybe if he could get to the three steps that led to the doors, where surprisingly, no one stood, he could use them to reach the kiosk faster. Just then a group of Russian soldiers entered and stood on the top step. A quick glance and Aleks estimated about a dozen. They pointed their bayoneted rifles at the crowd and yelled for everyone to move back. They were in full uniform, with round metal helmets strapped under their chins. The soldier on the end, with a big stomach, flat face, and handlebar mustache, shouted in a booming voice, "You are forbidden. The station is closed. Get out or we will shoot." He gave a downward wave and the soldiers cocked their rifles. There was a slight hesitation in the crowd, almost as if they had to consider it first, then there was a rush to get out.

Aleks moved with the crush of bodies out onto the street and toward the city center. He heard the sound of engines before he saw them. A convoy of Soviet trucks piled full of soldiers drove slowly toward them. The people moved out of the way in a wave that opened and then closed up again when the trucks were past. Aleks heard a yell, "Cowards! A little threat and see how they retreat."

Sliding past one person at a time, Aleks twisted his way to the right, toward the canal. There were fewer people here, and he drew in a deep breath of fresh air. Walking in the same direction as everyone else, toward Brivibas Iela (Freedom Street), he passed close by the opera house, a classic structure, all white with six tall columns along the front. People trampled the pink and purple flowers on the grassy lawn in front of it. As he reached Brivibas Iela, the crowd dispersed somewhat as people went in different directions. He turned toward the Freedom Monument, which stood in the middle of the walkway and rose over one hundred feet. The female figure, called Liberty, held her arms straight up over her head, holding three stars.

Aleks heard a sound like giant wasps. The planes came from the other side of the Daugava River. Six sets of three planes buzzed them and then turned back the way they came. Bombs exploded in the distance. Smoke rose from across the river. They must have bombed something at the airport, perhaps the terminal, perhaps Soviet planes left on the ground.

Aleks turned to a well-dressed, white-haired man walking by him. "Excuse me, sir, please, I just arrived. What's happening?" He kept pace with the man.

"Most of the Russian army is gone. German bombing is getting closer. And I hope they leave our city alone."

"Where's everyone going?" Aleks asked.

The man shrugged, "Out of the city. Trolleys

stopped running and the trains also. The only way out now is by foot."

"Where are you going?"

The man leaned toward Aleks and yelled, "To my daughter's house in the north end."

Aleks yelled back, "Good luck. And thank you."

"It's nothing," said the man. He tipped his hat and disappeared into the crowd.

The airplanes returned, lower in the sky. Big black swastikas were painted on the tails. The crowd increased its pace. Aleks reached the Freedom Monument. Instead of walking around it like the others, he walked straight up to it, turned around, leaned his back on the stone base, and stared at the sky.

Is this it? Are the Germans going to drop the next bombs right here in the heart of Riga? Are these the last minutes of my life? There were no more trucks in the streets, no tanks, no vehicles of any kind. A mass of swarming humanity flooded around him. His hand still gripped the gun in his pants pocket. *Six rounds. If I'm close enough, I could kill five and then myself if need be. Five Russians. For my father. I'll wait here until the people are gone. The crowd is thinning already. If I see Russian soldiers, I'll pull out my gun and shoot.*

But the Russian soldiers didn't come. And no one stopped to ask Aleks why he stood there as still as the statue behind him with his head back and his eyes on the sky and one hand in his pocket.

After circling Riga several times, the Nazi planes released the bombs. Aleks watched them fall. Then he heard them. Ka-boom, ka-boom, ka-boom. *They're here to oust the Russians. We'll be free of those bastards!* The bombs fell a few streets away, in the heart of the old city, straight ahead from where he stood. Aleks' ears rang. The planes flew away. The tallest point in Riga was the spire of St. Peters' Church, rising to over two hundred feet. Aleks watched and waited. The dark smoke came first, rising in angry clouds. All of sudden, the spire was engulfed in flames, shooting out on all sides. It wasn't long before the spire collapsed in a whoosh.

Aleks left his spot and walked toward the fire, toward the old city. The ringing in his ears prevented him from hearing anything else. The smell of acrid smoke filled his lungs. Much of old Riga was burning. Besides the church, the town hall and the Black Heads House were also bombed. Structures that had stood for centuries had turned into burning rubble in mere minutes. How ironic that they bombed St. Peters' Church on St. Peters' Day. He stood at the edge of the shadow of the burning church, heedless of the smoke and ash.

After an hour or so Aleks decided the bombing was over for now and walked away. There was not much chance of finding Max today. *It's odd that my contact has the same name as my dead brother.*

The ringing in his ears subsided and he could hear again. He walked back the way he had come and passed the Freedom Monument without a glance. He continued walking past multistoried apartment and office buildings. There were other people also walking the streets now, mostly men with vacant looks in their eyes. At Stabu Iela, he turned, went one block, then turned onto Baznicas Iela, stopping at a brownstone apartment building. He turned again to enter the arched walkway that went underneath the upper stories and into a courtyard. Inside the courtyard, stone steps led to a wide landing and double doors.

He didn't know if she'd be here. He hadn't heard from her since last year. He walked up three narrow flights of worn stone steps and knocked at the first apartment. The age-scarred wooden door opened right away.

She said, "I saw you on the street."

"Hello, Mother." He didn't smile.

They didn't touch in greeting. She lifted an arm and pointed inside, "Come in."

He walked into the main room. His eyebrows raised at the changes since his last visit. He consciously lowered them so his face showed nothing and sat down on an old burgundy sofa, partially covered with a mustard-colored blanket. She took a seat diagonally from him, on a green chair that had no cover to hide its worn fabric. On the wall opposite the sofa was a large fireplace that supplied the heat. The other furniture consisted of a short round table in front of the sofa, a tarnished brass floor lamp, and at the other end of the room, a small rectangular metal table and two metal chairs. Behind the kitchen table, wooden cabinets hung on the wall. Under them stood a small sink and stove.

He cleared his throat. "I didn't know if you'd be here."

She said, "Where would I go?"

"How have you been?"

"Surviving."

"I heard that everything in Riga was collectivized, even the market."

"Yes."

"Maybe now you'll get your fish stand back."

"Maybe."

As usual, he felt like he could not say the right thing. She looked the same as last year, maybe a few more wrinkles. Aleks had more gray hair than she did.

"Can I sleep here tonight?" he asked.

Her voice was a monotone. Her mouth barely moved. "On the sofa."

"Who's in the second bedroom?"

"It has no furniture."

"What happened?" She used to have beautiful handmade furniture that had been handed down through several generations.

"Bartered. Hunger does that."

"You bartered the furniture for food?"

"Yes, that and something better."

"What?"

Marina stood up, walked over to the cabinets and opened the doors. The first cabinet was packed full of cartons of cigarettes, several different brands. The next, crowded with Russian vodka bottles. The third one held canned food.

She said, "To get food, cigarettes and vodka work best. Hungry?"

"Yes." Aleks hadn't eaten since yesterday.

"Feel like home."

He went to the food cupboard and studied the cans of soups, vegetables, and fish before choosing a can of sprats.

"My favorite," he said.

"You always loved those little fishes the best. Me, I prefer herring."

"I remember." He opened the can with the mechanical opener that she handed him. His mother produced a fork and they both sat at the table. Aleks ate out of the can. She retrieved a carton of his brand of cigarettes and some matches and put them on the table.

"Thank you," The old gray ceramic ashtray sat on the middle of the table, clean, as if waiting for him. He lit up and dropped the used match into it. He inhaled and blew a cloud of smoke upward. Marina took out a bottle of vodka and two shot glasses, then poured. They touched glasses without a word. Aleks threw back his head and took his in one swallow. She sipped hers with a grimace.

She said, "Eat what you want. Sleep when you want. I need to go out."

"Do you think it's safe?"

She narrowed her eyes. "Safer than usual."

Marina filled a sturdy black bag with bottles of vodka and cartons of cigarettes, put it on the table, and went into her bedroom. Aleks poured himself another shot of vodka and lit another cigarette. The metal chair was uncomfortable even for someone with a military background. He moved his things to the pockmarked table in front of the sofa. His mother came out wearing a raggedy black dress. On her head was a black kerchief tied underneath her chin.

"Where are you going like that?" he asked.

"My nightly trip to the black market to trade for food. Requests?"

"More sprats? And stay away from old Riga. It's burning."

Aleks wanted to tell his mother not to go out, that the war would be over soon, that the Germans would be here in a few days, and there would be plenty of food again and the regular market where she owned a fish stand would be open. But he knew there was no point to telling her anything. She would say, "Pah." And then she would do what she wanted. He wondered if her money was still inside the mattress.

When she was gone, he went into her bedroom. One item was left, the old mattress, on the floor. She had shown him where her money was hidden last year when the mattress still sat on a beautiful oak frame. "You need to know where this is, in case something happens to me," she had said. The money was there. The pile seemed to be the same size and that was not surprising. Latvian lats were not worth anything better than mattress stuffing.

He fell asleep on the sofa after smoking a few

more cigarettes and drinking half the bottle. When he awoke, he saw that the door to his mother's bedroom was closed. Then he saw her black bag on the table. Next to it were a razor, a bar of yellow soap, and a white towel. Next to them were cans of sprats and various other fishes, salmon, tuna, and herring. He took the bath items. There was no hot water from the bathroom spigot, but the water was running. He had gotten used to the neatly trimmed beard. Shaving it off was hard going because the soap did not lather well with cold water. His face had numerous nicks by the time he finished. He looked at himself in the round mirror above the white porcelain sink and noticed blood oozing out of little cuts across his cheeks. A zigzag crack in the mirror cut his face in half diagonally. Without the beard, he felt naked. No, naked wasn't the right word. He felt unmasked. People could recognize him more easily now. He could be caught and shot if the Russians came back. He told himself he was safe while the Germans had control. But he didn't quite believe it. Aleks used the towel to wipe the blood. The spots darkened to the color of the ripped burgundy sofa. He laid the towel over the edge of the tub, went back into the big room, and waited for his mother.

She came out wearing the better dress from the previous day and said, "Good."

"What's good?"

"No more beard."

She took out two plates and cups, set the table, heated water, and made real tea.

126

"Sorry, Aleks. No coffee."

"Tea is just as good."

He savored the dark tea. If he had enough money to buy everything in the food cupboard, he could take it to Mija on the farm. He would take his mother there, too, to keep her safe, but he knew she wouldn't go. He ate another can of sprats. This time he put them on a plate and took his time, savoring each bite. Marina opened a can of green pea soup. Under Aleks' careful questioning, she told him in her clipped speech about life in the city under the Soviet occupation. They had not had fresh food for months. The canned food was smuggled in from Sweden, Denmark, Finland, or Great Britain. The bread from the bakeries was not worth waiting in line for, as they used a lot of sawdust in place of flour. There was no milk for babies and children unless you were lucky enough to find smuggled cans of condensed milk.

"Where is the black market?" he asked.

"Location changes daily."

"How do you know where to go, then?"

"It is whispered between us, decided each night for the next night."

The windows were open. No planes droned. No trucks roared. No trolleys moved. A few hardy souls walked on the streets. Aleks spent the day drinking tea and smoking and worrying. Marina went out again that night in her black clothes and Aleks finished the bottle of vodka.

The next day was the first day of July. As Aleks

and Marina ate breakfast, they heard music outside. They poked their heads out the windows. It seemed that the music came from an open window on a floor below them. A man held his radio out the window, waving it from side to side while the radio blared a recording of the national anthem, "Dievs Sveti Latvia" (God Bless Latvia). People on the street noticed the music, raised their arms and cheered. From a window across the street, a woman held out a Latvian flag. A man on the street shouted, "Our nightmare year is over." People started streaming out of the buildings, laughing and embracing. "We're liberated!" was heard over and over.

He wanted Marina to go out with him, but she refused to leave during daylight hours. Gradually, loud buzzing neared and drowned out the music. Aleks knew without looking up that they were the same kind of planes as the other day. Marina looked up at a clear blue sky marred by the vee formation of many planes. She said, "Germans."

"Yes, the Germans are here."

"Aren't we still occupied? Didn't they bomb us so that we would submit?" She left the window and sat down on the green chair. "Are they back to bomb us some more?"

Aleks looked up and said, "They won't be bombing. They're too high and moving too fast. You're right, we're occupied. But I don't think the Germans will be like the Russians. I don't think they will shoot me because I was an officer. I don't think they will deport people merely because they are successful. We will be safer."

"I pray you're right," she said.

The word "pray" reminded Aleks that he hadn't seen his mother's Bible, and he asked her where it was.

"I burned it," she said.

"Why?"

"It was cold. I had no other fuel that day."

Marina gave Aleks a key to the apartment, the same key he had used as a young boy. Outside, he breathed in the fresh air. Everyone he saw smiled at him and he smiled too. Women and men crowded the sidewalks. Many carried flowers. Aleks' first destination was the Freedom Monument, which was a common meeting place. Perhaps he would run into someone he knew.

German tanks and trucks drove down the main streets as if on parade. Soldiers in steel gray uniforms waved, smiling with bright teeth. The crowds welcomed the conquering soldiers with applause. Even strangers embraced each other. After the long winter of starvation and barbaric deportations and killings, the people needed something to celebrate. The joy of being liberated from Stalin overtook all reason. Mounds of flowers lay at the foot of the Freedom Monument. A woman with a small bunch of pink carnations handed one to Aleks so that he could lay one down too. Aleks walked on to the opera house.

Armored cars were parked around the square in front of it. People surrounded the soldiers standing by the cars. At the back of one car, Aleks saw a young blond soldier with a cigarette dangling from his mouth. The soldier handed a cigarette to a blond Latvian man and lit it for him. They looked like they could be brothers. As the match flared, the Latvian man cupped his hand above the German's so the match wouldn't go out. Their hands touched and then the cigarette end glowed. The German dropped the match on the ground and the two men stood and smoked side by side.

Aleks took a cigarette from the pack in his shirt pocket, lit it, and walked over to the two men. "Hello, there." The men nodded their heads and smiled. Aleks said to the Latvian, "By any chance are you Max?"

The man's eyebrows shot up. "How did you know?"

"You look like your father, Willy, except younger, of course."

"Who are you?"

"Aleks. We were to meet in the train terminal several days ago."

He nodded. "Ah yes, but it wasn't possible. Let me introduce you to Bernhard."

Max pointed to the German soldier. Bernhard and Aleks shook hands. Max asked Aleks, "Weren't you supposed to have a beard? I never would have recognized you."

"Yes, and I did have one that day. Here, let me show you my identity papers." He reached into his pocket but Max stopped him. "It's not necessary.

130

Today I trust everybody." He smiled broadly. "We must have been destined to meet here."

"Why is that?" asked Aleks.

"Bernhard is my second cousin. My grandfather was from Berlin, came here years ago for a job and stayed, married my grandmother, and never went back. My grandfather was a brother to Bernhard's grandfather. We've been in touch only by letters and pictures. We ran into each other by accident. And now here you are as well."

Max dropped his cigarette onto the sidewalk and ground it out with his shoe.

Aleks said, "Your father told me you were studying law, and at the top of your class."

"I was, until they closed the university last year. Maybe now it will reopen." Max turned to Bernhard, "Aleks is an officer from the Latvian army. My father said I can trust him."

Bernhard said to Max, "Do you think he would be interested?"

Max said, "I don't know, but it's safe to ask."

Bernhard turned to Aleks and said, "The Reich is looking for trained native soldiers to help with the war effort in Latvia. Interested?"

Aleks couldn't believe his luck. "Where do I sign up?"

CHAPTER TWELVE

$\mathcal{R}$ ationing of food and goods was reinstated in July. The black markets that had risen under the Soviets continued under the Germans. The Nazis were too busy waging war to bother with cultural life, and for the most part, did not interfere with organized religion. Riga University was reopened but closed again a few months later, no explanation given.

In Gulepils, the band of partisans disbanded when Willy and Harijs and Ollie disappeared about two weeks after the German invasion. Some said that they were living in the forests, vowing to fight guerilla warfare on their own until the country was free again. But no one admitted to knowing where they were. And no one knew what happened to Aleks. Not even his mother.

Mija hadn't heard from Aleks since he left for Riga. He'd always been good about staying in touch with his mother, so Mija sent Marina a letter. A reply came promptly. She hadn't seen him since the second of July. Aleks told her he was forming a Latvian Legion for the German Army, and he'd be in touch when he could. Mija wrote back and asked Marina to let her know if she heard from him.

Mija, Peters, and Feliks traveled to her house late one night at the end of July with two horses hitched to Feliks' hay wagon. The house was the same as on the day she had left it except for the mice scurrying in the walls. They loaded the wagon with canning jars, dishes, pots, and pans, Anete's afghans, clothes, towels, sheets, a few of Mija's favorite books, and the radio.

"What about the furniture?" Feliks asked.

"It would take too many trips," said Mija.

Peters said, "We shouldn't leave it. Feliks and I can make several trips. But I don't think we can move the piano unless we take it apart."

Mija said, "Then chop it up. I'm not leaving it for the Germans."

Feliks said, "What doesn't fit in the house, we'll store in my barn."

"We need to get the other radio—the shortwave—in our barn," Mija said. "And the antenna. It's on the roof, hidden under the stork's nest."

They even ripped the telephone out of the wall and took that along.

AT THE END OF AUGUST, they harvested the crops.

This year Feliks' helpers were only those living with them: Mija, Peters, Lize, Ints, Astrid, and even Anete and Hortense. This limited how much they had planted, but if they had involved others, they would have had to share the crops. The adults had decided as a group that the most important thing was to make sure there was enough food for the people living here. They needed enough to get through till the next summer, and without an unforeseen disaster, there would be just enough. As of yet, the Germans had not bothered the people this far out in the countryside.

The house was crowded. On the second floor, the twins' cradles had been moved into their parents' bedroom, but the girls would soon need something bigger to sleep in. The other bedroom on the second floor was set up dormitory-style for Mija, Lize, Ints, and Astrid with one double bed and two singles. Astrid and Lize shared the double bed. The two dressers along one wall were from Mija's bedroom, as was the double bed. The single beds were also from her house. There was almost no space to walk around. Anete and Hortense shared the maid's room on the first floor. Peters slept on a cot in the living room.

Lize and Ints had stopped asking where their papa was. Astrid stopped talking about her parents and Siberia about the same time. Peters didn't talk about family either. He had taken the position of a father to the children living here.

The vegetable garden yielded potatoes, tomatoes, carrots, cabbages, peas, and onions. They had focused on planting what could be canned or stored for the winter but still kept a small plot for perishables like lettuce. The women pickled the little cucumbers and the mushrooms, canned the tomatoes, and made jams and jellies with the fruits. Since there was no sugar, the men raided bee's nests for honey. As the summer advanced, Lize, Ints, and Astrid gathered mushrooms in the forest and all the blueberries and strawberries they could find in the wild fields beyond the farm.

Peters took Ints fishing almost every evening while Feliks completed chores like feeding the horses and repairing the harnesses. They ate some of the fish and the men dried and smoked the rest of it. They all grew muscles and looked healthy again and Ints' grown-up teeth starting coming in. Except for Laima and the twins, everyone was brown from being outside so much.

One afternoon each week Mija and Peters went by horse into town to pick up mail at the post office and to ask trusted friends for news of Aleks. The previous week, Mija had received a letter from the boarding school at Velsaine telling her that all students must report as normal. Astrid and Lize would go back to school next Monday. Ints would go to school again in the town and that would start in another week.

On their next visit, there were several letters for Mija. She opened the first one, from Marina, which was as brief as the previous ones. The slip of paper said "No news. Marina." The second one, from the elementary school, was a typed form letter addressed to "Dear Teacher" telling her that her services were no longer needed. She had expected this because the school had a German principal, and the rumor was that his priority was to fire all the native teachers and bring in new teachers from Germany. Mija sighed. Last year the students had to learn everything in Russian. Now they'd have to learn in German. Most Latvian adults were trilingual. Ints and Lize and the other young people, who grew up during the freedom years, struggled to catch up. She wondered if the students at the elementary school would have to share each textbook among four students as they did last year.

Mija's teacher friend Ester, along with her husband Edmunds, walked into the post office.

Mija held up her letter. "Look what I got."

Ester retrieved her mail and had the same letter. Ester invited Mija and Peters to come for tea to their apartment later that afternoon. They lived in town, not far from the post office.

Outside, Mija said to Peters, "Didn't Ester seem nervous?"

"Like a skittish kitten."

Ester still seemed troubled when they arrived for tea. She led them into the small living room that held a worn yellow-flowered sofa and two solid yellow chairs. Ester served a weak tea in pale blue china cups and saucers and apologized that she could not offer any sugar or sweets.

"Don't be silly," said Mija. "No one has those things anymore. The tea is lovely."

Ester said she didn't know how they would survive without her job. Their tiny garden plot behind the building didn't yield nearly enough food. Edmunds had lost his job over a year ago when the local government had been disbanded. Ester kept smoothing back her black hair, even though it was safely fastened into a stern bun at the nape of her neck. Edmunds kept clearing his throat and crossing and uncrossing his legs.

When the teacups were empty and Mija and Peters stood up to go, Ester whispered as if someone was listening at the door, "Please, sit, wait a minute. I need to tell you something."

Mija whispered back, "Tell us what?"

Ester closed the windows even though it was a hot day. She sat down again. "We're afraid."

"Of what?" Mija asked. She and Peters sat down again, leaning forward toward the sofa.

Ester said, "Bad things are happening in Riga. We heard they burned a synagogue full of 300 hundred Jewish refugees from Lithuania. The soldiers locked them in and set fire to it."

"No." Mija put a hand to her mouth.

Edmunds had been sitting without expression, his eyes moving from person to person, but now he looked away.

Peters said, "Where did you hear this?"

Edmunds turned back to them. "My father Samuel lives in Riga. He saw the fire, heard the screams, and could do nothing." He turned to his wife and said, "Ester, are you sure?"

"More than ever." She put her hands into her lap and clasped them tightly.

Edmunds set his teacup on the side table and continued. "They moved all the Jewish people into one section of Riga. My father is living in a three-bedroom apartment with fifteen other people. He sleeps in the kitchen, on the floor. They all have to carry a special permit to go anywhere, and they all have to wear a Star of David on their arm."

Peters said, "My god."

Edmunds continued, "It's a matter of time before the same will happen in the smaller cities, maybe even here."

"That's horrible news. How can we help?" said Mija.

"We understand you both were part of the original group of partisans, Harijs' group. Can you get my father out? Bring him here? He's an old man. My mother died last winter. He's all I have left."

Peters said, "Has he tried to leave on his own?"

"I went to Riga myself to get him two days ago, but soldiers were everywhere. They stopped us and examined our papers. I didn't have a permit to be in Riga and almost got arrested."

Mija asked, "Since when does one need papers to be in Riga?"

"These days, if you are Jewish, you need a paper to walk down the street. They escorted my father back to his building and accompanied me to the edge of the ghetto. They said if I came back, I would be arrested and jailed."

Mija said, "How does one know where the boundary of the ghetto is?"

"They're putting up a barbed wire fence. It's not finished, but there are guards everywhere," Edmunds said.

"Do they stop everyone?" Peters asked.

"I don't think so. There are too many. But once the fence is completed, he will never get out." Edmunds hands shook as he tried to drink more tea.

Mija said, "We'll think of something."

"Give us a few days," said Peters.

On the way home, Peters and Mija discussed connecting the shortwave radio to find out about potential help for Samuel but they decided it was still too dangerous.

"I wish we could find Harijs and the rest," Peters said.

"We either have to find them or help Samuel ourselves. I wonder how soon the soldiers will reach us here. I can't sit and wait anymore."

"I agree. I say we help Samuel ourselves."

"Yes. And soon."

Mija's horse, Biz Z, snorted and pulled up. She patted him and said, "What's the matter?" Big Z started walking toward the birch forest to the left of the road. A bearded Willy waved to them from the edge of the trees.

CHAPTER THIRTEEN

The next day, Nazi planes appeared in the skies over the farm. Feliks and Peters, threshing barley in the barn, didn't hear them. The grain was spread on the floor with one man on each side. They beat the grain out by swinging a flail over their heads and throwing it down in a thump, thump rhythm on the grain. This would be the barley for the beer.

The women were in the house. Laima and Anete and Hortense were canning the last of the tomatoes. Mija, Lize, and Astrid were playing with the twins in the living room. Ruta and Rita had started sitting up. If placed on the floor on their stomachs, Rita tried to crawl while Ruta rolled over and sat up.

Ints was outside in the barnyard feeding the lone pig. He heard the distant buzz and looked up into the bright cloudless sky. The planes were high, and he couldn't make out what kind they were. He ran to the barn to tell the men. They came out and watched from the shade of the barn. They counted five planes. Then the women came out of the house to see what the noise was. Lize and Astrid each held a twin in their arms and pointed for them to look up. As the planes circled, they moved lower.

Ints said, "Are they going to bomb us?"

Peters put a protective arm on Ints' shoulder. "I don't think so."

Mija said, "I bet they're going to land at the base."

Ints asked, "Why are they here?"

Peters said, "Maybe they're here to protect us. Don't worry. Everything will be fine."

Dinner that evening was strange. For once, Feliks did the talking. He rambled about how he was going to make beer from the equipment that was handed down to him through two generations. He went into detail about each step and described the brew pot and the hose and the bottling bucket. He finished by saying, "My homebrew is the best."

Peters said, "Not only have I never brewed beer, but I've never known anyone who brewed it. How long until the first batch is ready?"

"A matter of weeks," said Feliks, "but it will be at its best by Christmas."

Ints said, "Can I have some too?"

Mija said, "On Christmas Eve, we'll let you have a little taste."

Lize said, "What about me?"

Mija said, "Yes, everyone who wants a taste of

beer shall have one on Christmas Eve." The children cheered and the adults smiled. In the back of Mija's mind, she still saw the images of the Nazi warplanes circling the farm.

That night, Mija was awakened by a tapping on her shoulder and then a hand on her mouth. As her eyes adjusted in the dark, she saw Peters' face. He was holding an index finger at his mouth to signal silence. She nodded and he took his hand away.

He whispered, "Get dressed. Meet me downstairs."

"Why?" she whispered back.

"Aleks."

Mija's dress for tomorrow was laid out on the dresser and her shoes were on the floor next to it, so it didn't take long.

She followed him in silence to the barn. Peters pulled the door open enough for them to enter and left it ajar.

A portable light sitting on the barn floor was on, and Mija saw her husband. He was almost close enough to touch. He wore a German uniform with a Latvian Army insignia on the chest. His hair was cut short, and he was clean-shaven and healthy-looking, a much different man from the one who left her a few months ago.

"Where have you been?" she asked.

"Didn't Marina tell you?"

"She said you disappeared into the German Army on July 2. Where have you been all this time?"

"Germany. There was no way to get in touch. I landed in Gulepils this afternoon. We're going to reopen the base here for training purposes. I'm in charge of the base and the Gulepils region."

Mija locked eyes with Aleks and said, "Have you gone crazy?"

"Better me than a foreigner."

"Are you sure?" She clenched her fists.

"Yes."

"And when they tell you to kill other Latvians? What will you do?"

"I won't be put in that position. Don't you see? I'm more valuable like this."

She realized their discussion was hopeless but continued anyway. "They're killing the Jews."

"They're fighting a war. They're fighting against Stalin."

"Do you deny they're killing the Jews?"

"I haven't seen such a thing."

"Why did you come here?" What he was saying was so far against her own beliefs that she almost wished he hadn't come.

"I went to our house first. Do you know there's almost nothing left? I was frightened when I saw it. I'm so relieved you're all here."

"Are we in danger?" Mija's and Aleks' eyes were still locked. Peters hadn't moved from his spot behind Mija.

Aleks said, "As far as I know, you're not in any personal danger. But I believe things will get worse before they get better."

"What if you lose the war?"

"I'd rather be dead than have the Russians here again."

"Are there only two alternatives, the Germans or the Russians?"

"In Germany, I saw many things. And I read the secret pact between Hitler and Stalin. The Baltics were carved up even before the war started."

She didn't want to hear anything else. "Why did you come here?"

"You sound angry."

"I am." Mija clenched her fists tighter. "You disappeared. I didn't know if you were alive or dead. And now you show up in the middle of the night dressed like the enemy."

"I'm sorry I scared you. I came to help, but I don't have much time. My car is parked down the road a little, with my driver Johan. I swore him to secrecy, and the others who helped me."

"Let's get to it then." She unclenched her fists.

"I have legal papers here saying that Lize and Ints are orphans and that Feliks and Laima are their guardians. They'll be safer that way."

"I don't doubt that." How terrible, she thought. "What about me?"

"I have papers for you and Peters. Identity papers with new names. You both should go into hiding. You, Mija, so that in case things don't go well, you'll be safe from reprisals having to do with a husband in the

German army. Peters, because there is a decree coming out. Anyone between the ages of 18 and 45 will have to register for labor service. Anyone not registering will receive a fine and prison term. Thank goodness Feliks will be forty-six this year. The papers for Peters have a false name and birthday, making him the same age. Peters, it's the only way you won't be conscripted into the German Army. Your other choice is to volunteer for the Latvian Legion, and I will make sure you work for me."

Peters said, "Thank you. I'll take the false identity." Aleks handed him the documents.

Aleks continued. "The papers say you were both born in Riga. That way you can get ration cards if need be and travel in and out of the city. I kept your first names Emmija and Peters, for simplicity's sake. Your last names are both Ezerins. That is on purpose also, so you can pose as husband and wife, if need be."

Mija was surprised at the amount of thought and planning that Aleks had done, and her heart softened a little. She said, "How can I get in touch with you?"

"You can't. It's better that way. Will you please write a letter to my mother?"

"What should I tell her? And better yet, what should I tell our children?"

"Tell them what you think is best." Aleks walked up to Mija, put his hands on her shoulders and tried to kiss her. Even though she appreciated that he was concerned for their safety, she couldn't understand why he'd work with the Germans. In body, he was the man she married, but in principle, he was a man she didn't recognize. She pressed her lips together and didn't move her arms. He let go, walked slowly to the portable light, turned it off, and walked out of the barn, carrying the light with him.

Mija wiped her lips with the back of her hand. "He's not the man I married." She and Peters walked back to the house in silence. He held the documents in one hand and with the other, held Mija's hand.

Mija went back to bed and lay on top of the covers still dressed and made a plan. As soon as Lize and Astrid were back at Velsaine and Ints started school with Feliks and Laima as his guardians, she would get Edmunds' father out of Riga.

CHAPTER FOURTEEN

A filmy drizzle veiled the late morning light. Mija and Peters arrived at the Gulepils train station in plenty of time and sat at the rear of the last car, the only one carrying civilians. Within minutes, all the seats were occupied. Outside, soldiers stood in lines, waiting to enter the other cars. The process of loading them seemed interminable. Mija fidgeted with her purse, opening and closing it. Peters patted her hand and said, "Relax." She sat still and concentrated on whether they had missed planning for any contingency. Half an hour later, they still sat.

A soldier entered at the front and started checking each person's passport and ticket. He talked so fast, Mija couldn't make out what was being said. Her German was good, but not good enough to decipher such a fast clip from so far away. The first person, a man in an expensive business suit, handed up his papers. The soldier examined them and gave them back with a curt *Danke*. It was a slow process. As the soldier moved closer, Mija could hear the same two questions over and over. "Where are you going?" and either "What is your business there?" or "What was your business here?" With every second or third person, the soldier asked additional questions.

"It's taking too long," whispered Mija. Peters put his arm around her shoulder and squeezed lightly. He whispered back, "It'll be fine." Mija looked outside through the shrouded mist at the soldiers guarding the station doors. Standing ramrod straight and holding their rifles pointed at the sky, they resembled her son's wooden toy soldiers. She wondered if it was normal to have that many at such a small station. Her inclination was to get up and leave. Then she reminded herself of their mission.

The soldier finally reached them, and she took out their false passports and handed them over. The soldier asked, "Where are you going?"

As per the plan, Peters lied. "We're going home, to Riga."

"What was your business here?"

"Visiting my sick mother." Peters had the appropriate expression on his face.

The soldier said, "Sorry." As if tired from his work, he took a cursory look at their passports and gave them back. He wasted no time leaving, closing the door behind him.

Peters whispered, "See? All is well."

Mija could not think of anything safe to say. Peters kept his arm around her shoulder and was equally quiet. The minutes passed by like hours. Fifteen minutes later, the train finally left. The clickety-clack of the wheels drowned out conversation. Mija stared out the window, comforted by the warmth of Peters' arm.

Eventually, the sky lightened and the drizzle stopped, but pale gray cloud cover remained. They reached Riga four hours later. The civilians, including Mija and Peters, rushed to get off the train and into the terminal, then pushed through the exit doors leading to the street.

"What if we can't find Samuel?" Peters said.

Now that she was in Riga, Mija felt a newfound confidence. "We will find him. All we need to do is follow the directions Edmunds gave us. The delay in Gulepils worked to our advantage. Now we don't have to worry about what to do before five o'clock when everyone returns home from work. We'll be less noticeable."

PETERS TOOK MIJA'S HAND. She felt his sweat mingle with hers. As they crossed Lacplesa Iela onto Sadovnikova, they entered an older part of the city, one neither of them was familiar with. Mija and Peters had both memorized Edmunds directions and didn't need to discuss their route. They passed by a building on a corner that, according to Edmunds, was the Ghetto Guard headquarters and marked the edge of the Jewish ghetto. Here, many people wearing Star of David armbands walked with fast steps and averted eyes. A few blocks later, there were only a few others.

Mija said, "I wonder why there are no soldiers here.

"They must be concentrated at the entry points."

Four blocks later, at their target street, Liksna Iela, they turned left and found number twenty-two. Peters rang the doorbell marked number four. An old woman with wavy white hair stuck her head out a second-floor window. "What do you want?"

Peters said, "We're here to see Samuel Freibergs. We're friends of his son Edmunds."

"I'll be right down to let you in."

They entered a small vestibule and followed the woman up a flight of narrow wooden stairs and through a door that led into a small kitchen where an old man sat at a scarred wooden table. A small collection of Star of David armbands dangled from a hook on the coat stand by the door. A young woman held a baby on her hip with one arm and with the other hand stirred a pot on the stove. The room smelled like cabbage. Mija could see through the doorway into the next room where people sat on a sofa and chairs and several children played on the floor. The adults within view stared at the visitors, but no one spoke.

Peters said, "Is there a Samuel here?"

The man in the kitchen chair said, "Who are you?"

"I'm Peters and this is Mija. We are friends of Edmunds Freibergs."

The man said, "I never heard of a Peters. Ester has spoken of a Mija, another teacher. Are you her?"

"Yes. You must be Samuel. Edmunds looks a lot like you. It's a pleasure to meet you." Mija extended her hand.

Samuel stood to shake hands and said, "Why did Edmunds send you?"

Mija shrugged, "It's simple. To take you to him."

Samuel eyebrows lifted. "Really?"

"We don't have much time."

The old woman who let them in said, "Can you take me too?"

Peters said, "To Gulepils?"

"Anywhere. Eventually, I want to go to Daugavpils where my daughter lives. Please."

With merely a fleeting thought of consequences, Mija said, "Yes, we'll take you."

The woman's eyes lit up. "I'm Freda. Thank you, thank you so much."

Peters said, "But you can't take anything with you except a purse. And Samuel, take nothing but what you can put into the pockets of your jacket. Do you both have papers?"

Samuel said, "I have an old passport and the new one."

Freda said, "Me too."

"Bring only your old passports," Peters said. "Let's go. We don't have much time to get back to the train station."

The young mother at the stove turned and said,

"Can you help the rest of us get out?"

Peters said, "We can try to come back and take a few at a time."

"Thank you, the young woman said. "After the recent fire, there is little hope that any good can come of staying in Riga if you are a Jew."

Peters said, "We heard about the fire."

She nodded. "Yes, the Germans brought a new kind of hell."

Mija said, "We were horrified to hear. We had no idea, until very recently, of what was going on in Riga."

Samuel and Freda hugged everyone goodbye. As the four were about to go out the door, Samuel took an armband.

Peters said, "No, no armband. If we get stopped, we'll pretend to be visitors here for the day."

"And if they ask for our papers?"

"In Gulepils, no one has the new papers. We'll say you moved to Gulepils and the change of address form hasn't arrived yet. If we are lucky, no one will stop us. Walk tall, as if you know your purpose."

Mija walked arm-in-arm with Freda, staying next to Peters and Samuel, and the four smiled and chatted as if they didn't have a care in the world. The streets were crowded. Within minutes, Mija's face hurt from smiling, and her mouth was so dry, she could barely talk. But they were in luck this day. They walked past the exit guards and out of the ghetto without being stopped.

At the train station, Peters bought one-way tickets

for Freda and Samuel. They found the platform with the train bound for Gulepils and, as in the morning, boarded the last car, again the only one for civilians. Unlike the crowded trip to Riga, most of the seats were empty. Mija led the way to the last row. Freda sat at the window with Mija next to her. Samuel was at the window across from them, with Peters in the aisle seat. Mija asked Freda and Samuel for their passports and put all four together inside her purse, as she was the only one who spoke fluent German. As the minutes ticked by, the car filled to about half its capacity. Mija asked Freda question after question about her life in order not to think about what lay ahead.

Twenty minutes later, a soldier came and started checking papers. By the time he reached them, Mija's cheeks were on fire. She smiled as she handed over their passports. He checked each one carefully and then the matching person. Frowning, he said, "Where are the new papers for the old people?"

Mija smiled and then said, "They haven't received them. Many in the outlying areas have not. We came on the morning train from Gulepils, where they know of this trouble. Our papers were not questioned and we are merely going home again, sir."

The soldier dropped the passports in her lap and pointed a finger at her. "Do not try to travel anymore with these papers." He clicked his heels, turned around, and walked out of the car.

CHAPTER FIFTEEN

*I*n the middle of November, Mija and Peters moved to a deserted farm about an hour by horse from Riga. They stayed in the barn to avoid detection. They planned to move closer to the outskirts of Riga as soon as they could.

Peters prayed that his wife and boys were alive and thought about how cold Siberia was, colder than here by a large margin. He felt guilty for not being there, for not being put on the cattle car with them, not being able to find them or help them or save them.

So far, the shortwave radio had been no help. Today was Christmas and there was still no news. What he did hear was that Germans were killing Jews in all the bigger cities. In some cases, many thousands. There was never information directly from Riga. Partisans wouldn't dare send signals from the city. He worried about the chances of having his own transmission signal intercepted. They were in touch with Willy and the others using special codes that changed weekly. They planned to band together as soon as he and Mija set up a base of operations closer to Riga. Then it would be easier to go in and out of the city as needed. They had discussed hijacking a car or small truck, but then there would be the problem of finding fuel and maintaining the vehicle. Trains were no longer an option. As of last week, civilians had to have a special visa to be on a particular train at a particular time.

So far, they had only saved Samuel and Freda from the Riga ghetto. The second time Mija and Peters went to Riga, the ghetto was fully enclosed in barbed wire, and there was one way in and out, through the gate next to the Ghetto guard headquarters. Jewish people with work permits were allowed out to go to work in the morning and back in at night. They were counted each time. Anyone else needed a special permit from the police station. Mija and Peters had left empty-handed and disheartened.

Peters sat cross-legged on the floor in a corner of the loft, head hanging. The pressure from the headset hurt his ears. He jerked it off and threw it against the wall. A few minutes later, he heard Mija tethering the horse below. He rubbed his hands together and blew on them before putting his wool mittens back on. Upon standing, he felt the usual stiffness and jiggled his legs up and down to get the circulation going. He went to the loft opening, removed the thin wood covering, and waited for her.

"What's the news?" Mija asked, as she handed Peters a brown paper bag.

"Nothing new," he said.

She lifted one booted foot to the top rung of the ladder. Peters put the bag down, held onto her hands with his, and pulled her the rest of the way in. A gusty wind blew upward as Mija turned to re-cover the opening with the wood and an old hooked rug.

Peters smelled the package. "Smoked sausage?"

"Yes. They killed the pig. And there are two bottles of Feliks' beer."

Mija shuddered as she took off her wool scarf, shook her hair, and unbuttoned her coat. She was on the verge of tears but didn't want to cry. And as much as she dreaded it, she needed to talk. She stood there and talked and talked until the story of her day was told.

IT STARTED WITH A LONG horseback ride to see her children early that Christmas morning and ended with another long ride back in the cold of the setting sun. She hadn't been to the farm in two weeks. Feliks ran out from the barn to greet her. Her big brother, a tall, large, balding man, sobbed and gave her a bear hug. She hugged him back hard, not knowing why, but understanding that he needed comfort. Without talking, they walked the horse into the barn and Feliks closed the door behind them.

"What happened?"

"Ruta died."

Blood left her face as the news sank in. Tears streamed down Feliks' cheeks. She grappled with what to say. No words would be good enough. Finally, she asked, "What about Rita?"

"She cries all day for her sister."

"What happened?"

"We don't know. She had a bad chest infection and then the fever wouldn't go down." Feliks wiped his eyes. "She was coughing since the summer."

"I thought she was better last time I was here."

"She was. But then one day last week, she got worse and worse. Three days ago, she started with convulsions and then she died."

"Where?"

"She's here, in the barn, wrapped in a blanket, in the little coffin I finished this morning. I tried to make a grave close to the grove of white birches out back, but the ground is too hard." He wiped his eyes with the back of his hand.

Mija said, "I'll boil water and we'll soften the ground, at least for a shallow grave." She patted his shoulder and then hugged him. "I'll get started."

In the house, Mija gathered a somber Ints, Lize, and Astrid close to her in the kitchen and stood holding them without talking for a few minutes. She asked them to sit and wait. She walked into the living room where Laima sat expressionless in the same chair as last year when she was in labor. Rita had fallen asleep on her lap and her little blond head was propped in the crook of Laima's arm. Laima rocked back and forth, her face streaked with tears. They continued to fall as she patted Rita's back.

Mija said, "I'm so sorry."

Laima looked down at Rita as though she hadn't heard and continued rocking. Mija returned to the kitchen. Too nervous to sit, she stood, facing the children. "Where are Grandma and Hortense?"

"Back at our house," Lize said. "Papa took them. He came here with another soldier the day before Ruta died. He told us even old women had to do their duty, that they had to keep the house and cook for him and the soldiers living there."

Mija's legs gave way, and she dropped into the nearest chair. She stayed calm on the outside. There was no point in getting angry now. She would save that for later. "How many soldiers?"

"I don't know. Papa said something about soldiers in every room," Lize said. "Mama, he was dressed like the other German soldier. Why?"

"He's trying to help us the only way he knows how."

Ints said, "We did what you told us and pretended we didn't know him. His eyes looked sad and he acted like he didn't know us either. Why?"

Mija wiped her eyes and said, "War makes strange things necessary. And the other soldiers, they are not our friends."

Ints said, "I'm afraid." He started crying too.

Mija got up and put her arms around him. "Don't be afraid. In the end, all will be well."

Mija stood there holding onto her son. She told the girls they were old enough now at thirteen to take over the household duties, that they should help Laima and also help take care of Rita. Astrid said she was a good cook, her mother had taught her at an early age when she had to stand on a chair to reach the stove. Lize said she would keep everything neat and clean.

Lize asked, "What about school? We have to go back to Velsaine after the winter holiday."

"Yes," Mija sighed. "You must go back. There's no choice about that. Can you do what I've asked?" She looked from one to the next. "Remember, you must take care of each other."

Mija told Ints that he would have to be Feliks' big boy and help with the manly duties and with the animals. Ints nodded gravely. He had been holding a small wooden truck that Feliks had carved for him. He walked over to the jelly cupboard and shoved it into the bottom drawer.

Mija wanted to tell him no, don't put the toy away, you can still play. But she didn't.

It took several hours to boil enough water. Ints kept the fire stoked and put more logs in the potbellied stove as they were needed. Lize and Astrid filled the pots and watched them heat up. Mija carried the pots to the gravesite where Feliks dug.

When the hole was big enough, Mija helped Feliks carry the tiny coffin and place it in the ground. Everyone gathered outside, bundled up against the winter wind. A rogue cloud covered the sun for a few minutes. Old leaves swirled across the dark ground. Laima held Rita in her arms, her chin resting on top of Rita's head. Mija read from the bible. "The Lord is my Shepherd, I shall not want . . ." Then she said a prayer and asked for God's mercy and for the angels in heaven to take good care of Ruta. She sent the others back to the house and helped Feliks cover the grave with the hard earth.

MIJA TOLD PETERS, "They killed the pig the day before Ruta died. They thought maybe she wasn't getting enough of the right kind of food. But it was too late. Today is their birthday, and now Christmas will always be a day of sorrow."

"I'm sorry." Peters wiped his eyes.

Mija walked to the corner that was their sleeping area and sat down on the blankets and straw bedding. "I give up. I can't do this anymore."

Peters walked in circles. Mija started to sob and he went to her, sat down, and put his arms around her. Her shoulders heaved and she let go of the grief and anger that she had held back all day and the days before and all the days since the war started. He put one hand on the top of her head and with the other arm held her against his chest. Eventually, her sobs lessened.

She said, "I want peace and all we have is ceaseless war."

"It's not ceaseless."

"It feels that way. The years of freedom seem like

a dream. We were at war when I was a child and we're at war again. As a child, in spite of the horror, I had hope. I covered my fears with hope. Now I don't even have that." She cried quiet tears that streamed down her cheeks and came from the ocean of tears she'd held back for so long. "I'm going to drown."

"We're not near any water." Peters held her tighter.

"I'm going to drown in my tears."

"We will survive this."

"I don't know."

"We will get through this." He rocked her slightly, back and forth. She felt the strength of his arms and the warmth of his breath on her face. At the same time, there was a hollow ache inside. He touched his lips to hers, at first tentatively and then harder but still with gentleness. She pulled back.

"No, we can't. It's too late for us."

He said in a husky voice, "Don't speak."

"Peters."

"Don't speak. Don't speak."

He kissed her again. His lips were soft and tender, the same as she remembered from their teenage years. She melted into them and went to a different place, a place where no one could hurt her and where she didn't need to be afraid. Soon they were naked under the blankets and they found the wave of each other and rode the wave and no one else existed but the two of them. For a long time afterward, they lay as one, intertwined. She wanted to stay there forever.

Peters spoke first. "I love you."

She answered, "I love you, too, but we must not speak of it."

"Yes, we need to."

"In the beginning, you said don't speak of it. And we won't." Mija touched her lips to his to silence him and they lay there, kissing, touching along the length of their bodies, and feeling the warmth of each other. Gradually, they separated and were two, not one, and Mija was cold.

FOR THEIR EVENING MEAL, they shared one of the sausages and drank the two bottles of beer. As if what happened did not happen or perhaps it was merely unspeakable, Mija said, "I forgot to brush Big Z down and feed him."

"I'll go. You rest."

After he took care of Big Z, Peters went outside in the dark to walk and think. Snow started to fall in large, soft flakes. A memory from his childhood intruded, a memory of playing in the snow with his best friend Mija, a snowball fight on the way home from school. He stuck his tongue out and tasted the cold drops. He scooped up some snow and made a ball, which he threw toward the woods nearby. The snowball splattered against a tree. A muffled noise startled him and he stood still. But he didn't hear anything else. Maybe it was a rabbit, maybe his imagination. He walked the perimeter of the barn, his black cap and coat turning white. Nothing seemed out of the ordinary. Peters' footprints blurred as soon as he made them. For tonight, with the snowstorm upon them, they should be safe.

When Peters returned to the loft, Mija was asleep. He took off his cold, wet shoes and crawled under the pile of blankets next to her. The bottom layer was an old down comforter, which was still good enough to keep them from freezing. On top of them was a newer and thicker down blanket and piled on that were four woolen horse blankets.

Mija had her back to Peters. He put his arm over her and she muttered, "I'm frightened."

"It's all right," He stroked her shoulder and then snuggled closer. The wind whistled through the cracks, lulling her to sleep.

Mija jolted awake in pitch black to the sound of Big Z neighing. Big Z neighed again. She turned toward Peters and shook his shoulder.

CHAPTER SIXTEEN

*B*ig Z neighed again. Mija whispered, "Someone's down there." Peters reached for the rifle,
stowed under a pile of hay next to his head. He crept
to the opening and in one swoop lifted and moved
aside both the rug and the wood covering.

Pointing his rifle downward he bellowed, "Move
to the ladder! With your arms up! Quick, or I'll shoot!"

A female voice yelled, "My gott. Don't shoot." A
dim figure, swaddled in blankets, appeared by the
ladder below.

"Who are you?"

"Please. I all alone."

"Your name?" Peters kept the rifle trained on her.

"Dara. I look for food. Two days since I eat."

"How do I know you're telling the truth?"

Mija had crawled to the opening and peered down.
Peters tried to wave her away with a twist of his head.

Mija left but only to light a candle and take it to the opening. She held the candle low so the light diffused down. Peters glowered.

Mija said, "Take the blankets off so we can see you."

The girl dropped two blankets, took off a headscarf and a knitted hat. Then she removed three coats and two sweaters. She stood in a long-sleeved red wool dress, black wool stockings, and worn leather boots. Even in the dim light, one could see that she was skin and bones, with a smudged face, dark eyes, and dark shoulder-length hair down. She scratched her head with all ten fingers.

"Where are you going?" Peters asked.

"I go to Riga, to parents. Germans start ghetto in Riga, parents send me to Balvi, stay with aunt and uncle. Soldiers come. Take aunt and uncle. I hide in closet until next day. I take food tied in scarf. I stay near to woods. My food, gone. I looking for food. Is here near Riga? I not see horse until he make noise."

"Put your clothes back on," Mija said. "And then come up here. We have food."

Once in the loft, the girl gobbled up the piece of sausage and slice of pumpernickel bread that Mija gave her. Peters made a bed for her in a corner of the loft.

"Where do you come from?" Mija asked.

"I tell you, Riga." Dara ate the last bite of black bread and licked her fingers. "Is good food."

"I mean before that. Latvian is not your native language."

"Oh, Ukraine. Papa. He come to Ukraine for working on railroads and meet Mama. We come to Riga five years."

By the time Dara settled down and fell asleep, the light of gray dawn crept through the big crack in the corner wall. Mija and Peters were awake, talking quietly, side by side, with the covers pulled up to their chins. As they breathed out, puffs of white melted into the air. The cold penetrated everything.

"We have to move into the house," said Peters, "I'll chop some wood, we'll make a fire."

"It's too dangerous." Mija's teeth chattered.

"We'll keep a fire going at night to keep us from freezing."

"If we do that, we won't have Big Z to warn us of intruders." Mija shivered. She was colder than she'd ever been before.

"You're hot. Are you sick?" Peters felt her forehead. "You have a fever. We're moving into the house. No arguments."

Mija shivered again. "It's dangerous, and I can't be sick."

PETERS WOULDN'T HEAR ANY arguments about not moving. As he considered the situation, he wrinkled his forehead. The door to the one-story house was both locked and sturdy. He didn't want to chop the door open or break a window. The chimney would have to be their way in. When Dara woke up, he coaxed her into climbing up a ladder onto the roof. He climbed up behind her, held her hands and lowered her. Once she was all the way in, it was a short drop to the ground. Dara had no trouble opening the door to let them in.

In the main room, the fireplace was open on all four sides. One side had a brick ledge to use as a stove. A square pine table and four matching chairs sat not far from the stove, covered with a pretty tablecloth, white with embroidered flowers along the edges. A small blue vase, empty, sat in the middle of the table as if waiting for spring and for someone to fill it with wild daisies. A sink against the outer wall had a hand pump that fed from a well. There were two bedrooms, no bathroom. They would continue using the outhouse. One small bedroom had a double bed and one dresser. The other bedroom, even smaller, had a single bed and a small two-drawer chest. The furniture was dark pine and looked like someone had made it a long time ago.

The air felt colder inside the house than outside. Everything had been cleaned and put away, as though the owners went on vacation and would be back at any moment. In the cupboard that held the dishes, Peters found two jars, one with honey, the other with strawberry preserves.

Mija didn't complain or even talk as Peters and Dara helped her get from the barn to the house and into the bed in the larger bedroom. Every part of her body hurt, especially her head. All she wanted was to get warm. Peters covered her with the down comforters from both beds. Then he chopped wood and started a fire, not caring about the daylight. He made herb tea and added a teaspoon of honey. Dara sat by Mija's side and fed her with a spoon. This took a long time because Mija kept closing her eyes. Dara patiently waited for her to open them again. Peters moved everything except the horse into the house, even the shortwave radio.

Outside, everything was covered in a thick blanket of snow that kept falling. The good thing about that was that no one would be able to surprise them, at least not in the daytime. The woods started far enough away that anyone nearing would be visible as long as someone kept a lookout. Peters didn't shovel a walkway from the house to the outhouse or the barn because he wanted no indication that anyone was there. He slogged through the snow a different way each time so as not to make a path. He even balanced a steel washtub from the barn on top of his head, bringing it into the house and setting it between the sink and table. He kept the fire going all day and all night, until the next day after breakfast.

When he wanted to use the shortwave radio, he carried it to the barn and reconnected it to the antenna cable, which, as always, was disguised by the stork's nest on the roof.

That evening, Peters and Dara sat by the fire and she opened up to him.

"My parents very old when marry and not think they will have children. I was big surprise. Now they sick. Arthritis. Goiter. Gout. Worst is back troubles.

They need me take care. I need find them."

He patted her on the shoulder. "Yes, I understand. But right now, it's not safe. As soon as possible, we'll help you."

"I lucky to find you and Mija. I hope she better soon."

Mija was sick for several days. Peters and Dara made herbal tea for her every few hours and took turns sitting with her. Peters slept beside the fireplace. He had made himself a pallet with the horse blankets from the barn. Being right beside the fireplace, he felt when the fire needed tending and could do the job half asleep.

On New Year's Day, they took baths. Peters went first while the women waited in the bedroom. When it was the women's turn, Peters went to the barn with his radio.

Mija couldn't wait to get in the warm water. She just fit, and to get her head wet, she bent forward and dunked her head. The sliver of harsh lye soap they had found seemed like the creamiest cream to Mija, and her skin flushed as she dried herself. Clean clothes, woman's clothes from the drawers, a blue and green flowered dress, felt strange, but when she belted the dress, the fit was acceptable. Dara also wore clothes from the drawers; a navy dress with long sleeves that had seen much wear. They boiled more water and washed their dirty clothes. They scrubbed and scrubbed until their hands were red and then hung the clothes all over the house to dry. The coats, though, were wool. They carried them to the barn and laid them over bales of straw. They'd leave them there for a few days to air out and all the bugs would die.

There was still a problem with Dara. Her head was full of lice. The only remedy Mija could think of was to cut Dara's hair and then shave her head. Otherwise, she and Peters would soon have lice too. There was nothing to say they didn't have nits already incubating in their scalps.

Dara didn't like that idea. "I ugly if no hair."

Mija said, "Don't worry, your hair will grow in by the time anyone sees you. Besides, do you want to keep on scratching every minute of the day and give the bugs to us too?"

Dara relented.

Mija picked a spot outside, well away from the front door so no stray hairs with nits would blow into the house. Dara held the oldest blanket tightly around her neck so all the hairs would fall to the ground and not on her clothes. They would leave the blanket outside and bury it deep under the snow. Using a pair of scissors, Mija cut Dara's hair as short to the scalp as she could. Dara's scalp showed pink in the bright sunlight, scratched raw in some places. Mija used a bucket of warm water and lathered Dara's head as fast as she could. Using Peters' razor, Mija shaved, starting at the top of Dara's forehead.

"Am I hurting you?"

"No. I cold."

"I'm almost finished."

Moments later, a horse with one rider galloped toward them.

Mija said, "Go inside. Now."

CHAPTER SEVENTEEN

Aleks waited until well past the 8:00 p.m. civilian curfew. The dim streetlights cast a long, skinny shadow. His shadow shortened as he neared each light and became almost nonexistent as he walked past. He was dressed for the weather, wearing his gray army coat and wool army hat. His scarf was wrapped twice around his neck. The wind blew random snowflakes from the ground up to his face and soon his cheeks were red and his eyebrows were built up with tufts of white. He carried a little package in the crook of his arm. The sidewalks were cleared of most of the snow that fell earlier in the day but were still slippery in places, and he couldn't walk as fast as he wanted. The area around the Freedom Monument was unlit. He looked at the street sign. Instead of Brivibas Iela (Freedom Street), the sign said Adolf-Hitler Strasse.

Aleks didn't know everything, but he did know that the Germans living in Latvia were allocated larger food rations. The native citizens were restricted to 900 calories a day. He knew that the people in the country who grew their own food were lucky. And that those in the army were warm and fed.

He reached the familiar brownstone building on Baznicas Iela, stood in the walkway to the courtyard, and lit a cigarette. Now that he was here, he wasn't ready to go in. There was no difference if he blew out smoke or air, every breath came out as a white puff. He threw the butt into the snowbank on the edge of the sidewalk and made his way through the walkway. A skinny black cat ran in front of him.

At the door to the second-floor apartment, Aleks knocked and waited. He knocked again. Marina opened the door. She looked Aleks up and down but didn't say anything.

"Hello, Mother. May I come in?"

"Yes." She turned and retreated. Aleks closed the door behind him. His mother took a seat in the green chair. She was wearing a brown wool shawl that covered her head and shoulders. On her hands, she wore crocheted brown and yellow gloves. Her black dress came to mid-calf, and her black boots reached to the hem. When she sat, several inches of her pale white legs were exposed.

Aleks took a seat on the burgundy sofa.

"It's cold in here." He didn't unwrap his scarf.

"No wood. Maybe tomorrow."

Aleks set his package down on the coffee table and took off his gloves. Leaning forward, he ripped the brown paper off the package. There were four individually wrapped bars of Belgian chocolate and he handed one to her.

She said, "I don't like chocolate," and didn't move.

He laid the bar back on top of the other three and said, "Perhaps on a day when you have no food, this will help keep you alive." Marina sat up straighter. He continued, "I was going to ask you to give the other three to Mija and Lize and Ints if you see them. You can give them yours as well if you wish."

"Perhaps I can trade my chocolate for a piece of wood. I've not seen Mija."

"Ints is safe with Laima and Feliks. Lize was at boarding school but is with her brother for the winter holiday. I don't know where Mija is. I thought maybe she'd been here," he said.

"I've not heard from her since July."

Aleks was disheartened to hear this. He'd hoped to find out that Mija was safe. He'd even imagined that she might be here. She hadn't been seen in Gulepils for months. "Would you consider leaving Riga now? I can get you safely to Gulepils."

"Is there danger?"

"Not from the army, merely from starving or freezing."

"I stay. You stationed in Riga now?"

"No, I'm here for a meeting."

"What happened to the Jews?"

"What do you mean?"

"The ghetto. Only ghosts are left."

"Ghosts?"

"The Jews, they're gone. Thousands, maybe twenty thousand."

Aleks' mother wouldn't tell tales. "I don't know what happens in Riga. I'm in charge of the little area around Gulepils and the base there. And I arrived here this afternoon. What did you hear?"

"The Germans are butchers, no better than Communists. Pah!"

Aleks winced. "I'm doing what I need to do to protect my family. I'll see what I can find out."

"Don't come back in that uniform."

"I don't have any other clothes here, I'm sorry." Aleks stood up and unbuttoned his coat. He took some folded German money out of his pocket and bent over to lay it on the middle of the coffee table, next to the chocolate bars. "Happy Christmas, Mother. I hope you can get some wood with this."

She stared straight ahead. Aleks buttoned his coat and let himself out.

On the walk back to the Hotel Riga, Aleks came upon a group of three soldiers holding each other up and walking crookedly, but he saluted them anyway. They stopped and attempted to salute him back. The one farthest from him slipped and made windmill movements with his arms but fell down anyway. Aleks kept on walking.

The Hotel Riga had been commandeered by the German army. His room was on the fourth floor, one floor below the room he and Mija were in during their honeymoon. He still had a good view of the opera house.

He threw his coat on a chair. The snow on his eyebrows melted and ran down the side of his face. He stood by the window and stared. He replayed the honeymoon weekend with Mija and regretted that they hadn't left the room and gone to see an opera that Saturday night. He had never been to one. He thought about his mother and felt guilty because he was warm. Sleep was a long time coming.

Breakfast was an official affair in the high-ceilinged dining room that could hold five hundred. Aleks was escorted to his assigned table by a blond Latvian girl wearing a blue Tyrolian dress. His direct superior, Major General Kurt Lintelle, a tall, balding man, already sat eating but rose to shake hands. The Major General's silver hair grew in a semicircle above his ears all the way around, and the top of his head was shiny.

"Colonel Adamsons," he said, and clicked his heels together.

Aleks also clicked his heels. He had gotten used to this little ritual and didn't realize he did it. "Good morning, Major General. I hope I am not late." Aleks knew he wasn't late, he was fifteen minutes early, but wasn't sure why the Major General was already eating.

"You're in plenty of time. Please, help yourself."

Major General pointed toward the buffet table along the wall. Major General sat back down and waved his arm. A dark-haired waiter dressed in black came running. Major General snapped his fingers, "Coffee here," and pointed to the cup by Aleks' place. The table was set for four, but the other two chairs were empty.

Aleks helped himself to a boiled egg, some sprats, and a slice of pumpernickel bread. He passed by the smoked salmon, pickled herring in sour cream, and fancy breads.

Aleks sat down and Major General asked, "Not hungry?" He slathered butter on a croissant and bit off a large chunk.

Aleks shrugged. "In the morning, I'm not as hungry as later."

Aleks cracked open the egg with the edge of his knife. He noticed a chip on the rim of his coffee cup. "When I was here before, the china was much better. And there was silverware, not these aluminum pieces."

Major General swallowed what was in his mouth and picked up his cup. "Yes." He drank sloppily and waved to the waiter to refill his cup. "The good china and silver were sent to Berlin for safekeeping."

Aleks ate one bite at a time and sipped his coffee, waiting for Major General to talk. Aleks was soon finished. Major General was still eating. The room started to clear.

"We will have our meeting now." Major General said.

"Certainly, sir."

Major General stood up and Aleks followed him through the dining entrance into the grand entry hall and up the wide staircase to the second floor. All the rooms had been converted into offices and meeting rooms. They went into Major General's private office. Aleks became concerned. He thought he was coming to a group meeting of officers to discuss how things were going in the various sectors of Latvia and ways to improve the war effort. He had ideas about those things and had spent a good part of the car ride yesterday jotting down notes. Major General walked around his large mahogany desk and sat in his black leather chair. Aleks sat in the first of the two smaller chairs facing the desk.

Major General said, "Welcome to Riga." He retrieved a bottle of French brandy and two snifters out of a drawer and poured. Aleks wasn't used to drinking in the morning. He removed a silver cigarette case from his shirt pocket, opened it, and offered one to Major General. Major General took one and used the heavy silver lighter on his desk. He stood and handed Aleks one of the brandy snifters. Aleks rose also and they clinked glasses. Major General drank half of his in one swallow. Aleks took a taste. The thick brandy, with a slight flavor of apricots, slid down his throat easily. Aleks set the snifter on the desk and waited. Major General drank the rest of his brandy in one gulp.

"You're doing an excellent job, Aleks."

"Thank you, sir."

"We're going to need more like you in the coming

days. Yes, it won't be long before you're also promoted to Major General and have an office next to mine."

"I'd be honored, sir."

"We need your help."

"With what, sir?"

"First, we need to reduce the rations. We'd like to do that with a minimum of fuss and maybe even so that the people don't realize it."

"With all respect, sir, I'm not experienced in food rationing."

"Second, we need to continue taking care of the Jewish problem."

"In what way, sir?"

"The problem in Riga is under control. We've moved all the women and children and old people out. We've kept the able-bodied men for work in the warehouses. We've decreased the size of the ghetto by three-quarters. Now there are more apartments for our own. We've done the same in the other big cities in the Baltics. It's time to continue with the smaller cities."

Aleks wanted to ask where they moved the people but thought better of it.

"How can I help, sir?"

"I'd like you, first of all, to visit certain cities between here and Gulepils and tell them the plan."

"What is the plan, sir?" Aleks stubbed out his cigarette in the dark green glass ashtray. Major General did the same and opened a wooden box filled with cigars and offered him one. Major General made a big ceremony of lighting them. Aleks finished his brandy.

Major General poured them each another finger's worth and took another large swallow before talking again.

"Your job is to talk to the police chiefs and army officers in charge of the towns. Tell them first of the need to reduce rations to 700 calories. Second, all the Jewish people in the smaller towns must be imprisoned."

"Why, sir?"

"For their own protection, of course."

Aleks knew he would have to figure this out on his own.

"Is there anything else, sir?"

"We appreciate your work and you will not go unrewarded."

"Thank you. When should I start?"

Major General took a folder from a pile on the corner of his desk. "Today. Here's the list of towns and persons in charge of each. Start in your own town and work backwards. Visiting them shouldn't take more than two weeks. Type up a report for me. We'll have another meeting here two weeks from today. Oh, and one more thing."

"Yes?"

"From each town, make sure you get a list of the Jewish people, their names, dates of birth, and occupations. Include the lists with your report."

"Yes, sir. Thank you, sir."

Aleks finished the brandy and put out the cigar. He picked up the folder and saluted.

Major General said, "We have every faith in you."

"Thank you, sir. Goodbye." Both men clicked their heels and raised their right arms in a final salute.

CHAPTER EIGHTEEN

Aleks left the hotel with a reluctant step, holding his brown leather valise in one hand and matching briefcase in the other. A black staff car waited for him at the side entrance. His driver, Johan, an older soldier who had seen combat in the previous world war, stood beside the car. His thick black hair and pug nose made him look younger than he was. Johan was stationed in Aleks' house so he would be available as needed. He took the valise from Aleks and opened the rear passenger door. Johan stowed the valise in the trunk, got in, and waited for instructions.

"Back to Gulepils. I'm wondering, did you hear anything about a Jewish resettlement?"

"What do you mean, sir?"

"I heard that the women and children and old people from the ghetto in Riga were resettled."

Johan cleared his throat. "I also heard news but

am not sure what you mean by resettlement."

"Damn it, Johan, tell me what you know."

"Would you like to see where they've been resettled?"

"Yes, take me there."

"I want to see it too."

Johan turned at the next corner. A few blocks later, he turned onto Maskavas Iela. The north side of Maskavas Iela marked one side of the original ghetto. The area was vacant. There were no people inside the barbed wire, and the snow had not been cleared from the sidewalks. As the car drove past the empty streets and wooden houses, the word "ghosts" that his mother had spoken came to Aleks' mind. Maskavas Iela paralleled the railroad tracks and the Daugava River. Johan drove the car southeast instead of the northeast direction which would take them back to Gulepils.

Aleks said, "Where are we going?"

"I'm told it happened in Rumbala."

"Rumbala? There's nothing there to speak of."

"We'll see soon enough."

About eight kilometers from the center of Riga, Johan turned toward the small ramshackle Rumbala train station and drove past it toward the Rumbala Forest. At the edge of the white birch trees where the road stopped, Johan pulled over and turned off the engine. There was no other traffic.

The men got out of the car. Johan said, "Someone told me it's this way."

"Who told you?"

"His name is better left unsaid, but he's a career man like me. I believe he was a witness."

They walked into the forest, a mixture of birch, spruce, and tall pines. Shortly, they saw a clearing and a hill. Latvia, except for the area around the town of Sigulda, is rather flat. The uneven hill looked out of place. Aleks brushed away some snow and realized he was looking at a woman's coat. As he brushed more snow away, the pile became distinguishable. The hill was made of coats, all sizes, shapes, and colors. They walked around the pile through the next wooded area to a second cleared area with another hill. Johan took a turn at brushing away snow. This was a hill of shoes. A little further along, a third hill was made up of clothing. They rummaged through for a bit, not wanting to believe what they saw with their own eyes: skirts, big and little dresses, blouses, shirts, slacks, sweaters, slips, underpants, brassieres. Neither man spoke. They walked further into the forest. Soon there was another clearing, but it wasn't a hill. This was the largest cleared area. The ground was lumpy. The snow from the previous day had melted in spots. Some of the spots were dirt. Other spots were whitish. Aleks and Johan walked to the edge of the lumpiness and both bent down to brush away some snow.

Aleks stared into a woman's lifeless eyes. "This can't be." He reached down and closed her eyes. Standing, he looked across the killing field. Marina could have been right; there might be twenty thousand or more dead people in the expanse of shallow ground covered by a thin layer of dirt and snow.

Aleks was not a religious man, but he crossed himself. "May the Lord have mercy on their souls."

Johan said, "Amen."

Aleks thought, My god. *What kind of butchers did this? What have I gotten myself into?*

Johan said, "I'm sorry for your loss."

"Pardon?"

"Your people, the Latvian people that were slaughtered here. These people are innocent of any wrongdoing. I am ashamed."

"You, also, are innocent. You're merely serving your country."

They walked in silence back to the car. As they drove away from Rumbala Forest, Aleks took out the folder and a notepad from his briefcase and started making plans to do what he was told. What he had seen in the forest was so unthinkable that his mind could not hold it. He pushed the scenes of the hills and the killing field down into the place of denial where he had pushed so many other things. As long as no one asked him to kill innocent people himself, he would try to last through the war.

The town of Gulepils had about five thousand inhabitants. There was not a large Jewish population. Aleks estimated that there were between seventy and one hundred. Where was he going to put them? There was no separate jail in the town. There were three holding cells in the basement of the town hall. No one could squeeze all those people into such a tiny space.

His plan was to keep them safe until the war was over. He couldn't imagine making a ghetto in the small town either. There were several apartment buildings scattered throughout the town, but they were small, with two to four apartments in each. This wasn't a city with row houses. Most of the houses were one-story brick with two or three bedrooms. Each house had its own little yard on all four sides. There was the military base, housing several hundred soldiers, most of them airmen, in training. There was not even one extra barracks to be used, and he couldn't ask the Reich to decrease the number of men who rotated in and out every few weeks. He considered every street in Gulepils as a possible ghetto, going over each one in his mind's eye. None seemed satisfactory. He didn't want to displace the other people out of their homes either. He thought about the edge of town where there was a public park and a large lake at the far end where people swam in the summer and took out rowboats. The Gulepils Palace sat in the center of the park, an odd-looking English Gothic style structure made of bricks. A baron from Germany had built it in the middle of the nineteenth century, a three-story rectangular building, and on one corner loomed a hexagonal tower. It had been empty for years.

"Johan"

"Yes, sir."

"When we reach Gulepils, drive to the park. I'd like to look at the palace."

The palace was deserted but not locked. Aleks and

Johan walked through the cold rooms, all twenty-eight of them. Aleks couldn't get the images of the bodies out of his mind. Hearing rumors was one thing. Touching the dead body of an innocent civilian was another. He shivered.

He said, "It's cold in here." But it was more than the cold air. He was taught to fight and to kill and he understood that. He understood war, at least he thought he did, until now. What he had seen today was beyond understanding.

There were fireplaces in every room. There were no bathrooms or bathing facilities. There was no furniture. He would have to bring in army cots or let the people bring something from home if they wished. Yes, he would tell them to bring their own things. Then they would feel more like home. As they walked down stone steps to the basement, the sound of skittering rats filled the silence. The kitchen was here, with a fireplace that took up one wall. There was no running water, so they would have to use the well. If he had the barbed wire fence built around a large enough area, the residents would have plenty of trees to chop down for firewood. Even if they put a fire in every fourth room, they wouldn't freeze. Yes, this would be suitable. He would put the Latvian police chief of Gulepils in charge of enacting the plan.

Police Chief Sprotis was in his office in the town hall when Aleks arrived late that afternoon. Aleks went over the details with him, and Sprotis asked why the Jewish people had to be imprisoned.

"For their own protection." Aleks hoped he spoke the truth. Five days later, all eighty-three Jewish people in Gulepils, including Ester and Edmunds and Samuel Freibergs, had taken up residence in the Gulepils Palace prison.

CHAPTER NINETEEN

*M*ija stood in the snow where she had just finished shaving Dara's lice-filled head. A horse carrying a bundled-up man trotted down the lane toward them. Dara had run into the cabin as ordered. The man was alone and didn't look military. Mija hoped Peters would come from the barn soon. In any case, her gun was in her pocket and her hand was on it. The man pulled the panting horse to a stop not far from her.

He yelled, "I found you."

"Ollie!" Mija breathed a sigh of relief as she slogged through the snow toward him.

Peters ran out from the barn door yelling, "Stranger, hello."

"How?" Mija raised her eyebrows.

"Feliks."

Now Mija saw that Ollie had arrived on Feliks'

horse, Big Bertha. The horse neighed and stamped her hooves; steam rose from her nostrils.

"God, it's good to see you," Mija said as she hugged him. "I didn't know my brother was paying such close attention when I explained where we were."

Ollie pulled a torn piece of brown paper from his coat pocket and showed them the inky map Feliks had drawn. Ollie's mustache was covered with white and frozen like a thick icicle. He untied a small sack from his saddle and handed it to Mija. "From Feliks." Inside the sack was a well-wrapped piece of pork.

Mija hustled Ollie inside while Peters took Big Bertha to the barn. She set the frozen piece of pork on the butcher block beside the stove. A few vegetables already waited there in a row. The pork would add much-needed nourishment. Mija pulled a dishtowel from the shelf above the sink and gave it to Ollie. After he rubbed his hair and mustache, he put the yellow towel around his neck.

On Mija's call, Dara came out from her bedroom. A red-flowered kerchief was tied around her bald head and knotted in the back. Her cheeks showed the pink of embarrassment.

Peters came in and started a fire. "It will be dark in less than an hour. It's safe enough."

The four sat in a semicircle on blankets in front of the fire. "You have a nice place here," Ollie said, "much better than the places I've been living."

"Where have you been all these months?" Peters asked.

"Mostly in the woods, alternately sniping at soldiers and avoiding them. More recently, in Riga."

"And Harijs and Willy?" Mija asked.

A dark look came over Ollie's face. "Willy. He wanted to find his son Max. Harijs and I went with him to Riga, thinking it'd be safer sticking together. We stayed at my cousin Dzenis' apartment. We had to sleep on the floor, but at least he had wood for the fireplace." Ollie's voice cracked. He coughed and took a couple of deep breaths and stared at the fire. He ran one hand through his coarse dark hair. Mija and Dara looked away. Peters leaned over and stoked the fire. Ollie's mustache and hair were almost dry. He rubbed his face and hair with the towel again. His face was bright red from thawing out.

Ollie continued. "The second night there, the three of us were stopped by two drunken soldiers, before curfew. We were one block from Dzenis' apartment. The soldiers weren't satisfied with our documents, even though they found nothing wrong. They accused us of being Russian spies, of all things, and said we were under arrest. The three of us looked at each other, Harijs whispered 'run,' and we turned and ran for the nearest walkway to a courtyard. In their drunkenness, the soldiers were slow in taking out their guns, but they managed to shoot at us. A bullet grazed the back of my arm." Ollie pulled up his sleeve to show a jagged red scar. "Harijs was shot in the calf. He's recovering. Willy took a shot in his back and fell. Harijs and I turned in and ran through to the courtyard. Two women in a first-floor apartment saw what happened and one waited at the outside door. She let us in. Through the front window of their apartment, we saw Willy face down on the ground, trying to crawl away. The soldiers kicked him repeatedly, one on each side."

Ollie stopped talking and his eyes moved as if watching the scene again. He stared at the wall for some seconds and then sighed. "When Willy stopped moving, one soldier leaned over and touched his gun to the back of Willy's head and shot him. The second soldier added his own bullet. Blood oozed in a large puddle. The soldiers spat on him and then sauntered down the street as if nothing had happened."

Peters added another log to the fire and then asked, "What then?"

"We shouldn't have run. We should have fought them with our bare hands and killed them." With the back of his hand, Ollie wiped a tear. "Zana's a good nurse. She stopped our bleeding, then bandaged us up with a ripped sheet. The bullet that hit Harijs went clean through, but he still has a limp."

Mija said, "I knew a Zana when I went to school in Riga. She was studying to be a nurse. Zana Ziedins."

"Dark hair, dark eyes, short?"

Mija said, "Yes. She's a lovely person."

"Wait till I tell her."

"Tell her a big hello from me. What happened next?"

"We waited a long time to make sure no soldiers came back. In the middle of the night, Zana and Brita dragged Willy's body into the courtyard of the building, put him in a corner, and covered him with snow. At the first light of day, Brita went to tell Dzenis what happened and brought him to us. Zana gathered many of the tenants from the building together in the courtyard. We stood in a semicircle around Willy and held hands. A few people said some words of prayer. Even though they didn't know us or Willy, most were in tears. We had to leave his body there.

The next day, Zana smuggled out some antiseptic and bandages from the hospital where she works. A couple of days later, when my wound was healing well, Dzenis made arrangements for me to get a ride on a supply truck that had Gulepils as one of its stops. Harijs still couldn't stand, so stayed. Dzenis is one of the few in Riga who has a job. He escorts Jewish workers to and from the ghetto gate to the warehouses." Ollie's shoulders slumped and he covered his eyes with one hand.

Mija asked, "What happened when you reached Gulepils?"

Ollie sat quietly.

Mija stood up. "I'm sorry if I pushed for too much information. I think it's time to cook dinner."

Dara went with Mija. Mija put the pork into a pot of water and set the pot on the woodstove. Dara, with a small knife, pared and chopped up the two potatoes, two carrots, one onion, and one turnip.

When the stew came to a simmer, the women rejoined the men. Ollie had regained his composure and continued his story. "Willy's wife Selia and the two teenage boys were overcome, as you can imagine. They want to move the body to the family plot in Gulepils right away, but that might be impossible. With Max still missing, they are full of fear. No one knows if Max is alive or dead. We didn't find out much except this. He disappeared from Riga. His apartment had two new tenants living in it who didn't know anything about Max or his roommate, Victors. The landlord said they disappeared without giving notice. The best guess is that both Max and Victors joined the German army, but Selia hasn't even had a letter from Max, so who can say what happened."

"What about Harijs' wife?" asked Mija.

"Ilze left Harijs a letter saying she no longer wants to be married, and she moved back to Apene to take care of her parents. From the very beginning of the war, Ilze and Harijs fought about what he was doing."

Peters said, "I remember how unhappy she was."

The aroma of the pork made Mija's mouth water so that she had to swallow more than usual. When the stew was ready, she removed the pork and set it aside. She ladled the vegetables evenly into four bowls and sliced off one thin piece of pork for each. The rest would be rationed over the next several days. After dinner, Mija served tea with a little honey as a special treat. They sat by the fire. Mija sipped from the crockery mug, wanting the feeling of a full stomach and the warm sweet tea to last forever.

They found out from Ollie that here on the farm

they were well off compared to those in the city. Dara asked about the ghetto. Ollie told her that most of the Jewish people in the ghetto were no longer there, that they'd been resettled.

"Where? I want go too," said Dara.

"I don't know."

"Can you find out? I miss parents." Her big eyes were wide open.

"I'm sorry. It's so difficult to find out anything these days." Ollie leaned over and patted her arm.

That night, after the women were in bed, the men talked in whispers.

Ollie said, "Did you hear about Rumbala?"

"Yes, but I haven't dared tell Dara about it. Mija knows too. Dara's parents are probably dead."

Ollie said, "The only people left in the ghetto are able-bodied men and a few women. The men are used for manual labor in the warehouses, the women for seamstress work with German uniforms. My cousin Dzenis saved some of them. If someone gets sick, they are taken away and don't come back. Dzenis tries to get out the ones who are sick. I want to help the cause. So do Harijs and Brita and Zana, even if that means going underground. Zana is afraid to go to work anymore. She was raped one night by the German doctor in charge of the hospital. Brita used to be an opera singer. After war broke out, she worked in a bakery. As you know, there's less and less bread to bake as rations continue to be reduced. Brita was told last month that she was no longer needed."

Peters said, "Let's do it."

"I'm ready."

"First, we have to find an abandoned farmhouse closer to Riga and bigger than this log cabin. And Dara needs to be moved somewhere else. At fifteen, she's too young to be part of it."

Mija was up first the next morning. She pumped water from the sink, put on a kettle for tea and a pot of water for oatmeal.

Peters and Ollie were up before Dara. They told her about their nighttime conversation, and all three agreed that Dara needed to be moved. Peters asked her if perhaps Feliks and Laima could take her.

"With Aleks and the other soldiers living so close, that might be too dangerous. Also, Ints goes to school every day. Having Dara in the house may be too difficult a secret for him to keep."

When Dara woke up, the talk turned to the weather. It was snowing again, but not the soft kind of snow. Even though it was morning, the sky was gray, and it was dark enough that Mija lit the candle on the kitchen table. As with dinner the previous evening, they ate their oatmeal by candlelight. Pellets of icy snow darted onto the windows in a muffled rat-a-tat-tat.

Peters said, "We'll keep a fire going today. No patrols will be out in this weather."

Ollie asked, "Does that radio work in bad weather?"

"Lately, it hasn't worked at all, no matter the

weather. Do you know anything about them?"

"A little." *Let's take a look.*

Dara pumped water into a big pot for washing the dishes.

Mija said, "Dara, we need to find a new place for you to stay."

Dara's eyes darted like a scared animal. "I like here. I good." With a dishrag, she scrubbed and scrubbed at the inside of the bowl she was holding.

"Of course, you're good, but we want to keep you safe until the war is over. Then you can search for your parents."

"Not safe here?" She stopped scrubbing and looked at Mija.

"Not much longer. We're going to try to save more Jewish people from the ghetto. And try to find your parents and save them too."

Dara's eyes brightened and a smile formed, the first real smile Mija had seen on her. She was pretty when she smiled. Her black arched eyebrows and large brown eyes were dramatic; without the smile, she looked quite somber. "Where is safe?"

"Would you like to be with girls your own age?"

"Yes, I like. Is safe place?"

"My daughter is close to your age. Remember, I told you about her. She lives in a house in Velsaine with two other girls. They go to school in the daytime. You'll have to stay in the house all the time and make sure the curtains are closed so no one sees you. There's an attic you can sleep in. Can you could do that?"

"Yes, yes. They have books?"

"Of course. You want to study something?"

"I want speak better." Dara dried the bowls with care and stacked them in their place on the shelf above the sink.

Mija sipped the last dregs of unsweetened tea and handed the cup to Dara. "I'm sure they'll let you read their books and help you with speaking. As soon as the weather breaks, we'll take you to Velsaine."

Mija thought, Dara will be safer with the girls in Velsaine. *The problem is how to get there. We can't take her on the train. She looks Jewish, her head is bald, and she doesn't have proper papers. But. . . maybe Ollie can get fake papers. And a kerchief would hide the baldness well enough. Then I could take Dara on the train from Gulepils. It's an hour on the train. Could we take that chance, or should we take a horse and carriage from Feliks farm? In the carriage, it might take three hours to get there. We could be stopped by soldiers on the road as easily as on the train. Maybe the train is safer.*

Peters and Ollie returned from the barn. They had no luck with the radio. They hoped that when Harijs joined them, he'd know how to fix the problem. Snow fell and the wind howled all day. By late afternoon, an icy crust covered the windows. Mija felt like she was imprisoned in an ice tomb.

CHAPTER TWENTY

Several weeks of wintry weather passed before the sun came back. A few days later, the roads were passable.

Dara said, "I scared. Never ride horse before."

Mija said, "Don't worry. You'll be safe right behind Ollie. He's an expert horseman, and Big Bertha is a very calm horse. My brother trained her well."

"If you say, then I do."

Mija helped her get up after Ollie mounted. They had decided the safest thing to do was to disguise Dara as a boy. She'd dressed in some smallish men's clothes that were in the house. She wore three layers of pants and sweaters and socks and a pair of men's work boots that were too large, even with all the socks. The brown wool jacket came to her knees and the sleeves fell to her fingertips. She wore two pairs of thick black mittens. With her head covered by two black knitted hats that covered her eyebrows as well as her ears, no one could tell she was a girl.

At first, she held onto the sides of Ollie's coat gingerly. When the horse broke into a trot, she gripped him tighter, but she still held herself stiffly. Mija, sitting behind Peters, held onto his waist lightly. She was comfortable on the horse but not comfortable being so close to Peters. They hadn't spoken about that evening, the one before Dara showed up. She tried to think about something else and looked over at Dara. The poor girl looked terrified. Mija smiled at her, and Dara formed a small smile back as the horses trotted side by side along the snow-covered country road.

Ollie thought he could get false papers for Dara in a day or so in Gulepils, and that would be the priority. The papers would make her the son of Mija and Peters, matching her surname to their fake ones and her first name would be Daris. Mija hoped Ester and Edmunds would let Dara stay with them a day or two until they got everything organized for Dara's move to Velsaine. Mija thought about asking Ester to keep Dara longer but decided that would be too dangerous. Ester's apartment was too small and the risk of being caught too great.

The roads between the log house and Gulepils were deserted. Not many people would have reason to be out in the coldest part of the winter. Two hours later, they arrived at Willy's widow's doorstep. The house was on the first street at the edge of town, many blocks from the center. Selia opened the door cautiously, but when she realized who was there, she opened the door wide. "Come in, come in. The horses, put them in back, behind the house." Her brown hair, streaked with white, was pulled back in a bun, and she was dressed in black. She said, "I wish I could offer you some food . . ." as she led them into the living room.

Mija said, "No one has extra these days," and introduced Dara.

Selia said, "Please, sit." She pointed to the sofa and armchair. There weren't enough spots for them all, so Peters got himself a chair from the kitchen.

Selia asked, "What brings you here?"

Ollie said, "We have no news of Max, sorry."

Selia sighed, "I also don't have news." She stared at the floor.

"How about the war? Anything new in the past few weeks?" asked Peters.

"Nothing. I think everyone waits for the spring thaw. But—" Selia stopped and looked at Mija.

"What?" Mija asked. "Please, if you know anything that would help us . . ."

"I don't know if this will help, but you should know. You will find out from someone. Better from me." She hesitated. Silence hung over the room as if a dark presence had followed them. "It's about Aleks."

"Please, tell us," Mija said. She intertwined her fingers and held them in her lap to keep them from shaking.

"He got some kind of promotion."

"He left Gulepils?"

"I don't think so."

"Then what?"

"He's the big commander over the whole area. Even the chief of police has to get permission to do anything. And the army has taken the Jewish people."

No one spoke. The adults were afraid to ask. Dara furrowed her brows. Neither Mija nor Peters nor Ollie would ask the question they were thinking: Are the Jewish people dead?

Mija asked tentatively, "All of them? How many?"

"I believe so. Eighty. Maybe more." She shrugged and looked away.

Ollie asked, "Where did they take them?"

"To the park. They're in the park. Living in the old palace, with barbed wire all around."

"Even Ester and Edmunds Freibergs?" Mija was relieved that the people were alive but still held the arm of the chair even tighter.

"I believe so. They are surviving. There are many rooms in the palace, if you remember. They have the same rations as the rest of us. That's all I heard."

"Thank you, thank you for telling us," said Mija. She let go of the chair and unclenched her teeth. At least they were alive. And Aleks was alive.

Selia asked, "How can I help?"

Ollie said, "Dara and I need a place to stay for a couple of days. Then we'll be gone. Do you think—"

Selia interrupted him, "Of course, for a few days, yes. But my food, there isn't much."

Mija said, "Maybe Feliks and Laima can spare

something. What do you need most?"

"We have so little, anything is welcome. My boys go to the woods to hunt every day after school, but this time of the winter, on most days they find nothing. The rations we get are not enough for growing boys."

Ollie would try to get the papers for Dara today, or at least start the process. The war had turned his old friend Egils into an excellent forger, he told them. Peters and Mija would come back the day after tomorrow, on Friday, to make the trip to Velsaine. They said their goodbyes and left for Feliks and Laima's.

LAIMA SAID SHE WAS HAPPY to see them but even so had such a look of sadness about her. Peters told her how sorry he was about Ruta. Rita, in Laima's arms, started to cry when she heard the name of her twin. Laima patted her head, held her close, and rocked from side to side. Peters said, "I'm sorry. I should have thought before I spoke.

Laima said, "It'll take time. Feliks should be back with Ints soon. He takes him to and from school himself, in the sled, with Oscar."

Mija told Laima about their plan for Dara and asked, "Is your telephone working?"

"No one has telephone service anymore except the army. No, wait. Maybe the post office. Why?"

"I wanted to telephone the principal of Lize's school so she can tell Lize we're coming for a visit. If we arrive Friday afternoon, we can spend the weekend with the girls and get things settled. I don't want to show up unexpectedly. People always think you're coming with bad news."

"Maybe if you go to the post office."

"Yes, tomorrow we will do that."

IN FRONT OF THE POST OFFICE, Mija and Peters were stopped by two soldiers. One looked over Mija's papers, then Peters', then stared at him. "You don't look that old."

Mija said, "And I'm the lucky wife to have such a young-looking man for a husband." She smiled. "We've been married fifteen years now. Wasn't I smart to snag him?"

The soldier handed back both sets of papers to Mija. "I haven't seen you before. What are you doing here?"

"Visiting my husband's second cousin. Their baby died."

"I'm sorry, madam. Please, be on your way." The soldiers continued walking down the street.

Inside, Peters said, "I almost believed that you're my wife."

"War teaches people to be good liars."

The postmaster, old Ernests Puzulis, a white-haired gnome of a man, was happy to let Mija use his official telephone. He wouldn't take any money. "I've known you since you were born. I don't want your money. Make the call, now." Peters stood by the door on the lookout for soldiers while Mija made the call. Luckily, Miss Kronberga was in her office and would relay the news to the girls. Mija said, "Tell them I'm bringing a surprise and we'll be there on the afternoon train."

THE BIG CASTLE THAT HAD been turned into a school years ago now housed German troops, a hub for troop rotation, not a place where any soldier stayed long. Velsaine was less than half the size of Gulepils, and the castle was on the outskirts. Other than the troops at the school, no soldiers were stationed in the town, and the streets were not normally patrolled. The Germans had ordered the school to continue and made an additional mandatory order that all students who attended before must still attend. Classes were held in the building that used to be the Black Cat Restaurant. The former owners cooked, and the students ate all three meals there.

The students lived in various houses within the town, any place with an extra bedroom. Lize lived with Astrid and Edita in Astrid's parents' house. The clothing store was on the first floor. Many of the clothes that were in the store when the family was arrested were still on the racks; fussy ladies dresses and gentlemen's suits, things no one had use for these days. The second floor consisted of a living room, two bedrooms, a tiny kitchen, and a bathroom. Above the second floor was a small attic.

Eight boys lived in Peters' old house. Peters knew most of them. He and Ollie visited with them on Saturday afternoon while Mija spent time going over all the rules with the girls. The curtains were closed on all the second-floor windows.

Mija said, "Remember, don't touch the curtains for any reason. Can I trust you to follow all the rules?" All four girls nodded their heads. "This is very serious, what we're doing, what I'm asking you to do." She looked at each girl one at a time. All four girls seemed to be listening attentively. "Should I write down the rules?"

"No, Mama, you don't have to. We can remember."

"Good, it's better not to write anything down on paper that can be used against us."

"You mean in case we're caught?" asked Lize.

Mija held her breath. "You won't be caught. All you need to do is follow the rules."

The three girls were happy to have another girl join them. Mija had never seen the childish side of Dara and was surprised to see her laugh after she showed them how fast she could run up the attic stairs and hide.

CHAPTER TWENTY-ONE

*M*ija, Peters, and Ollie arrived at the train station early enough to take Mija's favorite seats at the back. Their papers were not questioned by the taciturn guard who seemed bored with his duties. Still, Mija was nervous until the guard left. As the train pulled away, she noticed their car was about three-quarters full of civilians dressed in drab brown and gray. Perhaps the war had removed the color from everything.

The landscape was grayish-white under gray clouds. Everything was covered with the snow of a normal February. On the horizon, ice-covered limbs on the birch trees formed a lacy pattern. There was not a bird to be seen. Not a plane was in the sky. Two rows ahead of Mija, a young couple argued. The girl had curly black hair; his was wavy brown. She thought it must be a lover's quarrel, but it was hard to hear over the din of the clacking wheels. Mija recognized a word here and there. "Selfish pig," spat out by the girl, was the loudest. She was so loud that most of the other passengers stopped talking. After a few moments, passengers returned to their own worries. Peters and Ollie discussed homemade beer. Ollie said they should make some next year if they could get the supplies and equipment. Peters said they could find out from Feliks the best way to make it. As they got closer to Riga, the clouds thinned to show a watery blue sky.

It was a short walk from the train station to the trolley stop. When the trolley arrived, there were only a few sullen-looking riders. The three friends debarked from the trolley at the corner of Adolph-Hitler Strasse and Matisa Iela, a few blocks north of the Freedom Monument. The snow piles on the street were dappled gray, dirtied by trolley wheels and army trucks. Peters and Mija followed Ollie across the street. She stepped with care to miss the slush. Wordlessly, they walked down Matisa Iela, a street lined with tan brick buildings. Though the clouds had gone, the sun did not warm, and the frigid wind blew icy darts through Mija's wool coat. The sidewalks were wet with a liquid film that was almost ice.

Ollie pointed to Dzenis' building. "Here, this is the one." The entrance was on the street instead of in the back like most apartment buildings. The trio entered through the brown wooden doorway. The three of them filled up the vestibule. The dingy stucco walls hadn't been cleaned or painted in a long time. The stone stairs were dark, almost black, worn in the center from years of footsteps. Dim ceiling bulbs, one per floor, lighted the way. The wrought iron railing was rusty in many spots. Ollie led the way up to the third floor and down a narrow hallway.

Dzenis, his wife Vera, and their son Maris were finishing supper. Vera busied herself clearing the table as Ollie introduced everyone. The bigger room was a living room, dining room, and kitchen all in one. Because there was no door in the frame, one could see the tiny bedroom to one side. There was a double bed with no space for anything else. The bathroom was outside and down the hall, used by the entire floor of six apartments.

Vera and Maris stayed in the background, sitting at the table, their backs to the visitors. Vera was teaching Maris the alphabet from a picture book, and he wrote the letters on a slate board with a piece of chalk. His little legs swung back and forth with each stroke.

Peters sat beside Mija on a small sofa centered between two windows against the outside wall. Ollie and Dzenis sat in the two faded chairs facing them. Behind them was the fireplace. To the left was the table. On the wall, behind the table were a kitchen sink and a stove, and attached to the wall above the sink was a single cupboard. The apartment had what they needed, except for space.

"Are you sure you want to continue with this dangerous business? Peters asked Dzenis.

"Would anyone care for a cigarette?" Dzenis asked his guests. The visitors shook their heads. Dzenis lit one for himself and took a long drag. "After Rumbala, about four thousand were left in the ghetto. There are no more old people, no children. Even with so many already dead, or maybe because of it, I can't stomach the idea of more death. They are helpless in that ghetto."

"What can we do?" Mija asked.

Dzenis' face looked much younger than his silver hair suggested. His eyebrows were black and bushy, and he was stick thin. Two lines dented his face, starting at the corners of his mouth, slicing diagonally down each side.

He sucked in another drag. "When I can get it, I smuggle in food and medicine. What they are fed is criminal, not enough for a mouse to stay alive. The conditions are so bad that even a healthy man can die from a cold. When I hear of someone too sick to work, I try to smuggle them out because if they cannot work, they are certain to be shot, often right on the street." He flicked a long ash into an overflowing ashtray.

"How do you get them out? Aren't they counted?" Peters asked.

A slice of frigid wind whistled through the window to the left of Peters. A brown towel that had been wedged against the bottom of the window had slipped to the floor. Peters picked up the towel and stuffed it back into the crack.

"They count them," Dzenis said, blowing a smoke

ring up toward the high ceiling, "but they don't check names. I have a friend who puts on a yellow star and joins the group. With a little planned commotion at the entrance, the one escaping pulls off his yellow star and walks away to a prearranged spot. Later, after the guard changes, my friend takes off his yellow star and walks back out of the ghetto, showing his legitimate papers and saying he was visiting. One time, my friend couldn't go at the last minute and I put on a star myself." Dzenis ground out the cigarette and lit another one. Wispy smoke hung in the airless room.

"What happens once they are out?" asked Mija.

"That's the problem. No more hiding places. No one else I can count on. People are too busy staying alive themselves—not enough food, not enough heat. Soldiers search your apartment for the least reason and need little provocation to throw you in jail or worse. A knock on the door can be fatal. As you can see, I can't hide anyone here."

"We're ready to do this," said Peters. Mija and Ollie nodded.

As soon as they set up a base of operations in an abandoned farm, or even a house, much closer to Riga, they would begin.

Dzenis said, "A place close to the end of the trolley line would be ideal."

One of them would check in with Dzenis every sixth day, on the first of his two days off. One or two of the men would pick up escapees at a designated spot on the prearranged day. The timing would be crucial.

"And then?" Dzenis asked, "What will you do with them?" The ever-present home-rolled cigarette hung from his lower lip.

Mija said, "First, nurse them back to health. We don't have medicine, but we do have some herbs. Perhaps Zana can get medical supplies. Then we'll take them to a safe place. We'll find people in the countryside willing to hide one person. And maybe that one will know another one. If I must, I will go knocking door to door myself."

Ollie looked at Dzenis. "Cousin, we will succeed."

Dzenis nodded as he took the stub of cigarette from his mouth and ground it out. He turned to his wife. "Vera, it's time for a toast." He stood up and motioned the visitors to follow him to the table.

Vera sent Maris to sit on the bed with his book. She set a small tray of shot glasses and a half-full bottle of vodka on the table. Dzenis poured solemnly and then passed one to each of them. They raised their glasses.

"To success." said Dzenis.

Mija was giddy from the combination of an empty stomach and the vodka as the trio walked up the street toward Zana and Brita's apartment. She slipped on a patch of ice. Peters grabbed her arm and saved her from falling.

"Whoa," he said. Mija's cheeks were flushed.

Peters asked, "Ollie, will there be food at Zana and Brita's, or should we find a restaurant and eat first?"

"Let's eat. A few restaurants are still open, mostly

filled with soldiers, though. Let's try Monk's. I know the owner."

The restaurant was in old town which had cobbled streets too narrow for trolleys or cars. They walked through a wrought iron gate to a stucco building with an arched wooden door. A small paper sign tacked to the door said, "Open today 11 to 4." Thick stone stairs led down to the cellar and reception area. The floor was also stone while the walls were covered with heavy wood. A single door of the same wood was the only break in the wall. No one was there to greet them.

Ollie said, "This building was a monastery a long time ago. The family history is that one of my relatives was a monk here, maybe 200 years ago." He knocked on the door. Presently, a short, bald man opened the door a bit and slid out, closing it behind him. He was dressed in black pants and a white shirt, buttoned to the top.

"Ollie." He smiled and reached out a hand. As the two men shook hands, the man said, "What a surprise. I thought you left Riga." He clapped Ollie lightly on the shoulder.

"I'm back. For a few days. Please, Ojars, these are my friends Peters and Mija. Do you have a table for us?"

"For my old friend, always. If you like the menu, that is."

"What's on the table today?" Ollie said.

"Food is so hard to come by. Haven't had fresh meat for weeks. Can't even get it from the black market. Oh yes, you want to know what we have. Sorry. It's such a worry." Little beads of perspiration appeared on Ojars' forehead. "Today we have a root vegetable stew, but you have to like turnips. Our other dish is rolled pancakes filled with a bit of cottage cheese and a dollop of wild strawberry jam on top."

"Wonderful," said Mija. "I haven't had pancakes in such a long time."

Ojars opened the door and led them into a long, wide hallway. Private alcoves were situated along each side. A waiter dressed in black walked by with a large tray smelling of turnips. He lifted the tray over his head and entered an alcove. The sounds of murmurs here and there; smells of vegetables and pancakes and beer filled the air. They walked down another long corridor, and at the end, Ojars pointed to the right. This alcove held a rectangular wooden table and three chairs on each side. There were no place settings. Ollie and Peters sat opposite Mija.

"Would you like some wine?" asked Ojars.

"You have wine?" said Ollie.

Ojars smiled. "For special customers. And relatives. What are we, cousins by some distant marriage? No matter, you're a special customer in any case. What will you have for lunch?"

"Pancakes," said Mija.

"Pancakes," Peters echoed.

"Same," said Ollie. "And wine."

"How about an appetizer? Smoked salmon? With a little caviar on top? On crackers? I've been saving them. I have a handful of tins left." Ojars wrung his hands and then wiped his forehead with the sleeve of one arm.

"I don't think we can afford such a delicacy," said Ollie.

Ojars waved a hand. "I wouldn't take money from you, old friend. Ollie, can I have a word in private?" New beads of sweat appeared where the old ones were wiped off. Ollie followed Ojars out of the alcove.

Peters said, "You look beautiful, the green of your dress complements your eyes."

"Thank you." Mija felt the blush in her cheeks.

"You were made to sit in elegant restaurants and eat rich food."

"I don't think so." She shook her head as if to dismiss that thought.

"Yes, my dear, certainly yes." Peters reached a hand across the table and covered Mija's. His hand was warm. After a few moments, she looked away and sighed. She was so tired of the prolonged war. Being separated from her children. Her husband working for the enemy. The realization that she broke her wedding vows. The additional realization that she didn't feel remorse. She thought of her family and Peters' family.

Peters interrupted. "What are you thinking about?"

Mija moved her hand out from under Peters' and fussed with her hair. "War. How horrible it is. How much work we have ahead of us. Our families."

Peters folded his hands at his side of the table. "I'm sorry."

"There's no need to be sorry. You have it worse. You don't even have the possibility of seeing your family until the war is over." Footsteps approached. Ollie was back.

"Well?" Peters asked.

"In a moment."

The waiter they saw earlier came in behind Ollie with a tray and set their places, first with heavy silverware, then with small white plates edged in gold. A large oval plate was covered with round crackers topped with tender salmon slices dotted with caviar. The waiter put down the plate and left with the tray. As Ollie reached for a cracker, Ojars came in with a small silver tray which held a bottle of wine and four crystal wine glasses. He set the tray down, opened the bottle, ceremoniously poured and handed them each a glass. He stayed standing and raised his own glass. "To the end of war and a free Latvia." The red wine was deep-bodied and smooth, the best Mija had ever tasted.

"Enjoy your lunch," Ojars said. He left, taking his half-full glass of wine with him.

"What did he want?" Peters asked.

Ollie pulled a piece of paper from his pocket. He whispered, "Things are bad. Ojars is being pressured to provide women for the German officers that dine here. He isn't going to cooperate. He's afraid of reprisals, that his silver and china will be confiscated and worse, that he'll be shut down and thrown in prison. He's going to shut the restaurant down himself. Sell everything on the black market and leave the country. Next week, the Monk Restaurant will be no more and he'll be gone."

"Where?" Mija asked.

"There's a man in Ventspils with a boat. For enough money, he'll take you across the Baltic Sea to Sweden." He handed Mija the slip of paper. "Here, you hold onto this. You never know when we might need it."

Mija read the name, Jacobs Lapins, and the name and address of a restaurant in Ventspils. She pushed the piece of paper down into the bottom of her purse. "What's the connection to the restaurant?"

Ollie said, "The owner is another cousin to Ojars. His name is Kristaps Barons. If we ever have to flee, he can be trusted."

"Who is this Lapins? Another relative?"

"No, a friend of Ojars and Kristaps. From their childhood. A real seaman."

CHAPTER TWENTY-TWO

*M*ija sat in the unheated train with her arms folded across her chest, rubbing them to keep the circulation going. A strong wind pushed the spring rain sideways onto the windows, obliterating the view. Not many civilians traveled by train anymore and soldiers traveled in the same cars with them. She had taken a seat in the back corner of the last car, hoping to be less visible to the enemy.

At Velsaine, a curtain of dusk had fallen. The rain had not let up. The streetlights were unlit due to energy conservation. She walked as fast as she dared the six blocks to Astrid's parents' clothing store. Staying close to the buildings, she held her black umbrella to the side in an attempt to ward off the wet drops. Where she had to cross the street, she dashed through puddles. Water splattered upward, soaking the hem of her dress.

The store was dark, as she expected. With Astrid's

parents in Siberia, there was no one to run the business. She went to the side of the building where the door to the upstairs apartment was. No one answered her knock. The girls should be there. Perhaps they were being careful. When no one came after the third knock, she turned the knob and the door opened. She ran up the stairs. At the second-floor landing, the door opened and all was dark. *How could that be? Where were they?* Mija felt along the wall of the living room until she found the switch to turn on the overhead light. She yelled, "Lize, Astrid, Edita, Dara." No answer. She checked all the rooms and the attic. Empty. Mija ran back down the stairs, holding onto the railing. She cursed herself for not letting Peters come along. She had told him, "You stay here and take care of business. I'll be back on Monday."

The rain slowed to a drizzle as Mija ran to the Black Cat. Maybe the students were at school late tonight, although that wouldn't explain Dara's absence. Dara was to remain hidden in the attic, always. Lights were on at the former restaurant, but the curtains were closed. Mija opened the door, dropped the umbrella in the foyer, and walked into the first dining room. Students sat at the tables, studying by candlelight. Most lifted their heads from their books to see who had come in and then returned to their work.

Mija looked around and said, "Does anyone know where Lize Adamsons is?"

Some of the students stared back at her with blank faces, making her even more uncomfortable. Finally, a pimply-faced boy said, "In the back." He pointed with his thumb.

"Thank you." Mija walked through the second dining room, also filled with students, all immersed in their books, heads lifting up to look at her, then turning down again. She reached the door to the back dining room. This was the smallest one, next to the kitchen, the same room where she and Aleks had dined with Peters and his wife and Astrid's parents.

The principal, Miss Kronberga, sat at a round table with all four girls—Lize, Astrid, Edita, and Dara. When the Germans took over the school, Miss Kronberga had been appointed principal. Mija had wondered how the woman was able to adapt and turn from communism into whatever the Germans demanded of her. Miss Kronberga stopped talking when she saw Mija. Lize saw her mother and opened her mouth, but no sound came out.

Mija swallowed hard, "What happened?"

Miss Kronberga looked at Lize. "Perhaps you should tell your mother why we're here."

Miss Kronberga pushed back her chair and pulled down on her brown skirt as if it was up too high, even though it fell halfway to her ankles.

"We didn't mean anything bad," Lize said in a quiet voice. "I already said I was sorry."

"Tell your mother why every student in the school is being punished and studying tonight until ten o'clock, why everyone's privileges for the weekend have been taken away."

"It wasn't just me." She looked down at her hands.

"All four of you?" Mija asked. Her hands balled into such a tight fist that her knuckles were white.

Dara said, "I sorry. I tired being in house all time. Is my fault." She put one hand up to her head, raked her crew cut, and sighed.

Astrid said, "It's not your fault, Dara. We all did it. And you shouldn't punish the whole school for it, Miss Kronberga."

"Tell that to the German soldiers, the ones who almost discovered your extra boarder," Miss Kronberga looked around at the girls and then at Mija. "Lize, tell your mother."

"We wanted to have some fun. It's boring, school all day, studying every night." Lize turned her head to look up at her mother. "I'm sorry." She hung her head down and held her hands together, fingers intertwined.

"What did you do?" Mija walked around to the empty chair between Miss Kronberga and Dara and sat down before her legs gave way to shaking.

"We got dressed up."

"And?" She looked straight at Lize.

Lize began, "We dressed up in fancy clothes and suits from the store. We weren't going to go anywhere. But then—"

Mija interrupted, "Suits?"

"Well, yes. Astrid and I got dressed up as ladies and Edita and Dara dressed as men. Dara, with her short hair, didn't look right in a dress. And it didn't seem right to make her be the boy all by herself, so

Edita volunteered."

"Where did you go?" Mija asked.

"For a walk."

"The four of you went outside like that?"

"Yes," said Miss Kronberga. "They looked like two men walking with two women of the night. Lize and Astrid had on tight dresses, high heels, and makeup."

"Who turned you in?"

Lize said, "A jeep with soldiers drove by. We told Edita and Dara to run back as soon as the jeep braked."

"Then what?" Mija wasn't sure she wanted to hear any more.

Lize looked up at her mother. "It was three soldiers, a regular one in the front driving the jeep, two others in fancy uniforms with all kinds of medals on them. One was . . . Papa." The word Papa came out in a whisper.

"What did he do?" Mija saw tears in Lize's eyes, and that Lize was trying hard not to let them fall. She reached across the table and patted her daughter's hands.

"As before, he acted like he didn't know me."

"And you?"

"I didn't betray him." A tear rolled from the corner of an eye and stopped at Lize's top lip. She used her tongue to lick it off and pinched her lips together.

"Betray" flashed in Mija's head like a movie marquee. She couldn't speak. She stood, walked around to her daughter, put her arms around Lize's shoulders and hugged her.

"What happened after that?" Mija asked.

"Miss Kronberga came," Lize said, "and rescued us."

"It's a good thing I saw them," said Miss Kronberga. "I was out for my afternoon walk about two blocks away when I saw them. I ran as fast as I could. I convinced the soldiers that they were my students. But they want to see all four culprits, the two girls and the two boys, tomorrow morning, in the former principal's office. When you came in, we were figuring out which two boys are about the same size as these two girls, to pass for them and who can be trusted."

"What a terrible position these girls have put you in, Miss Kronberga. How can I help?"

Miss Kronberga tilted her head. "If you come along tomorrow, perhaps you can help in the discussion. Do you think your husband will acknowledge you?"

"I can't say what he'll do, but I will come." Mija shivered, more from the dread of seeing Aleks than from being wet.

Lize said, "What about Alfred? He's about the same size as Dara, and there's a resemblance."

"But he has all those pimples, and she doesn't," said Miss Kronberga.

"Makeup," said Mija. "We'll put makeup on him, and if they ask, we'll say it's medicine for the pimples."

"That takes care of one," said Miss Kronberga.

"I'll tell them I dressed as a boy," said Edita. "It's the truth."

"That might work," said Miss Kronberga. "Yes, it will make the story more believable."

They called Alfred to the back. He was reluctant. The girls offered to help him with his homework. And Miss Kronberga offered him extra food rations for a week. And the plan was in place.

Miss Kronberga folded her hands on the table. "It's not safe for Dara to stay with the other girls. They are sure to be watched."

"We want her to stay. We won't do it again," said Astrid.

Lize said, "Please, let her stay."

Edita nodded her head and said, "Please."

"It's not safe," said Miss Kronberga.

Mija said, "Dara can come with me."

"Too dangerous," said Miss Kronberga. "They'll be watching you. She'll stay with me. I have a small attic with a high window. Dara will be safer there."

When the other students had been dismissed, Dara left with Miss Kronberga and Mija went with the other three girls back to the apartment. There was very little talking. Mija made a bed for herself on the sofa. It was a night of tossing and turning and second-guessing. She thought about how to prepare herself for the next day but realized that was an impossible task. Finally, she fell into a fitful sleep. The next day she had dark circles under her eyes.

AT ELEVEN O'CLOCK, they appeared as planned at the army building that used to be the school. They were taken to what had been the principal's office and told to sit on the wooden bench which was on one side of a rectangular table. The three girls, Alfred, Mija, and Miss Kronberga sat in a row, hip to hip. Alfred's face had been suitably made up, but even so, his red cheeks showed through.

Aleks and another officer walked in and sat on the other side in two leather chairs without a word. Aleks flinched when he saw Mija but said nothing. He took notes and didn't look up. The second officer conducted the proceedings. He asked for the names of the four culprits. Miss Kronberga did all the talking. She told the story in a calm voice, in as few words as possible, and acted contrite for her students.

Miss Kronberga recited the names of the four students and came to "Lize Adamsons," the other officer said, "Adamsons?" and looked at Aleks.

Aleks looked up and said, "It's a common name in this part of the country." He looked back down and kept on writing.

Miss Kronberga said, "Officer, I beg to ask a question."

"Go ahead."

"With all due respect, doesn't the Reich have more important things to do than hunt down students?"

The other officer said, "You are very bold to question the Reich."

"I'm sorry, sir. I'm not questioning, merely

wondering why you are so interested in students who are doing no harm to anyone."

"They made a spectacle of themselves. They should be respectful at all times. Proper decorum is expected, and if we don't start with the young people, all is lost." He lifted his hands and stared at Miss Kronberga.

She didn't flinch. "Yes, sir. Thank you, sir."

The officer then addressed Mija. "Madam, why are you here? You weren't on the list. Are you looking for trouble?"

Her voice started shaky, then smoothed out, "I came to visit my daughter Lize. They're all good students. They didn't mean anything. They've apologized and are very sorry. Weren't you a teenager once?"

If that made an impression, it didn't show in the man's face. After the questioning, Aleks and the other officer left the room. Mija's armpits were wet and she wiped the sweat from her forehead. The ticking of the round wall clock was the only sound. Finally, the two men came back. The other officer said, "The incident is regrettable. From now on, no students in the streets after school hours unless they are accompanied by a teacher."

"Agreed," said Miss Kronberga.

"You're dismissed."

Dismissed? Mija looked at Aleks. He was staring away from her, just as expressionless as the other officer. Had he really denied his daughter and wife?

How did that protect them? Mija was not twelve, and she could not hide in the cellar any longer. She pointed at him. "Sir, don't you know me?"

A dead voice said, "No madam, I do not."

Mija looked at his face, then into his eyes. If she stood up, she could reach across the table and slap him. His eyes showed her what she hadn't seen before. Fear. He was afraid. He was a scared little boy trying to act grown up. She wanted to scream that he was a liar, but no sound came. Inside, a soundless scream killed the remnants of anything she'd ever felt for him. And at that moment of realization, the inner scream stopped. She was left with one feeling as she stared at him. Pity. She turned her head away.

The soldiers walked out first and the others followed. They were several blocks away before anyone spoke.

Miss Kronberga said, "I hope that's the end of it, girls."

Their heads bobbed up and down as they said, "Yes."

Mija wished she could take Lize with her, but there was no way to do that without creating more trouble and danger. The Germans had mandated that students stay in the school in which they were enrolled. Even so, it was by the barest thread that Mija left her daughter there.

CHAPTER TWENTY-THREE

*M*ija sucked on her lower lip as she dug into the ground and planted another seedling. Her calloused fingers were creased with dirt, her nails embedded with it. She stabbed downward again with the dull trowel, making another hole. Beside her were several mounds of seedlings that she'd started inside—carrots, lettuce, cucumber, tomatoes, turnips. She also had a little pile of seed potatoes.

As she planted, she thought about the work they'd done. In the past year, their little group had saved thirty people from the Jewish ghetto. They'd gotten two out of the country. Mija was impatient to get more out, but without a car and the right papers, it was difficult. Part of the problem was finding farmers outside the city, where homes were less likely to be searched, who were willing to hide Jews and feed them.

Why did the world keep turning? Mija asked

herself as she stabbed another hole. Three years. The earth had gone around the sun three times since the war started. The war was at a standstill; the earth should stand still too. It seemed like they had been at war forever. One year of Soviet occupation, and now two years of the Germans. *How long would war continue? Until all the soldiers in all the countries everywhere killed each other?*

The bright sun had given her cheeks a glow. She stood up and stretched her arms high, made fists and tensed and flexed the muscles in her arms and legs to loosen the knots. The denim overalls were threadbare. So was the plaid flannel shirt, but it wasn't possible to get new clothes, for gardening or any other reason. Stores were not open anymore. The group of six partisans lived in the countryside just outside of Riga, in another abandoned farmhouse. To keep from being discovered, they moved every few months. Mija hoped they wouldn't have to move again before the vegetables came in, or at least if they had to move, that it was somewhere close enough so she could come back and tend the garden once a week.

She heard them before she saw them. Warplanes, one after another, an almost daily occurrence. As the planes moved out of sight, she stretched again and walked to the house.

It was her turn to cook dinner—potato and turnip stew again, with one dried mushroom, one clove of garlic, a little dried dill for flavoring. All was quiet; no one was home yet. Brita and Zana had taken their weekly trek to Riga to stand in line for food rations, which usually meant one small loaf of hard bread each. They would also find out if there was anyone for Peters to pick up tonight. They had taken the latest escapee, a man with a stomach ulcer, to a safe house last week and were ready for another. Or two or three.

Maybe Peters or Ollie would bring a rabbit or squirrel home. They hadn't had meat for weeks. The two men should be on their way home from the neighboring farm where they had taken food supplies and were checking on two of their previous escapees. She waved at Harijs across the front yard from her, in the doorway of the barn, keeping a lookout on the road, rifle by his side.

Inside, Mija stood at the kitchen sink peeling the vegetables with a small knife. She paused, wondering if she'd be able to kill a soldier with the knife in her hand. She stabbed a potato, splitting it into two. Yes, she could. Maybe she should keep a knife in her pocket next to the gun.

Later, when the stew was ready, a strong turnip smell filled the small farmhouse. Using the ends of a dishtowel, Mija moved the heavy black pot to the back of the brick stove that jutted out from the fireplace. Mija added a few logs to the fire, then went to look out the front window. The others should have been home by now.

It was the lavender hour. The sun had fallen below the horizon. The meadow across the road was bathed in a light that didn't belong to day or night. Brita and

Zana appeared around the bend in the road, running and waving wildly. Mija ran outside.

"They arrested Dzenis yesterday. He's in jail," Brita yelled.

CHAPTER TWENTY-FOUR

*O*llie went to Riga early the next day to find out what he could about Dzenis. He didn't return that night. The next morning, Mija was up early, as usual, and went about her business. With her back to the rising sun, she frowned at the weeds and pulled at them with ferocity. She threw another weed onto the pile.

A stork glided toward the barn roof. The bird's long red beak and legs were in clear outline, in contrast to the white body and black wings, which appeared ghostlike against the clouds. The bird landed next to the nest that hid the radio antenna. Three babies chirruped as the mother dropped pieces of food into their mouths.

Smoke drifted upward from the chimney, making a lazy S. That meant someone was up and had started a fire for cooking. Coffee would taste good, Mija thought, but of course, there was no coffee, only the bitter chicory that grew wild along the white birch trees that lined the dirt road. She went back to her weeds and didn't see Peters coming. The crunch of a shoe on a stray twig alerted her and she turned around. He carried two steaming mugs. Mentally, she crushed the stir of attraction. He handed her a mug and put warm fingers on her cheek to brush back the strand of hair escaping from the kerchief around her head.

"Imagine this is real coffee."

Mija sipped the brown liquid. "You're up early."

"It's almost time for me to relieve Harijs. I'm going to the short-wave radio first."

"Anything special?"

"It's been two years since the trains took my family to Siberia, and I still don't know where my wife and sons are. Someone somewhere must know something. That's always what I check on first. Second this morning is to find out something that would tell us why Ollie didn't return last night."

"I'm worried about Ollie too. He's always returned before, no matter what."

The skin below Peters' eyes was puffy and he had a stubble of beard.

Mija asked, "Sleepless night?"

"I dreamed I was on a train to St. Petersburg going to see Ingrida and the boys because they lived there, but the train broke down at the Russian border. I got off and started running on the tracks. Then I woke up. That was 2:00 a.m. and my mind's been racing ever since."

"Why didn't you wake me?"

"And make you miserable too? Besides, I would also have woken Brita and Zana if I'd gone into your bedroom."

"There could be a simple explanation. By the way, I tossed and turned myself last night."

"Aha, then why didn't you come get me?" He smiled. "It works both ways."

"Yes, you're right. Next time I'll peek in and check if you're awake. I could have used help with the weeding."

Peters laughed. "Weeding? No, thank you. I'm not so good at that. I'm liable to pull out all the healthy plants as well. Thank goodness you're so good at gardening or we'd probably all starve."

"If you change your mind, I can teach you easily enough. Nu, with no end in sight for this stinking war and more and more roadblocks to rescuing people, it's harder and harder to get a good night's sleep." Mija poured the rest of her drink onto the ground and frowned. "I'm more worried about Dzenis than Ollie. We've all heard the stories about prison life, the overcrowding, shooting prisoners just because they get too close to the barbed wire fence, illnesses running rampant, no medical care. We have to get him out."

"Yes, we may need to do that, although I believe the job is even harder than getting a Jew out of the ghetto. First, let's find out what happened. Maybe he just missed the last trolley and spent the night with friends."

"I suppose we can wait another day or two."

"You always were impatient." He gave her a friendly hug.

Mija watched Peters' back as he walked to the barn. The tan sleeves of the baggy shirt were rolled up to his elbows. The borrowed denim pants hugged his backside and were two inches too short. She didn't want to go into the house yet, so she walked to the barn after she was sure he'd gone up the ladder to the hayloft and the hidden radio. She put her empty mug down next to the barn door and went in to feed the horse. Maybe she'd take Big Z for a ride. He nuzzled her shoulder and then ate the hay she put into the trough.

A guttural scream came from above. An image flooded Mija's mind. She saw a body, either Lize or Ints, she couldn't tell which. They were dead. There had been a fire and the black shell of a body was all that was left. Another scream from Peters. "It . . . can't . . . be."

Mija made her way toward the ladder. Her feet were heavy. *Why did I leave them? Why did I think they would be safe without me? One or both of them is dead and it's my fault. I'm losing my mind. No, it's not my children. Why does my mind always imagine the worst? It's his family. Not mine. He was checking for news about them. And that's just as bad.* She lifted one foot, put it down. She lifted the other foot. In slow motion, she reached the ladder. She gripped the wood with both hands and put a foot on the bottom rung. She tried to yell, to make a noise, but her throat wouldn't obey. The sound that came out was a low growl. Up in the loft, there was more screaming, but she couldn't make out the words. She put her other foot on the second rung. Step by step, she worked her way up.

Peters was in the corner by the radio. His headset was on the floor and so was he, on his knees, sobbing, his head in his hands. "No," he said. His head dropped lower and lower. "No, no, no." Mija ran to him. He turned away and stood up with his back to her.

"What happened?" she asked. She put one hand on his shoulder blade. He was trembling.

"They're dead," he said. He took a deep breath and turned back toward Mija. Tears fell freely. Mija used both hands to wipe his cheeks.

Mija asked in a whisper, "Who?"

Peters whispered back, "My family." Mija wiped her hands on her overalls and wiped his face again. She searched her pockets for a handkerchief, but there was nothing but a gun and a knife.

"That can't be." Mija had always pictured his wife and sons safe in Siberia. They were away from the fighting. No one was bombing Siberia. Once people were sent to Siberia, they were forgotten by the authorities.

"They've been dead for over a year." Peters grabbed onto Mija in a desperate hug. She wrapped her arms around his waist.

"Dysentery. An epidemic went through the village and killed two-thirds of the people. Over a year and I didn't know." He gripped Mija tighter. "How could I not know?"

"My dear Peters, how could you know?" Mija laid her head on his shoulder and closed her own eyes. Peters sobbed. Mija held onto him tightly. He cried for a long time and Mija cried too. After his sobs subsided, Mija rose on her toes and pressed her lips to his wet cheek. "I'm so sorry."

The stork babies started chirping. The radio made a static noise and then noise from the headset drowned out the babies, another message coming across in code. Peters ran to the headset, put it on and sat on the floor close to the radio. Shortly, he removed the headset, let it fall beside him, and sat without moving.

Mija asked, "Well?"

"Nothing. The confirmation I asked for." Peters stood up and walked to the ladder.

"Where are you going?"

He cleared his throat before speaking. "Riga. To find Ollie. Get Dzenis out of jail."

"You said we should wait."

"Waiting doesn't get you anywhere."

Mija followed him down the ladder. Peters ran. She ran after him.

CHAPTER TWENTY-FIVE

"Hey!" Zana pointed at the men's bedroom door. "What's the matter? Peters looks like a ghost." Zana stirred the pot of oatmeal. "Breakfast is ready."

"No time." Mija ran into the women's bedroom and pulled a dress from the wardrobe. Then she rummaged for a pair of shoes from the pile at the bottom of the wardrobe and grabbed flat black T-straps. They were a little loose, so she grabbed a small cotton handkerchief, and using her teeth, ripped some pieces off, folded each piece, and tucked one behind each heel.

Brita moaned from her single bed, "What are you doing?"

"Go back to sleep."

Brita had late watch last night and had gone to bed at 4:00 a.m. when Mija got up.

The front door slammed as Mija grabbed her

purse from the top drawer of the dresser. She stowed the gun and knife in it. As she ran toward the front door, she said to Zana, "Going to Riga. Don't wait or worry." Mija slammed the door behind her and sprinted down the dirt road.

In the still air, she yelled at Peters' back, "Stop. Please. I'm coming with you."

He slowed, and when she was beside him, she took his hand and slowed the pace more, to an even walk.

"Do you have your gun?" he asked.

"Why do you think I'm carrying this ridiculous purse on my shoulder?" With her free hand, she patted his side pocket and felt the twin to her gun. Good, his gun was on the side next to her. The bulge was less noticeable with their intertwined hands right next to it.

"In case I run out of rounds, I have a small knife too."

"Where'd you get a knife?"

"Last time I visited the children, I removed it from a storage box. It belonged to Aleks' father. Who are we going to kill?"

"No one, not if we can help it. That makes us as bad as them."

"You look ready to kill." Peters walked faster. Mija slowed him down again by pulling against his hand. "What's the plan, then?"

"Already told you."

Peters was wearing the best clothes, gray dress trousers, a white dress shirt, and black leather shoes.

The clothes fit well enough, but he hadn't taken the time to shave.

Mija's dress was her favorite color, a dark green, which deepened the green in her eyes and flattered her light brown hair that she had twisted into a prim bun at the nape of her neck. The pieces of hankie wouldn't stay in their proper spot in the shoes. After pushing them down several times on the walk down the dirt path, Mija gave up and put them into the purse, resigning herself to blisters. By the time they reached the main road, her heels had red marks.

They crossed the wide street and stood alone at the trolley stop. This was the northern tip of Riga, the end of Brivibas Iela, where the blocks of row houses started.

Mija asked again, "What's the plan?"

"First, find Ollie."

Mija gritted her teeth in frustration and let go of Peters' hand. She wanted the semblance of a plan and was not comfortable without a framework for proceeding. *What were they going to do, walk around Riga for days hoping to run into Ollie?* There was not much traffic, a truck now and then. They had missed the 8:00 a.m. trolley and would have to wait almost an hour for the next one. A plane droned overhead. Mija looked up, saw the usual German insignia. Maybe one of these days she would see an American plane. Or British. Don't think about a rescue, Mija told herself. *We're dealing with Germans now and no other armies are anywhere close.*

She noticed a weed sprouting from a crack in the sidewalk and had an urge to pull it out. A gust of warm air blew a yellow flower down from a linden tree, and it landed close to the weed. Mija picked up the flower and smelled its sweetness. Peters took the flower from her hand, anchored it in Mija's hair, and patted her shoulder. The sound of an engine came from the north, a black staff car, one driver in front, one officer in the back. Without thinking, Mija jumped into the road and waved her arms. The car came to a stop in front of her. Before Peters could do anything, she had run to the side of the car and was talking to the officer. As he walked toward her, he heard a few words, "My husband's, Colonel Adamsons. My sister's in labor, it's an emergency."

The officer said, "Of course we will help you."

"Peters," she said, "get in the front."

As Peters got in, Mija introduced him as her brother-in-law. The officer in back said, "Your husband is well thought of. How far along is your sister's labor?" Without waiting for an answer, he said to the driver, "Turn around, Hans, go where Mrs. Adamsons directs."

"She's been in labor for hours. I think it's breech. If we don't do something, she might die. We never expected a problem, or we'd have gone to the hospital right away." Mija caught Peters' eyes and looked down at her purse, put her hand on the clasp and opened it slightly. The driver made a fast U-turn and stepped on the pedal. "Tell me where to go."

"It's not far. Hurry, please. It's the next right."

As the car turned, the tires rumbled on the stone road. As soon as they were out of sight of houses, Mija said, "Now." In a fluid motion, she moved away from the officer, put her back against the door, pulled out the gun, and pointed at his head. Peters, in the same amount of time, had pulled his gun and pointed at the driver, a blond boy with a clean, shiny face.

"Don't think about going for your guns, either of you," she said. "At this range, you don't stand a chance."

The German officer's eye twitched and he sputtered, "What's going on?"

"Stop the car. Now. Or I'll shoot." Her finger wanted to pull the trigger. She held the gun inches from his temple.

"Get out," she said. He obeyed and Mija followed. The driver and Peters got out of the front. "Take your guns out and throw them down. Now." Mija kept her gun pointed at the officer's head. The Germans didn't take their eyes off her and followed her orders.

"What kind of a woman are you?" said the officer.

"None of your business. Undress." The astonished Germans started taking off their clothes. "Faster. I don't need much of an excuse to kill you both." Mija shot her gun into the air above the officer's head and all the men jumped. "That's a warning. You don't want me to shoot again. I never miss my target." The Germans hurriedly took off their shoes, shirts, and pants. The driver fell down removing his trousers and turned red in the face as he got up. They stood in their underwear and socks. "Everything!" When the men were naked, she said, "Tie them up."

"With what?" Peters asked.

"Look for something in the car. Or use their clothes." Peters got the keys from the ignition and looked in the trunk. "Nothing here."

"Look in the glove box."

"Aha. Handcuffs. And keys. Three sets."

Peters handcuffed both men with their hands at their backs. "Now what?" he asked.

"Bury them alive?" Mija said.

"Too good for them."

A yellow line of liquid flowed down between the driver's legs and tears streamed down his face, but he didn't say anything. The officer stood straight-backed, but one eye twitched.

"Walk," she said. "Go. That way." She pointed toward the farm with her gun.

The naked men walked and Mija and Peters walked behind them, guns cocked, ready to shoot. When they reached the dirt path, Mija slipped off her shoes. The blisters on her heels were fully formed. She left the shoes behind. As they neared the farm, Harijs, still on lookout because no one had relieved him, came running with his rifle.

"What the hell . . .?"

"Put them in the barn, lock them in a stall, keep a guard on them. We'll figure out what to do with them later. We've got their car and we're going to Riga."

Harijs pointed his rifle at them, and the soldiers

walked even faster toward the barn.

Mija and Peters stopped at the house. Brita was still sleeping. Mija sat Zana down at the table and quickly explained what happened, eating bites of cold oatmeal between sentences. Peters stood silently by the door, his gun still in his hand. Zana's brown eyes couldn't open any wider as the story came to an end. Mija got a different pair of shoes, finding a pair that fit better. She wished she had a pair of silk stockings as a barrier for the blisters, but silk stockings, like her former life, were a dim memory. She grabbed the purse. "We may be back today, we may not."

Mija picked up the discarded shoes on the way back to the car. As they reached the pile of clothes, she said, "Do you want to be an officer or a driver?"

"The officer's clothes will fit better." These were the first words Peters said since he handcuffed the Germans.

"You're right. Put your clothes and the other clothes in the trunk."

As he changed, Mija said, "No, I think you need to be a driver. An officer without a driver will raise suspicion. You can be the driver to the officer's wife. It's true enough."

"I'll take off the decorations then," he said.

Mija got in the back seat and sat, waiting for Peters to transform himself. She took the new shoes off to take the pressure off the blisters. They had broken and were bleeding. The pieces of hankie came out again from the purse. She patted them onto the blisters. The white cloth turned dark as the blood oozed and stuck, clotting. She sank her heels back into the shoes.

"Where to?" Peters asked as he got in the driver's seat and turned on the engine.

"What do you think we should do?" Taking charge in this type of situation was new to Mija, and she automatically deferred.

"You started this, you got the car, you're in charge." Peters turned and looked at her. "I think you lost the flower in your hair."

Mija felt for it, but it was gone. "I lost more than a flower," she said. "Let's go to Dzenis'. Maybe his wife knows what happened to Ollie."

Mija stared out the window as they drove down Brivibas Iela. The hum of the motor sliced the air, the sky darkened, and there was a yellowish tinge to the clouds. The air outside the car was still, but with her window down halfway, a slight breeze blew on Mija's face. She opened the window the whole way and let the air flow full on. Raindrops landed on her cheeks. As the rain intensified, she rolled the window up three-quarters. Peters fumbled to find the switch to turn on the wiper blades. Thick drops fell faster and flattened on the windshield, obscuring his view. A rumble of thunder broke through the hum of the engine and Mija rolled her window up all the way.

"Don't turn down Matisa Iela. Stop at the corner right before it and I'll walk the two blocks to the apartment."

"It's raining."

"I know, but anyone looking out a window will be scared away by this big black car. We can't be seen."

Peters pulled over and parked. As Mija ran down Matisa Iela, she was pelted with hard rain. Thunder rumbled between lightning flashes. By the time she knocked on the apartment door, she was soaked through and chilled.

"It's me, Mija, let me in."

Vera opened the door. She got a towel for Mija to dry off and gave her a dress to change into. The dress was too short. Mija put her wet dress on the back of a kitchen chair and asked if Vera had a raincoat. Vera gave her Dzenis', which was slightly large. Mija buttoned the black buttons, tied the belt, and rolled up the sleeves. Vera didn't have an umbrella to loan her.

Maris was asleep in the alcove but coughed and the sound of phlegm rattling around in his lungs reminded Mija of her dead niece, little Ruta.

"He has a bad cold," Vera said. "You know how summer colds can be." We don't have the money to go to the doctor.

Someone knocked at the door in a signal, three quick raps, a pause, two quick raps. Vera opened the door to Ollie. He was wet too. Vera handed him the same towel Mija had used.

Mija told them what had happened today, about Peters' family, about the car she commandeered, and about the naked German soldiers who were now in the barn in a horse stall. Vera was as wide-eyed as Zana had been.

Ollie said, "I'm impressed. Now you can help me figure something out. I've been trying to put together a plan to get Dzenis out. That's why I didn't get back yesterday. I went to see two lawyers who weren't helpful. They shrugged and said, "What do you expect me to do against the German Army?" I tried to visit Dzenis. He's not allowed visitors. I lied that there was a death in the family. The soldiers didn't care."

Vera started to cry and told Mija about Dzenis. "He was arrested because he harbored a Jew, an extra one, on a day the partisans weren't scheduled to come to Riga. The Jew had an infected sore on his ankle and could hardly walk. We planned to keep him for one night and the next day Dzenis was taking him to you. But in the middle of the night, the soldiers came. Someone must have turned us in. With no place to hide, Dzenis and the Jew were handcuffed and led away. I'm lucky they didn't take me too." Vera started crying. "My poor husband, jailed. My poor son, if he doesn't get medicine, I'm afraid he'll die. We're all going to die."

Mija said, "Vera, you're not going to die. Neither is Maris. Neither is Dzenis. We will get him out. Pack up what you can—all your food. Put together any official papers you have. A small bag of clothes. We're going to get Dzenis and come back for you, and we're taking you away from here. Do you understand?"

Vera nodded.

Mija said, "Do you have any vodka?"

Vera retrieved a half-full bottle from the cupboard.

"Thank you," Mija said. "Be ready within the hour."

Outside, the rain had turned to a fine mist. Mija and Ollie walked to the car. She cradled the bottle.

"You won't be able to go in with me. They know what you look like," she said. "I'll do it myself. I have a plan."

CHAPTER TWENTY-SIX

At the central prison, a "Heil Hitler," the use of her husband's name, and a story about her imprisoned "brother" got Mija through the first door. Dzenis' name was looked up and she was sent down a long corridor where a door to the left led outside. Straight ahead was a second door with a guard.

She said, "I'm here about my brother."

"Political prisoner?"

"Yes."

"Of course. They wouldn't have sent you this way otherwise." He opened the door and closed it behind her.

A steep stairway led downward. The damp air reminded her of a vegetable cellar. The moldy brick walls caused her nasal passages to clog. She almost stumbled on the crumbly stone steps and grabbed at the wall to keep her balance. *This must have been built in the Middle Ages.* When she rubbed her hand against her raincoat, she left chalky marks on the black material. The only things that kept the stairway from being darker than night were occasional dim oil lamps attached to the walls. She reached a landing and a turn that led to more steps. *Good god, how far down is it?* She continued her descent. As she reached the bottom, she saw the outline of a soldier. Then she saw that he was standing next to still another door.

Oh my god, I don't want to be here in this small space with this German soldier. I should turn around and run back up. No, I am not a coward. I refuse to be frightened. I will do this. I will survive. Better, I will succeed.

Next to the soldier sat a small square metal table holding a black notebook and pen. Two metal chairs were pushed under the table. The tidy arrangement sat to the right, just far enough away so that the guard could stand between it and the door.

His words were curt and clipped. "I heard you coming. Give me your papers."

He was young, slim, and short. A few wisps of brown hair poked out under the brim of his cap. His arm was raised parallel to the ground as if to restrain Mija from coming any closer. His nails were clean, his hands looked soft.

She was so close that she could have touched his hand. Mija raised her eyebrows and said, "Don't you know who I am?"

"I have never met you. Where are your papers?"

"I don't need papers. I'm the wife of—"

He raised his arm, as if ready to invoke a 'Heil.' "I have my orders. No visitors without papers."

She gave him what she hoped was a stern look. "I'll wait, then, until your replacement arrives."

The top half of the door was all window. She saw a long hallway and, on either side, a line of cells. Mija pulled out the chair next to the door, causing the soldier to jump.

"You can't stay here."

The guard clicked his heels together and put one hand on her shoulder. Mija stepped back and his arm left her. She pulled out the bottle and showed him the label. "At least the Russians are good for something. Do you have any shot glasses?"

He made a face that she took for disgust "No, madam."

She sat down. He walked around to the other side of the table and faced her. His boot tapped against the stone floor. "You must leave."

Mija opened the bottle and lifted it toward him. His lips opened into an "O" as if to speak, but Mija spoke first. "This is good vodka, sir. Let's not waste it." She took what appeared to be a long swig, although she only let a tiny bit go down her throat. Handing it to him again, she smiled. "Sit down. For a minute." She winked and opened up her raincoat, revealing the tight dress.

His dark eyes widened. "I suppose a little won't hurt. But I will stand."

He clicked his heels, took the bottle, and tilted his

head. His Adam's apple bobbed as he swallowed. He coughed and his pale face turned red.

"Good vodka, no?" Mija took the bottle from his outstretched hand, took another pretend sip, and handed it back.

"Yes, this is good." He swallowed again.

She shrugged her shoulders. "Won't you sit?"

He didn't move.

Mija raised her eyebrows. "Please?"

He cocked his head and looked around as if checking to make sure no one else was there and then sat down. He held his back straight and placed his hands on the table.

Mija asked, "Where are you from? What is your name?"

"Scheid," he said, formally. "Heinrich Scheid. From Würzburg."

"First time away from home?"

"Yah."

At the mention of home, his shoulders relaxed and he put his hands together as if in prayer. As they passed the bottle back and forth, Mija found out that Heinrich Scheid was an only child, and his mother didn't want him to go to war. But he felt a duty to his homeland, and as soon as he turned eighteen, he signed up. He told his mother the day before he left for training. She made him promise not to take chances. When prison guard detail became available, he took it, for his mother.

"You're a good son, Heinrich Scheid," Mija told

him. When the bottle was empty, Heinrich slurred agreement to let her go through the door and look for her brother. If he was there, she could talk to him for five minutes. "Thank you, Heinrich," she said. "I see you are tired. Put your head down and rest for a minute."

"I am tired, madam. We work twenty-four hours between eight hours of rest."

"Are you finished soon?"

Heinrich looked at his watch, opened his eyes wider as if to focus, "That depends on how you think of it. Four more hours."

"Rest, dear boy."

Heinrich folded his arms on the table and laid his head in the crook of an elbow, letting his eyes shut halfway. Mija leaned over and patted Heinrich's shoulder. His eyes closed all the way. She sat and waited. After he didn't move for several minutes, she closed her raincoat and stood up.

Now, where are the keys to open the cells? What if he doesn't have any keys? Besides, I don't even know for sure if Dzenis is here. The soldier who looked him up could have made a mistake or even sent me on a wild goose chase. If he isn't here, I don't need keys. Come on, you don't know how long soldier boy will stay asleep. You need keys. Without them, you wasted a trip. She tiptoed behind Heinrich. There was a bulge in his pocket and a rounded piece of metal stuck out.

She squatted beside him. He made a little grunt and Mija froze. He turned his head from one side to the other. She waited. A line of sweat dripped down her forehead. She reached up and pushed the sweat back. He let out a small snore. Mija reached toward the ring, then hesitated. She let out a breath, then slowly inhaled. The mustiness in the air almost made her cough. Heinrich snored louder, and this gave Mija courage. She gripped the silver ring and pulled it out in one movement. The freed keys jingled and Heinrich moved. Mija felt hot sweat in her armpits. She stayed in a crouch until his snoring steadied again.

Her knees creaked as she stood up, but there was no movement from the guard. She stepped carefully toward the door so her shoes wouldn't make any noise. She turned the deadbolt, willing it not to squeak. Now for the door. The heavy door creaked once, louder than her knees. She waited and then pushed it just enough to slide her body in sideways.

The stench of unwashed bodies and human waste assaulted her, and she fought against retching. She held her index finger up to her lips as she walked down the corridor. All she needed was for them to start shouting and it would all be over. But no one spoke. And no one looked familiar. Cells that were meant for two were filled with at least six, maybe eight. There was one bucket in each cell, filled precariously close to the top with brown sludge. There were no toilets, no sinks, no beds. A few rolled-up blankets were piled in the corner of each cell. She was close to the end, where she faced another wall of brick and mold. Then she saw him. Dzenis was in the last cell on the right, standing between several others. His mouth had fallen open.

"Thank God," Mija whispered.

"Are you crazy?" he hissed.

"Yes, I'm a crazy woman. Be quiet."

"Whatever you say. And by the way, I'm happy to see you, I think."

"If we escape, then you can be grateful. Until then, you can reserve judgment."

"What are you doing?"

"Breaking you out."

The fifth key opened Dzenis' cell.

Mija said, "I'm sorry I can't let all of you go," and locked the cell again.

Dzenis followed her down the corridor. At the door, he turned and saluted those left behind. Mija closed the door, bolted it, and gently laid the keys on the table.

Mija whispered, "Fast, we need to get out of here and out of the city."

"After you."

They hurried up, up, turning on the landing, continuing up, seemingly forever. Finally, the air smelled lighter and purer. At the top, Mija said to the guard, "I promise you my crazy brother will not bother your orderly jail again. Many danke also from my husband, Colonel Adamsons. He will be proud of you."

A slight smile broke onto the guard's lips at the words "proud of you." He was a reserved looking man with a straight nose and black, unblinking eyes. He said, "I will take the release papers now."

Without missing a beat, she said, "I gave them to the guard below. He said that was the procedure."

The guard frowned and shook his head. "Those new boys can't get it straight. I'll have to report him. Go ahead, then." He clicked his heels and raised his right arm.

Mija nodded. She took Dzenis by one arm and rushed him through the outer door. He blinked as daylight hit his face. He coughed and phlegm rattled.

"You shouldn't be near me. I'm sick."

"Then it's a good thing I got you out. How fast can you walk? We don't want to bring attention to ourselves by running."

They were on a side street. She took a route away from the front of the prison. There were only a few civilians on the streets.

The black car waited at the same spot where Mija had left it, Peters still at the wheel. She opened the door to the back seat and motioned for Dzenis to get in.

"Hide on the floor. You're small enough to fit down there."

"You kidding? This car is huge. I could fit two of me down here."

"Let's go, Peters."

"I'm ready." Peters pulled away from the curb. "While I waited, several soldiers walked by. No one said anything, but they stared at me, and the car."

As the car turned the corner, the air filled with the sound of police sirens.

CHAPTER TWENTY-SEVEN

$\mathcal{M}$ ija said, "Faster, Peters!"

"For heaven's sake, I can't go faster than the car in front of me. We're doomed."

"Then pass them."

"Can't you see? There's no room."

Two blocks later, a police car turned onto their street and zoomed up behind them, sirens blaring. Braking at the last moment, it stopped inches from their rear bumper. There was no choice but to pull over.

Mija said, "Dzenis, get up from the floor, sit next to me as if you belong here."

She rolled down her window as a German soldier approached.

He peered at them and said, "Step out of the car, all of you!"

"Sir, you're making a big mistake." With her hand,

she made a downward motion to Peters and Dzenis that said, 'stay where you are.'

"You're in a staff car of the Third Reich, madam. Do you have permission?"

She said, "Of course. I am the wife of Colonel Aleks Adamsons." She pointed to Peters. "This is my driver." She pointed to Dzenis. "And this is my brother. You have no right to stop us."

The soldier looked at Peters and said, "Driver? I've never seen you before."

Peters' German was not perfect, but passable. He said, "I was formerly in the Latvian Army and am now in the German Army. I returned to Latvia two days ago from training in Germany."

"Your name?"

"I am Peters Ezerins."

"Your uniform is most improper."

Peters shrugged his shoulders and said, "I agree, but this is what they gave me. I was told there are no longer enough seamstresses. New recruits get old uniforms. I suppose the person who wore this before me died for the cause."

The officer raised his eyebrows. "Interesting story. No matter. I'm taking you all in. There's a missing staff car. I don't take chances."

A second police car arrived, and a second officer joined them. The first one briefly told him what happened. The second one agreed that the three would have to be detained.

The first officer said, "I will lead. You follow me.

The other car will follow behind you. Don't think about trying to escape. We would just as soon shoot you." The second officer nodded. From the look on his face, Mija didn't doubt him.

After Mija rolled up the window, Dzenis said, "Now we're in for it. We'll probably be shot."

"Maybe," Mija said, "but at least I stood up for you, my countryman, and for that I am proud." She felt calm. Her heart was not racing, her palms were not sweating. Her only regret was that if she died, her children would grow up motherless. But she had faith in Feliks and Laima to raise them as well as she would have.

Peters said, "I am proud as well, but Dzenis is right. We're probably dead. If not today, then soon. They are sure to find us out. Mija, we don't have much time. I want you to know I love you. I wish circum-stances were different. I wish——"

Mija interrupted, "That we were back in the park when we were teenagers. I wish so many things. And I love you too. If we get out of this——"

Peters finished her sentence, "We will continue our work. And when the war is over, we will be together."

"You're optimistic." A hint of a smile showed on her face.

"I learned it from you."

"That's all well and good but we need to minimize our trouble. We need to hide our weapons. Can you open the glove box up there?"

Peters' long reach barely opened it. He slipped his gun in. Mija slid her gun and the pocketknife over the seat and Peters stowed them also.

Peters said, "If anyone asks, we know nothing about any weapons."

They followed the officer's car into the parking area behind the prison. The soldiers led them inside. The men were led in one direction while another soldier took Mija by the arm in the opposite direction. He was gruff, not like the young guard she'd faced earlier.

"How long will I be here?"

"Until they let you out."

He pushed her inside what she thought must be a holding cell, and the door clicked behind her. She was locked in a space the size of a small closet. Perhaps it was a closet. A small opening in the top part of the door was covered with chicken wire. She was grateful for the air it let in. The bucket in the corner had been cleaned out but still stank a little. There was nothing else in the space, so she sat on the floor. Closing her eyes, she prayed silently. *Lord, if I die, please take care of my children. They didn't deserve any of this. Please, Lord, make sure Lize and Ints know I love them. Amen.*

The door clicked and opened. Mija stood up. A soldier she didn't recognize poked his head in, but he didn't look rough like the previous one.

"Are you Mija?" He whispered.

"Yes." He would get no more information than was necessary.

"My name is Johan."

Why did that name sound familiar?

"Aleks sent me."

"Really?"

"Yes, come with me, quietly. Don't talk until we reach our destination."

He took her arm and held it with a firm grip that did not hurt. She kept pace with him and soon they were outside. He led her into the back seat of a staff car.

He said, "Don't try to escape. We can only protect you so much."

She nodded. "You have nothing to worry about."

He got in the driver's seat, started the engine and pulled away.

"Where are Peters and Dzenis?"

"We can't do anything about them right now."

"Then take me back."

"Don't be foolish. You can tell that to Aleks. If he says to take you back, then you'll go back."

"Where are you taking me?"

"Not far."

She didn't know if she believed him. She anticipated being driven somewhere out of town, maybe far away, maybe even Gulepils. She realized she was wrong when he pulled up to a side entrance at the Riga Hotel. *How ironic. This is where Aleks and I had our honeymoon.*

Johan jumped out and opened Mija's door. As before, he gripped her arm. They went inside, up the grand staircase, to one of the second-floor offices.

Aleks sat behind a mahogany desk. He looked older, and his hair had noticeably grayed.

"Thank you, Johan. I will call for you when I'm ready."

Aleks pointed to one of the two chairs in front of the desk. "Please, sit. Tell me, Mija, what happened?"

"Nu, I don't know exactly what you're asking. What happened to us? What happened to me since we saw each other last? What happened to our children? The people who were shot for no reason except their religion? Or better yet, who did you kill to get promoted to Riga and get this huge office?"

Aleks grimaced. "I can assure you I've killed no one. This is not my office. You're lucky I'm here for a meeting. Let's start with today." He put his elbow on the desk and cupped his chin with his hand.

"It started like any other day in the past months. Or maybe years. Of war, that is. And then . . . I don't feel like going through my day with you, Aleks. I haven't seen you in a very long time, but you start up as though we just saw each other yesterday. I'm worn out. Take me back to prison."

"You don't want to die today, do you? If I send you back without answers, you will be shot. We don't have time to waste. Tell me the truth. You have five minutes."

"Peters and I, well, it was me really, commandeered a German staff car at the edge of Riga. I was tired of taking the trolley."

Aleks rolled his eyes, "I can do without your sarcasm. Who was in the car?"

"A driver and an officer."

"What did you do with them?"

"Right now they're safely locked up in the barn of the farm where we live."

"Who lives there?"

"Some men, some women. I will not name them."

"Are the Germans still alive?"

"Yes. I have not killed anyone." She raised her eyebrows and said, "Yet."

"You need to bring them back. Alive." Aleks clasped his hands together and laid them on the desk.

"Then what? Then they'll shoot me? No, I see no reason to tell anyone anything. Go ahead. Kill me. I'm not giving up the soldiers." Mija was surprised that she had no feeling except a deep calm. She had thought about the moment of dying many times during the past few years. She had thought about how she wouldn't cry or have regrets. Now that death could be near, she was ready. Except she did have regrets. But her goal right now was to get Peters and Dzenis out of jail.

"Mija, you're a stubborn woman. I can't help you if you don't cooperate."

"How can you help me? And besides, don't you already know where I live? You have spies all over the place."

"You overestimate my abilities, my dear wife."

"Don't call me that."

"Do you remember our honeymoon?"

"That was a long time ago. A lot has happened since then."

"And we don't have time to play games."

"Well, then. Can we make a deal?"

Aleks took a cigarette from his silver case and lit it with his lighter. Mija recognized the wedding gifts she'd given him.

He said, "I can only do so much. What do you have in mind?"

"A trade."

"Name it and I'll tell you if it's possible."

"I'll give up the soldiers. Maybe. No, I don't think I should give them up. They're my bargaining chip. How about this? You write up some false papers that show them leaving for Germany. Say they were called back for some reason."

"You would have made a good spy. Still could. I could help you."

Mija clenched her fists and met his eyes. "I am never working for the Germans."

He matched her stare. "And when the Russians come back?"

"I'll fight until we're free."

"Mija, we're too small. It's not going to happen. You'd better resign yourself to it."

"We had our freedom. We can win it again."

"We had our freedom for a handful of years. No one is coming to help."

"Once the war is over, we can demand it."

"From who? Our little country will be eaten up. If

not by the Germans, then the Russians will swoop in again."

"I want you to be wrong."

"I've spent my life studying war. And history. You know history. You teach it. You have to know I'm right."

Something shifted in Mija. She loved her country. She wanted the peaceful life she'd known between the two wars. Until today, she'd believed it might be possible. But now, hearing Aleks' words, doubt exploded within her. She had survived three years of occupation and there was no telling when it might end. Was she willing to stay in a country where she'd have to live under complete domination of another?

"Aleks, I know you're right. But I want you to be wrong." She sighed.

She looked away. "I will not live under communism."

"We don't always have a choice."

She turned back to him. "There is always a choice, Aleks. There are always choices, even when we think there aren't any. I have a choice right now. I can walk away."

"And then you will be shot in the back."

"By you?"

"Don't be ridiculous. Let's talk trade."

"I changed my mind. I want Peters and Dzenis out of prison. They committed no crime. I want the car back too. And you can't have the Germans."

"You're crazy, Mija. I can't do that."

"Then go ahead, put a bullet in my head. Make it quick." She looked away from him, at the wall with its picture of Hitler. She had an urge to spit on it.

Aleks picked up his telephone and dialed. He took another drag on his cigarette and blew the smoke out in small puffs that made rings. "Send Johan in."

He hung up the telephone. They sat in silence until Johan knocked on the door.

"Come in."

"Take a seat. We are at an impasse. Perhaps you can help."

Johan sat in the chair next to Mija and looked perplexed. "Me? I know we've had plenty of talks about things, but advice?" He shook his head. "I'm a lowly driver."

"You're a lifelong military man. You know the German Army better than I. I'm merely a Latvian puppet."

Johan sat up straighter and listened as Aleks summarized what had transpired and what Mija's demands were. Then Johan sat for a few minutes without speaking.

Finally, he said, "The army is losing more and more men. The tide of war may be turning against Germany. The prison system is in shambles. The guards would sooner shoot any more prisoners than find a space for them." He cocked his head to one side. "There might be a way. I have a long-time friend, stationed in Germany. He's a much higher rank than I am. I helped him once or twice."

Johan sat for another minute before speaking. "First, the staff car Mija wants. My friend can make up orders sending it to Gulepils. From Gulepils, I can make up papers saying there was an accident and it is out for repair."

Aleks said, "Excellent."

"It will need altered plates. I've done that bit of work before."

"You're a genius."

"No, I'm not, but I've seen a lot."

Mija said, "What about Peters and Dzenis?"

Johan said, "That's easy. I can do what I did for you."

Mija furrowed her brows. "What's that?"

"I'll take papers that Aleks makes up, giving him custody and permission to move them to the Gulepils prison. Aleks? Is that agreeable with you?"

Aleks frowned. "It will have to be. But Mija, you need to promise me something."

"What?"

"You will stay out of sight until the war is over. Papers will say you're in prison in Gulepils. I can tell them you are with the Jews. But if you're caught again, there'll be no saving any of us."

Johan said, "I have one more idea that might help. I can fill out an affidavit that on the way to Gulepils, that all three, Mija, Peters and Dzenis, tried to escape and I shot them, pulled their bodies into the woods, left them for the animals to feed on. The higher-ups in the prison system love stories like that. No one will question it."

Mija said, "Grisly. Has that happened already?"

Johan nodded. "A close version of it. Like I said, I've heard a lot. I'm curious, Mija. What do you intend to do with the German officers?"

"I won't kill them, but I will make sure they leave Latvia."

Johan nodded, "By the way, they were both involved in what happened at Rumbala. As far as I'm concerned, you can do what you will."

Aleks said, "Johan, you're a good man."

Mija said, "Thank you, thank you both."

Aleks said, "Will you go back to Feliks' farm and stay there?"

She shook her head. "I can't promise that."

"Mija, I hope we can work things out after the war."

Mija was surprised to hear Aleks' words. She shook her head. "I don't know. So many things have happened."

CHAPTER TWENTY-EIGHT

The partisans gathered in the living room of the farmhouse sitting in a circle on the floor by the fireplace, as there were not enough seats for all of them. Dzenis and his family were also there.

Dzenis said, "We all need to disappear. The margin of danger outweighs anything else."

Zana said, "I agree your family needs to disappear. But I am staying. I have no one and nothing to lose."

One by one, the rest agreed to stay.

Mija spoke last. "I have children. And that's my biggest reason for staying. While we're occupied, I will not stop fighting. Dzenis, where can we take you?" She reached over and tousled his son's hair. He reminded her of Ints at that age.

Dzenis stroked his beard. "I think the best plan is for us to go to my aunt and uncle's in Zilupe. It's far enough away."

Peters said, "Ah, Zilupe. That gives me an idea.

Why don't we take care of the German soldiers at the same time? Zilupe is not far from the Russian border. We can release them close to the border, force them into Russia. There they can fend for themselves."

"That's brilliant," Mija said. "Why didn't I think of that?"

"You've had enough brilliant ideas lately." Peters smiled.

Ollie said, "I agree. We'll keep them handcuffed and tighten the ties on their legs. For good measure, we'll stow them in the trunk. They'll be happy to run into Russia."

Brita said, "I can't believe we got the car back and with a full tank of petrol."

"Johan is the best German I've ever met," said Mija.

Harijs said, "We will leave tonight. Ollie, will you come with me to share the driving?"

"Who appointed you the driver?" asked Peters.

Harijs shrugged. "After what happened, you need to lay low. This place isn't safe anymore. I don't even think you should stay here tonight."

Mija said, "Sadly, I agree with you." She sighed. "Still another garden I have to leave behind."

Peters patted her shoulder. "It's too late to go anywhere tonight. Tomorrow we'll move. I don't think we need to go far. Just so it's not here."

Dzenis said, "All right then, it's settled. Let's get started. The faster I get my family away from here, the better."

HARIJS AND OLLIE returned the next day, and the partisans gathered in the living room once more.

Harijs started. "We sure scared Dzenis' aunt and uncle, arriving in the middle of the night like that. We almost got shot for robbers."

Mija said, "Any other problems?"

"We saw a convoy of German trucks on the way, rumbling toward us. I stared ahead and kept on going. Believe me, my heart was in my throat until they were well out of sight."

Peters said, "What happened at the border?"

"It was near daylight when we arrived," said Ollie. "At first they were glad to have their legs untied. They weren't so happy when they found out where they were going. I had to threaten to shoot them."

Harijs said, "They begged us to undo the handcuffs. We traded the handcuffs for tying their wrists behind them with the rope. That way they could undo each other eventually, and we had enough time to get away. I'm not sure they got to do that."

Zana asked, "Why?"

Ollie and Harijs exchanged a look. Ollie said, "Here's the truth of it. They went down the road toward the border at a fairly fast clip. We waited to make sure they didn't try to come back into Latvia. Then we heard shots. Could that have been a hunter? We'll never know. I'm guessing no one has to worry about those two anymore."

CHAPTER TWENTY-NINE

Mija stood halfway between the log cabin and the barn, staring at the empty stork's nest on the barn roof. The storks had flown to warmer climates months ago, and she missed them. Instead of the whir of stork wings, she heard the drone of warplanes. One, two, three, four, five, in a V formation. They were high up and soon gone. Dark scallop-edged clouds cut into the blue sky, and the horizon was dotted with the uneven squiggles of barren birch trees.

With every breath, the frosty air bit into her lungs. She wiggled her fingers and stamped her feet, then started walking toward the barn again. Her clunky shoes crunched a path in the new snow, feet disappearing underneath.

The faded gray of the barn's wooden exterior loomed in front of her. She heard Big Z neigh and hurried in. Gathering an armful of hay, she went to the horse.

Her arms ached for her children. She hadn't seen them for weeks. They'd changed so much since the war started. Ints had grown by inches and Lize had matured into a young woman. Ints hair had turned a darker blonde, like Mija's, and he had her green eyes. Lize was short, like Aleks' mother, slight, with Marina's wavy brown hair and light brown eyes.

With the snowfall, going to her brother's farm would be treacherous. Passenger trains no longer ran. There was no petrol for the black car hidden under the hay in a corner of the barn and with the ever-increasing troop movements in and out of Riga, driving that far was too dangerous anyway. She would have to go by horse, if she went. But in the snow-covered landscape, she could easily lose her way.

Big Z nuzzled her arm, and she petted his head absentmindedly. She talked softly to him. "Sorry, no apple today. I know you want to go for a ride. Maybe tomorrow." He snorted softly, as if he understood, and kept munching the dry hay. She leaned the side of her head against his neck and put her arm around his mane.

Had the struggle been worth it? She patted the horse's head. They had saved forty-two people. But what about the close to four thousand still there with no medicine, no fuel to heat their apartments, threadbare coats, sick and starving? Since Dzenis was gone, everything was that much harder.

BIG Z NEIGHED AND brought Mija back to the present. The wooden barn door creaked and Zana entered cautiously. Zana was always worried about something and flitted about like a nervous bird.

"Close the door and come in," Mija waved. "Need something?"

"I wanted to tell you supper's getting cold. Peters cooked."

"Something he brought home this afternoon?"

"No meat. Cabbage soup. But it's good." Zana smiled and patted her stomach.

Mija screwed up her face, "Cabbage again? Nu, it's better than nothing. I'll be in soon."

Zana scampered out and banged the door behind her. Mija ran her fingers through Big Z's mane, gave him a pat, walked to where the car was hidden behind bales of hay, and sat on a bale in the front. Taking off her shoes, she rubbed her toes. She wished she had some light. This time of year, in late afternoon, night closed over everything like a roller shade.

The barn door creaked again and Peters entered. He held a lighted candle in one hand, a little pot in the other, and with one foot he pushed the door closed behind him.

"I brought soup."

"I was coming."

"Cold cabbage soup is not good." She took the proffered pot. The handle of a spoon stuck out under the lid. Holding the pot by the handle, she tested the side with her other hand. Not too hot, she determined, and settled the pot on her lap. She warmed her hands on the sides for a minute before lifting the lid. The rising heat warmed her nostrils. The soup was thick with pieces of carrot, onion, potato, and cabbage. She put a spoonful into her mouth.

"Hmm," she said. "I guess I am hungry."

"I'm going up to the radio, back soon."

"Thanks for the soup."

With the candle, Peters lit a kerosene lamp. He put the candle and its little stand next to Mija. "There's hardly any kerosene left, and this is the last candle. We'll have to stay in the house after dark."

Peters was in the loft for a long time. The clicking and clacking of the radio signal device started and stopped as Peters sent messages and then waited for a reply. Full of soup, Mija leaned against the pile of hay bales at her back and closed her eyes. She brought her legs up and folded them underneath so that her toes could warm up against her thighs.

"Hey, sleepy girl."

Mija's opened her eyes and stared into Peters' face, inches from hers.

"Nu, why are you scaring me?" She sat up and he moved away.

"Bad dream?"

"No, no dream. What's the news?"

Peters sat down next to Mija and took her hand in his. "You should have put your mittens back on when you finished eating." He rubbed her hand between his.

"I'd rather hear it straight out."

Peters sighed, "They've taken them."

"Who? Straight, I said. The whole thing, and be quick about it."

"The ghetto. Cleaned out, loaded up into cattle cars at the main station in Riga. No more people in the ghetto. Straight enough?"

"Did they kill them? Another Rumbala?"

"Don't think so or they wouldn't have put them in cattle cars. But I don't know for sure." Another sigh escaped as he continued to rub her hand. Then he placed her hand on her lap but didn't let go. Mija put her other hand on top and they both leaned back into the bale, arms touching.

Peters said, "What are you thinking about?"

"I need to see my children. Tomorrow is Christmas. I'm going to take Big Z and leave at first light. I have some dried cherries from the summer. They'll love such a special treat."

"They'll love seeing you. And I'm going along." He nodded his head. "Big Z can carry both of us. No argument. At first light, we go."

"No argument. It's a good idea." She smiled.

"It's settled then. Let's go inside the house where it's warm."

It was snowing again. The fat flakes fell straight down and covered their heads as they plodded to the cabin.

Peters said, "We'll take the main roads. There won't be troop movements tomorrow. We'll have to be careful near Gulepils, though, and take the long way around to the farm."

"Yes," Mija said, half hearing him as she pictured herself with her children, sitting in front of a warm fire.

MIJA LAY WIDE-AWAKE in bed, curled up on her side. Zana and Brita were asleep in the other two single beds. Mija turned from the wall to the window. She heard Brita roll over and sigh. Zana snored lightly. Mija wondered if the three men snored. All six were inside. When the dark days of winter had arrived, they stopped having a guard outside during the middle hours of the night.

Why wasn't morning here yet? Mija heard a noise. *Planes? Can't be planes. It's not coming from the sky. Tanks? No, couldn't be. An army jeep!* Mija jumped out of bed and shook one, then the other. "Wake up, get up, get dressed. Quick, quick. Someone's coming."

Brita said, "Go, Mija, wake the men. We'll go out the window and meet you in the woods." She pulled herself into a sitting position, leaned over and shook the snoring Zana, put her feet on the ground, and reached for her clothes in the dark. They had drilled for just such an emergency.

Mija already had her clothes on—the thick woolen men's pants and sweater she had set aside to wear on the trip—and had stepped into her shoes. She pulled her coat on as she ran to the other bedroom. The men were up and getting their pants on. Ollie had heard the jeep too.

"Go, go, go," Ollie said as he opened the window. Mija jumped out first.

As planned, Mija ran to the edge of the grove of trees behind the house. She stopped, wrapped her scarf around her head, and dug out her mittens from the pockets. She could see the windows of both bedrooms, now closed. The fresh snow shimmered in the dim light. The other two women must already be inside the woods, she thought. Two figures ran toward her. Must be two of the men. Where's the third one?

She heard a neigh from the barn as the two men reached the edge of the woods. She said, "Psst. Over here." She could see headlights come around the bend toward the house as Ollie and Harijs reached her.

"Where's Peters?" she asked.

"Gone to the barn. We couldn't stop him," said Ollie.

"Good god, they'll kill him."

Ollie put an arm on her shoulder. "Come on, we have to get to the meeting place."

"Not without Peters."

"Yes, he wants it that way."

The jeep reached the front of the house. They could see the headlights coming across the snow. Car doors slammed and something, possibly the butt of a rifle, pounded against the front door. Mija saw Big Z walk between the barn and the house, unsure of where to go.

Harijs touched Mija's shoulder, whispered, "I see him too. Wait until the soldiers go in the house."

They heard the sound of glass breaking, then muffled yelling. Mija let out a long low whistle and the horse perked up his ears. One more whistle, short, and he trotted toward the grove, found Mija in the darkness, and nuzzled his head into her hand.

"You two take Big Z and go meet the women. I'll wait for Peters," she said.

"That's not a good idea," said Ollie.

"What's Peters doing?" Mija asked.

"Destroying the radio and the codes," said Harijs.

"Shouldn't he be done by now?" she said.

"He said something about being a decoy, so we could get away," said Ollie.

"Did you know about this before?" She stared at the men's stony faces. "I'm waiting for Peters."

"You have to go with us. It's better for all but one to get away than for all to be shot."

Two soldiers ran in front of the headlights toward the barn. Mija couldn't move, couldn't breathe. Ollie pressed on her arm, gave a slight pull, "Let's go."

"No."

"Yes." He gave a more insistent pull. "Your children. Don't you want to see them again?"

Mija took a deep breath as if she just woke up, picked up the horse's reins with one hand, and followed Ollie and Harijs. They heard a shot. Mija stopped. Ollie said, "You can't do anything but get yourself killed if you go back. Keep walking."

"You're a bastard," she said.

"At least they didn't bring dogs," Harijs said.

With her free hand, Mija fingered the little paper bag of dried cherries in her pocket. She switched the hand holding the horse's reins, felt inside her other pocket, and ran her fingers over the smooth, cool metal of the gun. The pocket knife was next to the gun.

The group met up with the other two women and went on as planned, across farmland to the next field and to the next grove until they reached the next deserted farm some five kilometers away. They had planned for this months ago. Hopefully, the buildings were still deserted. They hurried since it was getting lighter, and any minute someone watching, even from far away, would be able to pick them out in the snowy fields like flies on white bread.

Since they'd been here last, the farmhouse had burned to the ground. The small horse barn, with four stalls and a walkway, was intact, but there was no way to heat it. Here they were, no food, no heat, and with a horse to feed as well. Inside the barn, they sat in a circle in a stall. Big Z stood behind Mija.

Mija said, "Maybe Peters shot the Germans." No one responded. "Maybe he will bring some provisions in a pack. Maybe we can go back to the house." Even as she spoke, she didn't believe her words. The cold and silence pervaded like a fog. A single set of tears fell from Mija's eyes. She felt the hotness rolling down and forced back the rest. There was no time to cry now.

Ollie said, "In a few hours, if all is still quiet, I'll go outside and get some wood, melt some snow for water, maybe catch a rabbit."

Harijs said, "With the dissolution of the ghetto and now that we've been found out, we need to split up. We've done what we can."

Zana said, "I was thinking that myself. I wish I had a place to go, but none of my relatives has room or food."

Brita said, "You come with me. I have relatives in Sigulda. They will take us in."

"I don't want to be a burden."

"You'll come with me."

Ollie said, "If your relatives can't keep you, come to Gulepils and stay with me. One way or another, we will take care of each other."

Harijs said, "We're in this together, to the end."

Mija's mind was back at the barn, with Peters. *Why were they acting as if he didn't exist anymore?* She thought about her options and barely heard the conversation.

The others decided to rest for an hour or two. Ollie put Big Z outside as a sentry, and all five lay down in a row in the middle of the floor, one man at each end. Mija did not fall asleep. She couldn't hold back the tears any longer and used her hands to wipe them away. Finally, the others were asleep. Slowly, carefully, she sat up, stood up, and slipped out without waking anyone. She tightened the knot in her scarf and tucked the back inside her coat collar. She patted Big z, untethered him, mounted, and took the reins. "Let's go. We're going to get Peters.

CHAPTER THIRTY

$\mathcal{B}$ig Z slogged along in snow up to his knees and Mija worried that they were lost. The terrain was the same in every direction, white fields interspersed with woods at scattered intervals. She started by following the tracks they had made to the hideout, but the tracks soon disappeared. As they neared the next forest area, a bigger one than the others, she wanted to go to the left around it, but Big Z neighed and resisted. She let the reins go slack.

"Nu, do you know the way to Peters?" His ears pricked up. "Go, go to Peters." Mija let the horse take over and concentrated on scanning the horizon for movement. *Could someone be hiding in the woods? Did they see her, a solitary woman on a horse?* The gun in her coat pocket would only help if she was up against one person, and she was always aware of how far the gun was from her hand. Big Z was sure-footed and her hold on the reins was the lightest it could be without dropping them. Her knuckles rested on the saddle.

Mija smelled the smoke before she saw the billowing stack over the next rise. *Please don't let it be the barn. God, please, don't let it be the barn.*

"Faster, faster," she spurred the horse, lifting her hands and holding the reins tighter. Big Z stepped even higher in his efforts to increase his speed. The house came into view and was burned almost to the ground. The barn was intact. When they reached the barn door, she pulled one foot out of the stirrup and brought her leg around to dismount. In her haste, her other foot got stuck and she almost fell, catching the edge of the saddle at the last second.

"Wait here." She patted Big Z and ran into the barn through the open door. Big Z followed her in.

"Peters, I'm here." No response. "Peters, I'm back." She ascended the ladder and saw him right away, inert on the floor. "Oh, God." She felt his forehead, which was cold but not that of a dead man. Next, she felt his wrist. His pulse was very weak. His coat was a bloody mess and there was a bullet hole. She unbuttoned it, pulled his shirt out of his pants, and examined his abdomen. Just below his heart, there was a coagulated mass of blood, and the bleeding seemed to have stopped. She turned him slowly on his side so she could examine his back. He moaned.

"Thank God, you can feel." She pulled up his shirt. The bullet had gone clean through.

Peters moaned again, but this time said, "Back."

His voice was hoarse, the word a whisper.

"Your back hurts?"

"Soldiers." His eyes opened in a slit.

"Back, soldiers. Oh! Soldiers are coming back?"

"Um."

"Why?"

"Car."

"They want the car?"

"Yeh."

"Why didn't they take it with them?"

"Petrol." Peters seemed a bit more alert.

"Ah. They're coming back with petrol."

"You go," Peters said. "Danger."

"Not without you."

"You go." His eyes closed. "Go." He moaned again.

She said firmly, "Don't talk."

Mija left him and went to the vegetable cellar behind the barn. The small jar of honey she had hidden under the potatoes was still there. Back in the loft, she dipped two fingers into the jar and smeared the honey over the wounds, the abdomen. and the back, covering the damaged areas. Then she ripped a strip from the length of the cleanest horse blanket. After pressing the shirt flat over the honeyed middle, she wrapped the strip around twice and tied it at the uninjured side. She put the half-empty honey jar into her coat pocket with the dried cherries and licked her sticky fingers. Then she threw the horse blanket down the opening.

"Peters, wake up. We have to go down." She

moved his head from side to side and patted his cheeks. "Come on. Wake up."

His eyes opened a little. "Can't. Go."

"Not without you. Get up."

Peters lifted his head a few inches. Mija moved behind him, put her hands under his armpits, pulled him to a sitting position, then dragged his body to the edge of the ladder. She maneuvered his legs down the opening until they hung straight down. She slid herself down over his legs until her head was at the level of the top step. Mija wiggled him down the steps, one by one. His heaviness pushed against her chest until she thought they would both fall the rest of the way. Finally, at the bottom, she could no longer hold him up, and he slithered into a heap.

"Get up," she said to the motionless body. "Please, dear God, please." Big Z nuzzled Peters' neck, and his eyes flickered. Breathing hard, Mija put her arm around his shoulders, sat him up, and pulled at him to stand. Once she had him upright, he reeled forward, leaned his face into the saddle, raised a hand, and held onto the mane.

"Good, Peters, good. Now let's mount."

She put his foot into the stirrup and said, "Get up." She said it two more times before Peters moved. He put an arm up over the saddle. Mija pushed him up until his leg went over. He slumped forward and closed his eyes.

Mija used a horse blanket to cover Peters' back and tucked the ends under his waist on both sides. She removed his foot from the stirrup and let it hang freely so she could get on the horse behind him. Once astride, she positioned Peters more centrally, took the reins, and clicked for Big Z to go.

She turned the horse toward the smoldering ruins of the house and stopped by the big oak tree. Dismounting, she tied Big Z loosely and ran to the house. Using a corner of her coat, she picked up a red-hot piece of wood at its cooler end. She ran across the snow to the barn. Inside, she put the hot end into the straw in front of the car and blew. Nothing. She pushed more straw onto the wood and blew again. A wisp of smoke wormed upward. She blew until it was a flame. Then she walked with the horse and prone rider to the vegetable cellar.

"Stay," she said. She filled one sack with potatoes and left the rest. Big Z was already carrying two adults. She couldn't burden him with more than one sack. She didn't want to feed soldiers with her hard labor, but there was no choice.

"Sorry," she said to Big Z as she mounted. She tied the sack onto the saddle horn. Big Z handled his load well. As they reached the main road, she heard an explosion and turned to see a fireball. There must have been some petrol in the car's gas tank after all.

If there wasn't snow, they could travel to Feliks' farm using shortcuts over fields. With the pure white landscape, that was impossible. If she went back to where the others were, it wasn't far but was the opposite direction from Gulepils. Besides, there was no medicine, no heat and lots of danger. Better to go to her brother's where Peters would have a fighting chance.

It was Christmas Day. Could she trust that there would be no troop movements and risk staying on the roads? She had to. She couldn't afford to get lost on white fields of snow. Peters body was still. The blanket had come untucked and his arms swayed with the rhythm of the horse. *Please don't die, Peters. Not like this.*

As the horse plodded along, Mija talked out loud. "Where have the years gone? Remember when we rode our horses to the big lake at the edge of the forest beyond the far end of Gulepils?" She patted his back. "It was a cloudless summer day, after the planting but before the first hay-gathering. I'd never been allowed to go there before, but you knew the way. I was seventeen, right before you went off to university. The lake was the largest one I'd ever seen, and in the middle, there was a wooden platform that people could swim to and dive from. You dared me to race you to it. Halfway, I got a cramp in my calf. You didn't hear me yell, and no one was close by. I swallowed water and started coughing. Then I panicked and flailed my arms and made things worse. I thought I was going to drown. Finally, you looked around to see if you were winning and came back for me. You put one arm around my head and swam like that back to the shore, where I coughed up a bunch of water and threw up my breakfast. I was mortified and wanted to disappear, or at the very, least sink back into the water. Peters, you saved my life. It's my turn to save yours. Don't you dare die. You were right about no troop movements today. And everyone else must be smart enough to stay inside in this weather. Thank God there's not nearly as much snow on the roads as on the fields. And the wind has died down too."

Mija stopped at midday. She dismounted and led Big Z through a row of birch trees and down a slight rise to a stream. Using the thick end of a downed branch, she cracked the ice and broke open a small area. "Here, Big Z, take a drink."

While the horse lapped at the water, Mija took Peters' hand, which felt like ice but still had a pulse. She opened the honey, put some on her index finger and smeared it on his lips. His tongue came out just enough to lick the sweetness. She gave herself a little bit and then gave a bigger measure to the horse. Big Z licked her fingers. She washed her hands in the flowing stream and then took a drink herself. Using her cupped hands, she brought water to Peters' mouth and held it close. After some prodding, he slurped at it.

"Well, Peters, we've got to get moving." He grunted.

All afternoon, Mija kept up her dialogue. She kept repeating the same story of how he saved her. She interspersed that with little tidbits like, "It's a good thing it's a sunny day or we'd freeze to death." As they neared Gulepils, she steered clear of the main part of town and went around the long way down the dirt road. The journey took longer than she expected. The snow was higher here, and sometimes it was hard to tell where the road was, but she felt safer. They arrived at Feliks' as darkness settled down like a purple blanket, and a yellow moon broke over the horizon. Peters had not stirred or made a sound for some time, and that worried her. Lights showed through the cracks in the curtains of the house, and a black line of smoke rose from the chimney.

She dismounted, ran to the door and banged two long raps, three short ones. The door opened, and all of a sudden everyone was hugging her. Laima, Feliks, Lize, Ints. Little Rita jumped in too. Behind them were Astrid and Dara.

Mija pointed behind her. "Peters is hurt, on the horse." Feliks ran. Laima tried to shoo the children back in, but they protested. Mija insisted, "Go in, I'll be right there."

Feliks lifted Peters carefully and carried him in. As he entered the house with his burden, Ints walked out with his coat on.

Ints said, "I'll take the horse to the barn, feed him, and brush him. The animals are my job." He stood tall.

Mija looked at her son who was so young and so old at the same time. She gave him a close hug. "Yes, that's a good idea. But don't linger."

She put her hand on his head. "Where's your hat?" Ints took a knit hat out of his coat pocket and put it on. "I forgot," he said, and took the reins.

Inside, Feliks put Peters on the single bed in the maid's room, the same bed where Laima had given birth to the twins. Laima unbuttoned his coat and shirt and examined him.

"He's alive," she pronounced. "The wound, what did you put on it?"

"Honey was all I had. I'm sorry." Mija, cold and exhausted, sat on the one chair in the room and rubbed her hands together.

"No time for sorry," Laima said. "Honey is an old remedy for wounds and prevents infection. His pulse is very weak."

"What can I do?"

"Fill a big pot with water, put in strips of linen from a ripped up sheet, boil for five minutes. Then bring them to me. Do you have any more honey? We don't."

Mija handed Laima the jar from her coat pocket. "There's not much left."

Laima took the jar. "It will do for now."

Mija sent the girls to find a sheet. The pot was set to boil while Mija and the girls ripped up the sheet.

Mija took the bag of cherries from her pocket and set it on the table. "Leave some for Ints," she said as the girls scrambled to take seats. They counted out the precious pieces one by one. Lize looked like such a woman now.

The girls were full of questions on how the rescue operations were going. Mija told them about the Germans coming, recounting every detail of the escape. She didn't mention the ghetto in Riga being liquidated because she didn't want to alarm Dara. Dara still kept a very short haircut and dressed like a boy. Astrid flipped her red pigtails and said that after the war, she was going to Siberia to find her parents. Astrid had been writing them letters once a week, sending them to the bigger towns in Siberia, in rotation, since she had no idea where they might be. So far, no response. The girls all said they didn't want to go back to Velsaine after the winter holiday. They wanted to stay here on the farm with Laima and Feliks.

"How will you do your lessons?" Mija asked.

"Ourselves. We will borrow books," said Lize. "Or maybe you can get us books. Or maybe Miss Kronberga will come here to live and start a new school. Or we can go to the regular school in town. Or wait till the war is over."

"You have lots of ideas, Lize." Mija gave her a hug and Lize's eyes brightened. Mija had lots of ideas, too, but didn't share them. She hardly shared them with herself. She let the seeds of possibilities germinate just under the surface. Until she knew if Peters would survive, she wouldn't think too far ahead.

Ints came in through the kitchen door, and the girls gave him his share of the cherries. Mija used tongs to take the strips of cloth from the boiling water and laid them out to cool. No one mentioned Aleks. Mija wondered if they'd seen him, but she didn't ask. At the moment, that was of little consequence. The linen strips were ready, and she carried them to Laima.

"Nu, how is he?" she asked.

"Can you bind his stomach like you did with the

blanket? Some fresh bleeding occurred recently, but it's stopped now. I'll be back with some herb tea."

Mija bound Peters' wounds and then sat beside him on the bed and stroked his head. She talked to him softly. "Don't die on me. I need you. Please." She kept talking to him softly until Laima returned.

"Why do you look so worried?" Mija stood up.

Laima shrugged and sat at Peters' side. She spooned a small amount of tea into his mouth. Some of it dribbled out. She moved his head to a better position. His face was all the more white through his dark beard.

"Those wrinkles on your forehead tell me there's something wrong. Come on, don't keep anything."

"It's been hard."

"I know," Mija said.

"You more than anyone." Laima sighed. "The immediate problem is that I have nothing to treat the wounds with."

"What do you need?"

"Several plants would work."

"I'll go get them," Mija paced the floor while Laima spooned tiny amounts of liquid into the side of Peters' mouth.

"But where will you look? In the snow?"

"Are there any taller plants, something that would be above the snow? Perhaps in the forest?"

"Ah, I don't know. I don't want you to risk your life going out there."

"Are there troops close to the farm?"

"Not that I know about."

"Okay, then. Where? What?"

Laima wrinkled her forehead. "You know that tall plant that grows close to water?"

"Which one?" Mija turned and paced back.

"I don't remember the name right now."

"I thought you knew all the plant names."

"It's not one I've used much."

"Describe it then," Mija put her hands behind her and intertwined her fingers.

"Tall, up to my chest, with rough bristles and little bell flowers. I've seen it by the banks of the stream close to where the mushrooms grow, you know that copse, the biggest one between here and your house. Bees love that plant."

"What color flowers?"

"Bluish, toward purple." There was still a good bit of liquid in the cup, but Laima put it down on the pine nightstand. She fussed with the brown and blue patchwork quilted comforter and pulled it up to Peters' chin. "I'll wait a bit to give him more."

"What part of the plant do you need?"

"The roots, but I don't know how you'll be able to get them out of the frozen earth." Laima shook her head.

"I'll take Feliks along."

"In the morning then. I need as many roots as you can dig up. We need to peel them and mash them and put some on fresh every day until he's well."

CHAPTER THIRTY-ONE

With his right hand, Aleks gripped the butt of the small silver pistol. With his left, he stroked his fingertips across the barrel. He double-checked each chamber to make sure the rounds were still there and then slid the gun, pointing downward, into the side pocket of his old tan pants. He opened the closet door and took down his old brown sweater from the shelf.

His clothes were the only things left in the house when he had come back. The brown sweater was the first thing Mija's mother had knitted for him thirteen years ago. He pulled the soft wool over his head and straightened the sleeves over his thin cotton shirt. The sweater, slightly loose and a little long, covered his hips and hid the bulge of the gun. Aleks looked around the room, the bedroom he and Mija had shared for most of their marriage. There was not much left of the past here. The pale green walls were bare and in need of paint. Three picture nails were still in place in a row above the bed, and below the nails were light rectangles showing where pictures used to hang. Instead of white lace curtains, the windows were covered with black paper. Instead of sleeping in a double bed under a down comforter, he slept on a cot covered with a scratchy army blanket. An oil lamp on the plain three-drawer dresser gave the room its only light. Aleks checked his watch; 5:00 a.m.

He extinguished the lamp and walked down the stairs. He was surprised to see a line of light gleaming from the crack at the bottom of the kitchen door and knocked once before opening it. Even so, Johan jumped backwards from the stove.

"You're up early," said Aleks.

"Couldn't sleep. I made coffee. You?"

"Same. I'm going for a walk."

"In the snow?"

"A short walk. By the stream. Where the snow is melted." Aleks stood, arms hanging straight down, beside his pockets. "A walk in the cold keeps a body healthy. Besides, maybe I'll find some mushrooms." He forced a smile.

"Are you all right?"

"I'm fine. Just kidding."

"Oh. Do you need me to take you somewhere when you get back?"

"Not today."

"Would you like coffee?" Johan reached for another cup.

Aleks raised a hand. "Not now."

Johan looked quizzical. "That's unusual."

"My stomach's a little upset, that's all."

"You don't seem yourself this morning."

"I'll have coffee later. Keep the pot warm."

"Sure."

With a wave of his hand, Aleks left the kitchen. He selected his frayed navy woolen jacket from the long line of coats on hooks lined up in the hall and went out the front door. The sentry, Otto, a big balding man wearing a fur hat with ear flaps, offered Aleks a cigarette. Aleks lit both with his lighter. While they smoked and talked about the weather, Aleks examined the dead rose bushes on either side of the door. With Mija not here to take care of them, they had withered into spindly branches. The garden had died as well. He hardly remembered where the plot had been but could distinctly remember the smell of dill in the salads of fresh cucumber and sour cream.

Twelve soldiers lived in the house with Aleks. As the commander, Aleks had his own room. Four slept in what had been his daughter Lize's bedroom, four in his son Ints', two in the small first-floor maid's bedroom behind the kitchen, and two in his mother-in-law's attic bedroom. The soldiers had put army cots and the barest of barracks furniture in the house.

Hortense and Anete had been housed on the sunporch, but they were no longer here. Hortense had died of influenza, or maybe because she wanted to die, several months after Aleks' mother-in-law died suddenly. Anete had been sitting in the living room on her favorite chair by the fireplace knitting another afghan. She stopped all of a sudden, stared ahead, and said, "Oh, it's you." Then she slumped over, dead. They were buried on the grounds behind the barn, not far from the dog's final resting place.

Last night, Aleks had taken a single sheet of paper and a pen up to his bedroom. He sat on the cot, laid the paper down and thought for a while, selecting his words carefully, forming the note in his mind before putting pen to paper. Finally, he wrote:

DECEMBER 25, 1943

Dear Mija,

The situation is hopeless. Today I was ordered to kill all 83 Jewish people in the Gulepils castle prison and then bury them in a mass grave in the woods. I am to do it tomorrow. I'm sorry.

Love, Aleks

HE COULDN'T THINK of anything else or anything better to say. He folded the note carefully and slept with it under his pillow. This morning, when he had dressed, he moved the note to his pants pocket.

Aleks stubbed out his cigarette and said good-bye to Otto. He walked to the empty barn first and strode to the far corner where his journal was buried. The ground was hard. He used his gun to stab at the dirt.

He unearthed one corner of the journal and pulled the frozen mass out. He turned the pages until there was no more writing. The last page was numbered "30" in the upper right-hand corner in his neat script. He took the note from his pocket, set it on the page, closed and reburied the book as best he could.

Once outside, he walked behind the barn. There was a stork's nest lying on the ground, resting sideways against the building. The last snowstorm must have dislodged it. Aleks knew Mija would say this was bad luck. He would add that the omen caught up to reality. He turned away and walked to the stream.

Stars twinkled in the purple haze of the early morning sky, but the moon was nowhere. Stars were abundant and the snow glistened. The stream had a thin crust of ice along the edges where the current was weakest. Aleks lost his footing when he stepped on a large mossy stone on the bank. One foot slipped, crunched a hole in the ice and dropped into the stream up to his ankle. Water flowed around his foot and seeped up the sock and soaked the bottom of the pants leg. He pulled the foot out and kept on going, keeping his eyes on the ground to avoid any more moss.

He arrived at the woods before he wanted to, but there he was. This was the same area where he and Lize had gathered mushrooms and where he and Mija had lived when the Russians were after them. Other than the footprints he made, there were no other marks on the snow between the stream and the trees. His breath came out in white clouds as he labored across. Once inside the mass of trees, walking was even more difficult because of hidden, fallen branches. Aleks slipped and fell on one knee, twisting his ankle in the process—not the wet one, the other one. As before, he got up and kept on going. He was determined to find the spot with the large fallen tree trunk upon which he and Mija had sat and eaten most of their meals and where she had nursed him back to health during those three weeks.

He thought that perhaps he had gone in a circle and was back to where he started. But no, there was a long, high length of snow he had missed. He brushed the snow away with his bare hands to uncover the wood of the trunk, was unaware that the feeling in his fingers was gone or that one ankle was swollen or that his wet foot was numb. With broad sweeping strokes, he uncovered the length of the log and sat down on it, in the middle. He breathed in deeply but couldn't smell anything. He heard small noises, but there was nothing within his line of sight. Any number of animals could be here. Perhaps a winter rabbit looking for berries. Or maybe a deer looking for leaves under the snow. Mija would know. Would Mija know to get the journal and read it? Did it matter? He reached for the silver cigarette case and lighter in his coat pocket. There were three cigarettes left and he took one out, tapped it, lit it, took a drag and blew the smoke straight out. With his other hand, he turned the cigarette case over and looked at the inscription on the back:

DECEMBER 25, 1926
    To Aleks   Love, Mija

SHE HAD GIVEN THE case to him on their wedding day. He turned it back so he couldn't see the inscription. When there were no more cigarettes, Aleks took out the gun and held it between his bluish palms for a minute as if to warm it up. Then he brushed some dirt from the barrel. He gripped the handle tightly and touched the tip of the barrel against his temple. After some seconds he changed his mind and shoved it into his mouth.

CHAPTER THIRTY-TWO

It was still dark when Mija went to the kitchen to make tea. Laima was already there, a pot of tea waiting.

"Is Feliks up?"

"I'll wake him soon. Hungry?"

"I'd love some tea."

"And you'll have some breakfast." Laima set a plate of brown bread slices and a jam jar in front of her. "You can't dig for the roots without strength."

Mija sat on the chair, spread her bread with a thin layer of the jam, and took a bite. "Mmm. Boysenberry, my favorite. Any chance of sugar for the tea?"

"I used the last of the sugar in the Christmas pudding. I wish we'd known you were coming, I would have saved some."

"Ah, well. Next time I'll try to telephone ahead." Mija smiled.

Laima laughed. "Don't bother. Our phone lines were cut."

"Sabotage?"

"Who can tell?"

"Let me take some of this food to Peters."

"You sit and eat. I'm going to wake Feliks. Then I'll take care of Peters."

MIJA AND HER BROTHER left in the muted light of the Latvian winter morning. The top layer of icy snow crumbled under the horse's hooves. The fields were dark gray against the mauve sky. Mija felt her gun through the coat pocket, jutting against her thigh, and decided she'd better tell Feliks.

"Feliks, I've got a gun in my pocket."

He said, "Good. If you see a deer, shoot it. We need meat."

"I also have a pocket knife."

"Even better. If you kill a deer, we'll use the knife to gut it."

"What happened to my pacifist brother?"

"Necessity, pure and simple."

"Have you seen Aleks?"

"No."

They rode in silence until they were near their destination.

"Do you know the plant we're looking for?" Mija asked.

"Nope."

They rode past the wooded area and kept going to the stream. Mija saw holes in the snow that looked like tracks. They led from the woods to the stream. But she didn't break the silence. Dead and dormant vegetation covered the banks on both sides. She alit from the horse and gave the reins to Feliks. She walked the bank and soon found the plant they needed. Feliks dismounted also and let go of both sets of reins. He removed the bag of tools from his horse and prepared to dig. The horses sauntered to the edge of the water to drink.

Feliks had brought one pick to stab with and one shovel to dig with. He wouldn't let Mija help. Her eyes kept going back to the tracks. What kind of animal could have made them? A deer? The holes were too big, though, and upon closer examination, didn't have the right characteristics for a four-footed animal. A human? What would a person be doing here? Feliks' pick thudded in a rhythm as he hoisted it over his head and thrust down. Mija walked to the bank where the tracks started. She saw faint footprints on the bank. The prints came from the other direction, the direction of her old house. *Was someone in the woods or were the tracks old and frozen, made days ago?*

A shot rang out.

Feliks yelled, "Let's get out of here before we get shot."

"I'm going to go see what's going on." Mija removed her gun, cocked it, and ran, taking the same path as the tracks she'd been examining. Feliks ran to the horses, took their reins, then let go of them, and stood waiting. Mija screamed. He raced into the woods. The horses followed Feliks, first Big Z and then Big Bertha. Once inside the edge of trees, Feliks followed the sound of her voice.

"God, Aleks, no. God, Aleks, no."

His old coat lay on the ground close by and his cigarette case was beside his body. Mija picked up the case and looked at the inscription. She screamed, "How could you?" And then hot tears started and she fell on her knees, not knowing what to do or how to feel. She breathed in the cold air and stood up, holding back the tears.

"My god," said Feliks and he shook his head. "What should we do?"

Mija got up and walked up to the body. Against the reality of the scene in front of her, she thought, maybe it's not him and examined his left hand. The missing tip of his thumb confirmed any doubt. Her eyes moved to his wedding ring. She removed it and pocketed that as well. She had no idea why she wanted it. She also took the gun he had used. Another gun could be valuable.

Mija stamped a foot, clenched her hands into tight fists, and screamed, "Why didn't you come out and show yourself? You didn't have to die! What am I supposed to tell our children?" Then she let out a wail. Feliks hugged her. "Go ahead, get it out." After her screams were spent, she cried on her brother's shoulder. For a long time.

Mija wouldn't let Feliks take the body back to the farm. She did not plan to tell the children about this now. The ground was too hard to dig any kind of a grave. Mija covered the top of Aleks with his coat. They found enough downed branches to cover him.

Mija said, "In the spring, you can come back and bury him. What's left of him. If you want."

"We could have a proper burial then, like we did with Ruta," Feliks said.

"You can, I won't be here."

"Where are you going?"

"I don't know yet."

CHAPTER THIRTY-THREE

The unfamiliar streets of Ventspils confused rather than inspired. The houses were too far apart, the shadows too long. Mija stopped at the corner, standing in the fog under a dim streetlight. She reached into her coat pocket to pull out the hand-drawn map. The man's brown wool jacket reached down to the middle of her thighs. The sleeves were too long, and it was large across her shoulders. The brown of the coat and brown of the wool pants and brown of the boots all ran together making her slim silhouette appear taller than five-eight. She wore a plain black fedora with her hair tucked up under it. A plaid scarf of brown, black, and tan wrapped around her neck completed the costume. Before unfolding the map, she pushed up her coat sleeve to look at her watch. Almost 8:00 p.m. She was to be there at eight o'clock sharp.

The map was hard to read so she moved the paper

closer. There must be a street missing from the crude drawing. Refolding it, she crossed the street in the direction she was already going and went straight. Two blocks later, she saw the street sign she was looking for, turned right, and strode along the Venta River toward the harbor.

A man emerged from the doorway of a building up ahead and turned toward her. She could see a burgundy kerchief around his neck. She pulled a similar burgundy kerchief out of a coat sleeve and wrapped it once around her other scarf and tied it. She avoided the man's face, looking past him to the water of the Baltic Sea where the low moon cast a white shimmering line. Boats of different sizes, moored in an irregular pattern across the harbor, bobbed with the waves.

As the man reached her, he stopped and coughed. She stopped as well but didn't turn her head toward him. He said, "God Bless Latvia." She said, in her lowest voice, "Where Baltic heroes trod." They faced each other and shook mittened hands.

He jutted his chin. "You're a woman. You're supposed to be a man named Peters." He pivoted to the side as if to turn and walk away.

"Please, wait." She talked to his side. "Peters couldn't come. I have his identity card as well as my own. I was told you are a good man, Jacobs."

"Don't use my name. And I don't like surprises. I don't know you." The dark man shook his head. His full beard was stippled with gray. He started to walk away.

She followed him, pulled up to his side, and touched his elbow. "You can trust me. Please. Give me a chance."

He stopped and she stopped with him. He asked, without looking at her, "Do you have the money?"

"When we're on the boat, then I hand over the money. That's the agreement." She stood taller, lips pursed. A horn blew from the harbor in the distance.

"This is dangerous stuff, transporting fugitives. I need to see the money." He crossed his arms in front of him.

Mija talked fast. "We're not fugitives. We're a little family. The Germans shot Peters. He's recovering but has a long way to go. My daughter is fifteen. It's not safe for her. The soldiers . . . surely you've heard what happens. And there is my son." Then her voice softened as she said, "Do you have children?" Mija moved a little closer, stared into his eyes, and willed him to look at her.

"I'm a seaman, no children." His black eyes looked past her. Except for the kerchief, he was dressed in black from top to bottom, and he could be death itself come to meet her. Mija kept her eyes on his. His arms uncrossed as he glanced at her. "I have a sister. Let me see your papers."

Mija removed a mitten, unbuttoned her coat with nervous fingers, and dug out the papers from the inside pocket. No words were exchanged as he looked over them and handed them back. "Meet me here, ready to go, 2:00 a.m." Before she could respond, he disappeared around the corner.

She walked in the opposite direction. Her fingertips were numb even through Peters' thick brown wool mittens. Inside the mittens, she balled the fingers of both hands into tight fists. The windows of the houses were all dark. She kept to the sides of the buildings. The only people she'd seen were a few civilians. Does Ventspils have a curfew? What if she got arrested and thrown into jail for being out after curfew? They had arrived in the city a few hours before the pre-arranged meeting time. She put one hand to her lips and blew air into the mitten, repeating the motion with her other hand. The walk hadn't seemed so long when she was coming the other way.

She turned the corner where she'd left the horse and carriage, but they were missing. She looked at the street sign. This was the right street, but the carriage was gone. Her heart hammered against her chest, thud, thud, thud, faster and faster. Maybe she forgot the street names, maybe she got them mixed up. She walked around the block. No carriage anywhere. She had picked this spot because the area was full of deserted warehouses. What felt comforting about it before was now frightening. Anyone could have come along and . . . She stopped herself from thinking further.

The fog was gone and so was any cloud cover. Multitudes of white stars lit up the ink sky. She did not need a street lamp to see her watch, which showed 9:00 p.m. On foot, she couldn't cover the whole city by herself. She shouldn't have left them. She should have taken them and the carriage with her, or at least taken them closer to the meeting place. She took a deep breath and started walking without knowing where she was going. No, she thought. She had to stay close to where she left the carriage and turned around.

The old watch she wore was once her grandmother's, the one thing of value that she hadn't sold. Everything else had been sold on the black market in Riga. She had been amazed that anyone still had money, but she asked no questions. The silver cigarette case and matching gold wedding rings fetched the most. In one day on the back streets beyond the central market, she raised what she needed.

Unfortunately, there wasn't enough to take everyone. But Feliks and Laima said they didn't want to go anywhere. The country they grew up in was enough for them, and they would face the outcome of the war together. The girls, Astrid and Dara, stayed with them too. Laima and Feliks would help them search for their families once the war was over.

Feliks had said, "The war can't last forever. When peace comes, you can come back."

"Perhaps." She turned to Laima. "I'm going to miss you just as much as Feliks. You've been a sister to me." She looked at both of them. "I'll never forget what you've done for me and for Lize and Ints."

Laima hugged her. "Remember the song festival?"

"Of course. I'll always be grateful that you pushed me to go."

"Latvians sing. That's what we do. We will rise again and have many more song festivals. And one day, we will be free again."

Mija hugged Laima hard. "Yes, we will."

That early morning when they'd left, she hugged each one staying behind, saying, "Until we meet again." Lize and the girls promised to write to each other faithfully.

Ints had been the quiet one. After they were on their way in the old carriage, with Mija and Ints sitting up front wrapped in blankets, and with Mija holding the reins to Big Z, Ints tugged on her coat sleeve. "But what about Papa?"

Mija took in a sharp breath at the painful question. She said, "Papa will take care of himself."

Ints asked, "When will I see him again?"

Mija looked at her son and saw tears in his eyes. She said, "You miss him. It's all right, you can be sad. We're all sad."

"War," said Ints. He grabbed onto her arm.

"What about war?"

"War . . . makes me sad." Two big tears rolled down his cheeks. He wiped them with a coat sleeve. "Mama, can I hold the reins?" Mija handed him the reins and put her arm around his shoulder.

"Can we stop at the old house for a minute and say goodbye to Papa?"

"No, I'm sorry." She gripped his skinny shoulder tighter.

"Why not?"

"We're going in a different direction."

"Please, it won't take long." He turned to look up at her.

"There's another reason."

"What?"

"The soldiers are there, the ones that aren't our friends."

"Oh." The horses' hooves clopped and the carriage wheels creaked. Ints said, "I'm never going to be a soldier."

It had taken them ten days to reach Ventspils. With a horse and carriage, travel was limited to the daylight hours, and in the northern winter, those hours were short. They were lucky that it hadn't snowed. But the wind was capricious, changing from one moment to the next from blowing like a blizzard to disappearing altogether. As they neared the coast, there was less and less snow cover. Each day of travel, as the sky darkened in the late afternoon, they looked for a farm to stop at for the night. They weren't welcomed with open arms, but most of the time, they were given a corner of a barn to sleep in, as long as it was for the one night and they were gone by daybreak. It wasn't that people didn't want to help, but rather that they were afraid. Mija understood that. As she lay in the cold hay with her family, she tried hard to be grateful that they were out of the worst of the cold and tried hard not to be angry that they weren't inside a warm house.

She walked around the block three more times. She saw no one, not man, not beast. *Why was everyone else smart enough to stay in some kind of shelter on this bitter night?* Desperation overcame her. She knew she wouldn't be able to live without the precious cargo in the missing carriage. She put her hand inside her coat pocket, felt the gun, and wrapped her hand around the grip. She let her feet take her where they would.

After some time, she became aware that she was back at the harbor. Everything looked the same as before, except the moon was higher in the sky and smaller. *Why, oh why didn't I make a contingency plan?* Her toes were numb, and she tried to wiggle them as she walked. When she drew in her breath, her chest hurt. Maybe if she sat for a minute and rested. She entered a covered doorway, sat on cold stone, and pressed her back against a painted black wooden door. She pulled up her knees, wrapped her arms around them, let her head fall forward, and closed her eyes. Maybe if she rested, she'd have a clearer head and know what to do.

Visions of the past came upon her. Her wedding day, how happy she was, how her legs trembled as she said the vows. The day Lize was born. The labor came early and Aleks wasn't there, but her mother was. She was walking down a corridor now, in an office building. Lots of people walked in both directions, everyone was in a hurry. Everything was a brown tone, like a sepia photograph. She didn't know why she was there or where she was going. *Was that Aleks? Yes. He walked toward her, but he didn't see her.* He was going to walk right by. "Aleks, is that you?" He stopped, took off his fedora, and held it in his hand. He wore a brown suit, brown tie, and a white shirt.

"You look good," he said.

"So do you. How are you?"

"I'm happy," he said, and he smiled at her.

Clip-clop, clip-clop. "What's that," she asked.

"I think it's for you," he said, and he put on his hat and started walking past her. Goodbye," he said.

She wanted to follow him but couldn't. She was paralyzed. She heard the noise again, clip-clop, clip-clop, and then a neigh. Then everything went black.

"Mama!" Ints tugged at her arm. She woke up. Momentarily dazed, she didn't realize where she was or remember what happened.

Lize yelled from the front of the carriage, "Come on, Mama, get up! Thank God we found you."

Mija couldn't feel her feet or hands, but she let Ints pull her up, and somehow the frozen stumps of her feet carried her to the carriage. All of a sudden, she was aware and wanted to know, "Where have you been?"

Lize said, "Soldiers drove by the carriage in a patrol car. They didn't see us in the back—at least they didn't stop—but we couldn't take a chance on them coming back. We've been driving around all night looking for you. We've been past here twice already, but Ints just saw you now."

"Let's go. It's not far," Mija said.

Ints jumped up to where Lize held the reins. "Mama," he said, "get in the back and warm up. You look frozen."

Mija was too cold to argue. She crawled into the back. "Go two blocks and stop at the corner." They're alive, she thought, thank God, and she fell into an exhaustion of unawareness. No dreams broke into the weariness that filled her.

She felt someone tugging on her shoulder and opened her eyes and saw Peters. "Come on," he said. "It's time."

Mija could feel her fingers and toes. Her whole body felt light. "Then let's go."

She climbed out and then helped Peters. He held himself upright against the carriage with great effort. Lize and Ints stood on either side of him and held onto his arms. The man in black was standing in front of them. He said, "What about the horse and carriage?"

Mija said, "Big Z can take care of himself, don't worry." One at a time, she took out four small bundles tied in scarves from the back. She handed the smallest one to Ints. The next one went to Lize. Mija herself held the other two. Then she untethered the horse from the carriage. To the man, she said, "You can have the carriage." To the horse, she said, "Go, Big Z, go home to Feliks," and she clicked her tongue. The horse looked at her and tilted his head. "Go to Feliks. Go." At the next click of her tongue, the horse trotted off. He looked back once before turning the corner and Mija waved him on.

"Let's go," the bearded man said.

They followed him past the houses and the harbor, down a path toward a lighthouse. Soon they were walking on soft sand, which made the trek slow going as they made their way down the beach. At the water's edge, the man directed them to climb into a small wooden rowboat. They couldn't get in without getting their feet wet. Peters and the children sat at one end, Mija at the other. The man pushed the boat further into the water and jumped into the middle seat. Rowing with an assurance that came from long practice, the man navigated into the open sea, to a tugboat moored far out, far away from any other boats. He stopped and tied the rowboat to the tug. Mija thought they would be dumped into the sea as the rowboat swung up and down in the waves. They had to climb a rope ladder on the side of the vessel. Ints went first, Lize second, then Mija. Next was Peters. He managed to get up the ladder but fell over the edge at the top. Mija caught him and helped him sit down on the deck floor. The man threw the bundles up to Mija, then came up himself.

"You can sit below," he told them and pointed in the direction of a narrow stairway. "There are chairs."

"Where's the crew?" Mija asked.

"I'm the crew. It's better this way."

Mija opened her coat and took out the bundle of money from the inside pocket. The man opened the envelope, rifled the bills, and stowed them in his own coat pocket. He nodded.

When everyone was settled in the tiny storage hold below, Mija climbed back up to the deck. The anchor had been pulled up and sat in a wet pile. The engine turned over with a loud vroom and then settled into a softer noise, more like a purr. The boat pulled away. Mija held on to the side and watched the wake. Waves rolled toward Latvia as the boat headed toward Sweden.

Ten hours. Ten hours and we will be free. She wiped the tears from her cheeks as she sang the Latvian national anthem, "Dievs Sveti Latvia."

ABOUT THE AUTHOR

V. Z. Byram was born in a displaced persons camp in post World War II Germany of Latvian parents. They immigrated to the United States when she was three. She received her MFA in Creative Writing from Goddard College, has won numerous writing awards, and has taught literature and writing as an adjunct professor. She lives with her husband in Fort Myers, Florida. *Song of Latvia* is her first novel. Visit her website at www.vzbyram.com.

CPSIA information can be obtained
at www.ICGtesting.com
Printed in the USA
FFHW022013131119
56054487-62018FF